LAST TAKE

DI RYAN HALE CRIME THRILLERS
BOOK 2

R. K. LYNOTT

LAST TAKE
Published worldwide by Alibi & Ink Books.
This edition published in 2026.
ISBN 978-0-473-77463-9

This novel is entirely a work of fiction. The names, characters and incidents
portrayed in it are the work of the author's imagination. Any resemblance to
actual persons, living or dead, events or localities is entirely coincidental.

rklynottbooks.com
Alibi & Ink Books

For Finn and Elise, my favourite little accomplices, who make every day a plot twist.

CHAPTER ONE

———

GENIUS DEMANDS PERFECTION.

Cyrus Wilde strode onto the empty set. The studio lights glowed a sickly amber, sharpening the contours of the foam-and-plaster rock face of the ritual pit carved into the stage floor. He trailed his fingertips across the ornate handles of a rack of prop daggers and swords, the gleaming blades reflecting his dark form.

His performance yesterday on this very set had been a tour de force. A masterclass. The dungeon of Ravendeep Castle felt almost sacred to him now. Consecrated through his art.

The crew had watched in awe. They always did when he delved deep. He didn't just portray Lord Caspian Drest. With every thought, every breath, he became him. He recalled the wide eyes and hushed whispers when the director had called cut.

Five pages in one take.

Feeding off their admiration was as natural to him as breathing. Their energy fuelled him. He drew it in like a psychic vampire and transformed it into something extraordinary. They contributed so little, yet he gave back so much.

He was sure an extra, dressed as a temple priestess, had dabbed at her eyes afterwards. Tears that recognised his greatness.

The heels of his leather boots clicked on the stage, the sound swallowed by the cavernous set. He rolled up the sleeves of his cotton shirt to the elbows and loosened his silk cravat. Method acting required certain allowances after hours.

"Come out then," he called. The words bounced off corrugated steel walls disguised as ancient stone. "No need to be shy. We both know you're not here for my autograph."

A figure emerged from a polystyrene alcove, their features blurred by the shadow of a hooded cloak. The voice when it came was flat. "You're late."

Cyrus leaned against a prop altar and picked at the wax drippings from yesterday's shoot. "Spare me the dramatics, ducky." He waved a hand at the figure's cloak. "I'll turn up when I feel like it. Everybody knows I'm the reason this shit-show is still solvent." He frowned, hearing his Midlands accent creep through the polished vowels. "If you insist on meeting in the middle of the night, why not at the scene of my recent triumph?" He threw his arms wide and then dropped them back to his sides. "So have you carried out my instructions?"

"You've made this more complicated than it needs to be," the figure replied.

Cyrus smirked. Maybe, but he didn't care. "Complications keep things interesting, don't you think?"

Silence stretched between them. The figure remained still.

Cyrus drew air slowly through his nose, held it in his expanded chest, then released it in a huff.

"Look," he snapped. He hopped up onto the raised edge of the ritual pit. The gaping maw covered in fake blood stains was somewhat ruined by the circle of neon green screen at the bottom. "You know why we're here. I gave you a job to do, and to be frank, you haven't delivered. We both know I can make your life difficult."

"Is that so?"

"Don't play dumb." Cyrus let his impatience seep into his tone. "I'm the one who owns you."

"Funny. I was about to say the same to you. If the evidence got out about what you're up to? Mutually assured destruction."

Cyrus's smirk faltered. He masked it by jumping off the side of the pit. "Bold words. But let's not pretend we're equals."

The figure took a step closer. "Perhaps you're not as indispensable around here as you imagine."

"You think they'd recast me based on your accusations?" Cyrus's laugh rang out. He paused for a moment to admire the way it reverberated through the set, then he leaned forward and poked his finger into the figure's chest. "Get it done. No more excuses."

"I'm suggesting you reconsider your approach."

"My approach has served me well enough. Let's see... a lead role in the most popular show on TV. The face of a trio of luxury brands. The media hounding me for a sniff of a sound bite." He counted off his points one by one on his fingers. "I didn't get here by being humble."

"Or honourable."

Cyrus bristled. "Honour's a luxury in this industry. Status is what counts."

"To some, perhaps." The cloak shifted. "Anyway, I think you'll keep my secret."

"I'll keep it if I feel like it. You exist to do what I tell you and to keep your mouth shut. When I want your opinion on my career, I'll—"

Cold steel kissed his stomach before heat bloomed beneath his velvet doublet. His fingers brushed the dagger's hilt protruding from his abdomen. Sticky warmth seeped through the fabric and coated his fingers. He staggered back, and the rough lip of the pit bit into his hip.

"For fuck's sake!" The curse came out wet.

The figure stepped into a shaft of amber light and twisted the blade.

Cyrus's knees hit the foam rock floor. He tried to laugh, but only managed a choked gurgle. "Should've... seen it coming."

The hooded head tilted. A gloved hand yanked the dagger free. Cyrus's scream echoed off the soundstage walls, but he knew there was no one near the set to hear it. His phone skidded across the floor as he collapsed, the screen lighting up with Astrid's text in reply to his latest custody threat.

Darkness pooled at the edges of his vision, and his last thoughts shifted from the pain.

To the big season finale next week he'd never film. Freddy's fifth birthday next month. Who would feed the fucking cat left alone in his trailer?

The last thing he tasted was the tang of iron filling his throat, and the last sound he heard was a soft voice in his ear.

"I know you'll keep my secret because the dead don't talk."

CHAPTER TWO

DI Ryan Hale hated politics.

He hated the false promises, the kissing babies and the incestuous old boys' club of favours owed and granted.

Most of all, he hated when politics parked its arse between him and his job.

"Has the warrant come through yet?" Ryan asked DS Fiona Bennett as they sheltered from the needling rain between a tall manicured hedge and their van. The expectant faces of the rest of his team peered out at him through the open sliding door.

Fiona grimaced and pulled the hood of her raincoat further down her face. "Nothing so far."

"Any word from Lee?" DCI Lee, their boss, was on a spa day with her wife, but Ryan knew if the station could reach her, she'd call him, cucumber slices be damned.

Fiona shook her head.

At both ends of the van, uniformed officers huddled in their patrol cars and awaited instructions. The armed response team was already en route from Derby at Ryan's request.

He turned to the rest of the team. "Okay, here's the situation. We received an anonymous tip about domestic violence and a firearm, so we need to proceed with extreme caution. Digit, get the drone up. I want eyes on what's happening."

DC 'Digit' Asare nodded without looking up as he attached the rotor blades to the drone with nimble fingers. "Should be up in the air in one minute and forty seconds approximately."

DC Cal Pine adjusted his earpiece. "What if old Peasley shoots at the drone?"

"Then we'll know he's armed," Fiona replied dryly.

DC Sheri Dewan, the newest and youngest member of the East Midlands Special Operations Major Crimes Unit, studied the sprawling Georgian estate through a gap in the hedge. "Any intel on the layout of the house?"

"None so far," Ryan replied.

A sudden gust of wind whipped rain into their faces. Digit shielded his equipment. "Wind speeds are at the upper limit for safe drone operation," he announced.

Ryan gave him a pointed look. "Can you get it up or not?"

"Oh, I can get it up," Digit replied earnestly.

Cal sniggered.

Digit paused, then nodded. "You're reading a double entendre into my words regarding my penile erectile function. I can assure you my penis performs as expected for an adult male of my age and health status."

That was enough for Cal to double over laughing. When he got himself back under control, he slapped Digit on the back. "Never change, mate."

"Just launch the drone, Digit," Fiona said.

Ryan pinched the bridge of his nose. Only an hour ago he'd been in the nice, dry incident room.

Now, rain dripped down the inside collar of his raincoat while he squatted outside the residence of the esteemed local

MP, who, according to a staff member, had threatened his wife with a shotgun.

Just a typical Tuesday.

A black Toyota Corolla pulled up across the road.

Ryan swore under his breath and stomped over to the nearest patrol car. He banged on the fogged-up window, and the officer inside rolled it down. He pointed to the car.

"Get rid of her. I want a cordon put up at each end of the road to prevent any more civilians entering the area."

Sophie, his sister-in-law and senior reporter for the Derby Observer, looked over at him and waved.

Ryan ran a hand through his wet hair as the drone buzzed into the air behind him. "And don't take any of her bullshit about reasonable access to report on matters of public interest. Tell her it's for her own safety."

If Sophie had already arrived at the scene, the other vultures that called themselves reporters wouldn't be long swooping in behind. It would take them no time at all to realise they were outside the MP's house.

Lee would be pissed when she found out.

"Sir," Sheri called out. "The background report has come through."

Ryan marched back to the van. "Give me the highlights."

"Gerald Peasley, 53 years of age. Labour MP for North East Derbyshire since 2019," Sheri said, reading off her phone. "Comes from family money and is well connected in Parliament."

Ryan and Fiona groaned in unison. The day had just got better.

"Wife's name is Patricia, been married for eighteen years. Two children, both at boarding school. No prior reports of domestic incidents, but the wife has been to hospital with suspicious injuries. Nothing official, though."

"Weapons?"

"Two firearms registered in his name. A Purdey 12-bore sidelock ejector and a Rigby Highland Stalker in .308."

Cal whistled. "Fancy bastard."

The drone's feed flickered onto Digit's screen.

"Thermal imaging has picked up two figures in what is likely a conservatory. One is sitting and the other is line dancing."

"What?"

"Or maybe pacing around in an agitated state?"

Ryan sighed. "Right. We'll breach when Shania Twain plays, shall we?"

"Do you want me to activate audio?" Digit asked. His hand hovered over the keyboard. "Though we might struggle to hear any music through the glass."

"No, Digit. Visuals are enough."

Through the driver's window of the van, Ryan saw Sophie arguing with the officer. She got in her car, slammed the door and sprayed gravel as she took off down the road.

His phone buzzed in his pocket. Lee's name flashed on the screen.

"DI Hale." He stepped away from the van.

"Ryan, I need you and the team back at the station immediately. We've got a high-profile missing-persons case that's just landed in our lap. He's a big-shot television actor. The brass wants all hands on deck."

"We're in the middle of something here—"

"I don't care if you're in the middle of tea with the Queen. This takes priority."

Ryan lowered his voice. "We believe Patricia Peasley is in danger. Her husband..."

"Peasley? As in the MP?" Lee's tone sharpened. "What the hell are you doing at Gerald Peasley's house?"

Ryan explained the tip. A heavy sigh crackled through the phone.

"Listen, Ryan. Send a pair of uniforms to do a welfare check and get your team back to the station. Now."

"But—"

"The MP won't open fire on uniformed officers, and try not to piss off any more important people on your way back. We have enough shit on our plates."

Ryan ended the call just as Digit called out, "Sir, the heat signatures have moved through the house, and the garage door just opened."

"Can you get a visual on the vehicle?"

Digit's fingers flew over the keys. The image on his screen zoomed in. "It's a black Audi SUV. Registration matches Peasley's."

Fiona studied his face. "You're not considering stopping him?"

"If he's got Patricia with him, we need to intercept him."

She hesitated. "Without Lee's authorisation..."

Ryan knew what she didn't say in front of the team. His neck would be on the line if this went sideways.

"He could take her somewhere more isolated. We can't risk it. At least he'll know we're watching him."

Fiona nodded grimly.

Ryan waved the uniformed officers over and then turned to his team. "Cal, Sheri, take the unmarked car and block the drive."

Cal grinned. "On it, boss."

"And Cal."

The DC froze halfway out of the van. "Yeah?"

"If you start twittering, so help me God..."

"It's tweeting. Well now, the platform's called X. It's—"

Ryan held up his hand. "I don't care."

As the team sprang into action, Ryan grabbed his radio. "All units, the suspect's vehicle is leaving the property. Intercept and contain. Exercise caution; he may be armed."

Headlights pierced the gloom, and the Audi rolled into sight down the gravel drive. Cal's car screeched into position across the exit and forced Peasley to brake. The MP leaned out of his window. "What the devil is this?"

Ryan approached the driver's side. Fiona flanked him. "Mr Peasley, step out of the vehicle, please."

Peasley's eyes narrowed. "On whose authority? This is an outrage!"

"Police matter, sir. We need you to exit the car."

The MP slammed his fist on the steering wheel and threw the door open. "Whoever you are, you'll regret this."

Almost a guarantee.

Ryan's gaze shifted to the passenger side. Patricia Peasley sat with her face turned away. "Mrs Peasley, are you all right?"

She slowly faced him, and his breath caught. A dark bruise marred her left eye, the skin swollen. She forced a tight smile. "I'm fine. Just a misunderstanding."

"That looks painful," Fiona said. "Do you need medical assistance?"

Patricia shook her head. "No, no, it's nothing. I walked into a cupboard door. Silly me."

Peasley scowled. "There you have it. Now, if this farce is over, we'd like to be on our way."

"Not quite." Ryan signalled to Cal. "Search the boot."

"Hey!" Peasley protested. "You have no right."

"We have reasonable grounds," Ryan replied coolly.

Cal pulled on a pair of gloves and opened the car's boot. He frowned. "Just golf clubs back here, boss."

Ryan saw a flicker of something cross Peasley's face. Was it relief?

"Check them," he told Cal.

"This is a gross misuse of police resources," Peasley shouted. He made to move to the back of the car, but Ryan stepped in front of him.

"What do we have here?" Cal said. He pulled a rifle out of the golf bag with a fluffy head cover jammed over one end.

"I can't imagine that's a very accurate putter," Ryan said to Peasley.

Shrugging, the man looked down his nose at him. An impressive feat given he was a good half a foot shorter. "I'm taking my rifle to be professionally cleaned, as is my right. The head cover and golf bag protect it from damage while I transport it."

Ryan leaned in the open window.

"Mrs Peasley," he said, "my name is DI Hale from Chesterfield Station. If you encounter any more cupboard doors, you can always call the station and ask for me. Day or night."

Her eyes darted to her husband and back. "I don't know what you're talking about. You're making a big deal out of nothing. Gerald and I were just going for a drive." She looked away.

"See?" Peasley sneered. "Now, unless you're arresting me, we're leaving."

Ryan felt the situation press down on him as his options dwindled. "Very well. You're free to go." He motioned to Cal to put the rifle back in the boot and radioed for the patrol cars to reverse.

Peasley straightened his jacket and stabbed his finger in Ryan's direction.

"This is harassment, DI Hale. You can expect a formal complaint to be made to your superiors."

Patricia turned back to face her husband as he dropped into the driver's seat with a huff. Her gaze slipped over to Ryan.

Ryan fancied her eyes held a silent plea, but he couldn't act without her help.

The Audi sped away down the lane.

Fiona exhaled. "Could've gone better."

Ryan rubbed his hand over his face. "We had to try."

"Pack it up," he called to the team. "We have a misper."

Fiona touched his arm as the rest trudged over to the van. "You did the right thing."

"Doesn't count for much if we can't do anything to protect her," Ryan replied, his eyes fixed on the spot where the Audi had disappeared.

CHAPTER THREE

Ryan slumped in his chair, shoulders damp from the rain. The incident room hummed with quiet activity as his team tapped at keyboards and shuffled paperwork. He'd deserved the lengthy reprimand he'd received in DCI Lee's office for disobeying orders. At least she hadn't done it in front of the team.

He'd need a big win on this missing persons case to get back into Lee's good graces.

As if summoned by his thoughts, DCI Lee strode into the room.

"All right, team, eyes up." She dropped a file onto an empty desk. They turned to the front of the room as she pulled a photograph from the folder. "We've got a high-profile case requiring immediate attention."

"DCI, your skin looks great," Cal said. "Did you get the hyaluronic acid face peel? I hear it's—"

"Save it for someone who cares, Pine." Lee taped a head-shot to the whiteboard of a dark-haired man with sharp cheek-bones, piercing blue eyes and an icy gaze.

Sheri gasped.

"Cyrus Wilde," Lee said. "He's an actor, and he's been missing for three days."

"Never heard of him," Ryan muttered.

Cal's eyebrows shot up. "You've never heard of Cyrus Wilde, the actor who plays Caspian Drest on the hit TV show *Crown of Shadows*?"

Ryan shrugged.

"No great surprise since it doesn't stream on Sky Sports," Fiona said.

"Statistically speaking, DI Hale, it's not unexpected that you're unaware of the show," Digit interjected. "You lie far outside the show's 18-to-40-year-old demographic."

"Hey, easy on the far."

"It's only one of the most popular shows on television," Cal continued. "Come on, you must have at least seen the eunuch meme?"

Ryan sighed.

"No? Have you ever been online for fun?"

Lee shot them a look implying they'd both be eunuchs if they didn't stop talking. "*Crown of Shadows* is filming its third season at its purpose-built studio outside Buxton. Having a studio of this size in Derbyshire is a significant investment in the region. Millions of pounds and tourist revenue are riding on the show's success. According to witnesses, Wilde was last seen early Saturday evening."

Ryan glanced around the room. Fiona and Digit appeared indifferent to the star-studded element of the new case, but Sheri and Cal leaned forward, hanging on every word.

"The network initially assumed Cyrus had gone off somewhere to sulk," Lee said, "but it's been three days without contact, and the production team is worried about his safety."

"More likely worried about losing money," Cal said.

Ryan frowned. "An adult misper? Hardly seems like Major Crimes territory."

"It normally wouldn't be," Lee agreed. "But with the high-profile nature of this case, there's been significant pressure from above to assign additional resources."

"Right." Ryan crossed his arms. "First thing we need to do is understand the players."

Sheri shifted in her seat and tucked a strand of dark hair behind her ear. She cleared her throat.

"Something to contribute, DC Dewan?" Lee asked.

"I know quite a bit about the show and the cast." She sank down as if she hoped the floor would swallow her. "I'm quite active on the *ShadowCast* subreddit."

Cal lounged back and put his hands behind his head. "Didn't peg you as a card-carrying 'Crown Crazie'. Thought you'd be too busy reading proper books on your lunch break and posting insights on a Substack."

Sheri rolled her eyes. "I'm not obsessed, but I enjoy the show and follow the entertainment news surrounding it." Her cheeks flushed. "They pulled in over twelve million viewers for the season two finale." She sat up straighter. "It's a guilty pleasure, but so what? Everyone needs to turn their brain off sometimes."

"Go on," Fiona said.

"Cyrus has a reputation on the subreddit for being difficult and manipulative. The main storyline about him at the moment is his custody battle with his ex, Astrid Belmont, over their son Freddy. It's all over the tabloids."

"What a prince," Fiona said.

"It's messy. He abandoned Astrid when she became pregnant, but instead of crawling back like he expected, she hooked up with Isaac J. Emerson, the showrunner. They're married now. There was a wedding photo spread in Vanity Fair.

There's also rumours about a big storyline cliffhanger this year," she added. "Caspian, Cyrus's character, is in the thick of this 'trial by blood' story arc. The fan sites reckon the next run of episodes is all about him. People are invested. If he got fired and they had to recast, they could lose a lot of viewers."

Cal whistled. "Bloody hell. The off-screen drama sounds as unhinged as the actual show."

"It is," Sheri agreed. "There's a lot of tension on set, and rumours suggest Cyrus is causing disruptions."

"So we're stepping into the middle of a celebrity soap opera," Ryan said.

"Essentially," Lee replied. "But with the media sniffing around, this needs a delicate touch." She glanced at Ryan as she emphasised 'delicate'. Probably she already regretted handing him the assignment.

Ryan clenched his jaw. "Has Sophie been poking her nose in?"

"Someone saw her in Buxton, questioning crew members."

Ryan tapped a finger on the desk. "What do we have? Any evidence of foul play?"

"No," Lee said. "But given the circumstances and the lack of contact, we need to treat this seriously. Start by speaking with the cast and crew. Mr Emerson is expecting you at the studio. Keep me updated on any developments."

Once she'd left, Ryan said to Sheri, "Your knowledge might give us an edge. Once we get back from the studio, I want you to compile a dossier on the key players and any information you have about recent gossip connected to Cyrus."

She blinked. "Of course, Sir."

"Digit, dig into Cyrus's background. See if anything stands out. Financial issues, known associates, enemies."

Digit made a note.

"Cal, start the boards," Ryan said. "And no Hickey Dock or whatever it's called."

"You're trolling me, right?" Cal shook his head. "How can you not know TikTok?" He headed for the whiteboards.

Ryan ignored him. "Fiona, I need you to coordinate with local law enforcement in Buxton. See where they are with their investigation and make sure we're not duplicating efforts."

He looked around at his team. "Remember, despite the celebrity angle, this is a missing person case. Let's keep it professional and avoid getting caught up in the hype."

As everyone settled into their tasks, Fiona turned to Sheri. "So the show's worth a watch then?"

"It's good if you like elaborate plots, medieval intrigue and people being stabbed in the back. Both literally and figuratively."

"Sounds like an hour upstairs," Ryan said as he started his report on this morning's incident. Did the word 'pompous' have one 'p' or two?

Fiona came up beside him. "Are you all right?"

"Why wouldn't I be?"

She gave him a look he knew well. It said, *Cut the crap.* "High-profile missing person? Another case with paparazzi and big headlines."

He sighed. "I can handle it. Cyrus will probably turn up drunk in a casino before the end of the day."

"Would be nice for a change."

One could only hope. As Fiona left to call the Buxton station, Ryan couldn't shake the feeling this case would be anything but straightforward.

CHAPTER FOUR

RYAN ALMOST MISSED THE SMALL SIGN FOR SILVERHEATH Studios as the windscreen wipers fought a losing battle against the Derbyshire drizzle. He turned the Range Rover onto a narrow road snaking down into an old limestone quarry.

The green fields fell away, replaced by sheer, pale cliffs. A vast, man-made amphitheatre carved into the earth. The cliffs were streaked dark with water and disappeared into the mist that clung to their heights.

"Blimey," Cal murmured from the back seat.

"I've seen these rock faces so many times on TV. I wish the rain would stop so we could see them better," Sheri said from her seat next to Cal.

Cal twisted in his seat, craning his neck. "On telly, it always looks all moody and cinematic. This is more... car wash special."

Sheri let out a laugh.

Fiona glanced back from the front seat. "Welcome to the Peak District. If it's not raining, it's about to."

Ryan steered the SUV around a tight bend, and the headlights swept across a distressed metal sign for 'Silverheath Studios'.

Nestled deep within the quarry's embrace lay the studio complex. Corrugated steel hangers and prefabricated blocks sprawled across the flat pit, connected by angular covered walkways. A severe Victorian building of weathered limestone dominated the entrance, clashing with the modern glass extension tacked onto its side. A high fence topped with razor wire surrounded the perimeter. Small signs mounted on the fence warned of quarry edges, restricted access, and prosecution of trespassers.

"Lovely," Fiona remarked.

"Got to keep out the riff-raff," Cal said.

Ryan eased the SUV up to the security gate. "Unfortunately for them, not today."

A broad-shouldered figure emerged from the guard hut and strode towards the Range Rover. The man's uniform was pressed under his open raincoat, and his security badge gleamed despite the gloom. Somehow, the rain seemed to avoid him.

"Identification," the man demanded.

The greying buzz cut and the man's rigid posture suggested he took his job seriously.

Ryan reached for his warrant card, but Fiona leaned across first. "Hello, Vance."

The guard's eyes flicked to her, a look of surprise crossing his face before he masked it. "Fiona. Didn't expect to see you here." His gaze shifted to Ryan. "Who's this then? Your new bloke?"

Fiona laughed. "God, no." Her eyes widened. "Ah, I mean this is Detective Inspector Hale. My boss." She turned back to Ryan. "DI Hale, this is Vance Mitchell."

The man puffed out his chest. "Head of Security for Silverheath Studios."

Ryan remembered he'd met Vance many years ago. He hadn't been impressed.

Vance's eyes returned to Fiona. "It's been a while."

"It has. You keeping well?"

"Can't complain," he replied, though his tone suggested otherwise. "You sure he's not the reason you left?"

Fiona's cheeks coloured. "Vance, it was years ago and there was no bloke, in this car or otherwise. We both decided to part ways, remember?"

"Did we? Funny, I recall it differently."

Cal snorted, and Sheri elbowed him in the ribs. "What?" he whispered to her, loud enough for everyone to hear. "Bit awkward, innit?"

"We're here on police business." Ryan held out his warrant card, keen to move this along and save Fiona any more embarrassment.

Vance checked the card and grunted. "Mr Emerson is expecting you." He tapped the side of the car and pointed. "Park in the front car park, and I'll escort you to the reception office."

As Vance returned to the guard hut, his ramrod posture was even straighter than before.

Cal leaned forward, a grin plastered across his face. "He seems great. Why ever did you break up with him?"

Sheri whacked him on the arm.

Fiona sighed. "It's none of your business, and it was just a short-lived thing."

"Still hung up on you, by the looks of it."

"Drop it, Cal," Ryan ordered.

Cal raised his hands. "Just saying."

The gates swung open. Ryan drove through to the car park and pulled into a guest space outside the glass entranceway.

Off to the side were half-built set pieces resembling castle ramparts and medieval villages.

"This place is mental," Cal said. He pulled out his phone.

Before Ryan could stop him, he'd posed for a selfie, angling the phone to capture a half-built turret in the background.

A hand snatched the device from his grasp. Vance must have followed them from the gate at a trot.

"Studio policy forbids unauthorised photography," he said as he pocketed the phone.

"Oi, give that back!" Cal protested. "Mate, my followers are going to riot if I don't post today."

Ryan stepped between them. "Mr Mitchell, return the phone. My officer needs to be contactable at all times."

Vance smirked. "Rules are rules. Can't have behind-the-scenes snaps leaking online. He can have it back when you leave."

"I'll make sure he deletes the photo, and I'll personally guarantee he won't take anymore," Ryan said. "But I need to be able to get in touch with my team on site."

For a moment, it seemed Vance might argue, but then he took the phone from his pocket and handed it back. "Fine. But any more breaches, and I'll report it to your superiors."

"Understood."

Cal erased the image and showed Vance the screen. "Happy?"

Ryan sighed. "When this is over, we're having a chat about why social media and active investigations don't mix."

"All right, all right," Cal grumbled. "I'll tell my followers I'm on a digital detox."

"Half the site's a dead zone anyway," Vance said. He pointed to the towering quarry walls. "Signal's patchy at best.

You'll see folks wandering about like zombies, phones in the air, hoping for a bar or two."

"Inconvenient," Fiona said.

"Adds to the place's charm," Vance replied. "Now, if you'll follow me."

He strode away, leaving an uncomfortable silence in his wake.

"What a dick," Cal muttered.

"We might need that dick before this is through. Try not to antagonise him," Ryan murmured as they followed Vance through the glass doors.

"Hey, I meant to say on the way over. I've been looking at Cyrus's socials," Cal said. He held out his phone screen so the others could see Cyrus Wilde's photo grid. Rows of brooding monochrome portraits and artfully lit red carpet appearances. He tapped a finger on a photo and enlarged it. "This shot in the Shadow Queen's throne room was posted at 23:42 on the night he went missing. Caption says, 'Greatness thrives in adversity,' which sounds like the type of poncy shit he says. But," he scrolled down the feed, "it's a repeat, and he never does repeats. He uploaded the original photo earlier in the month."

Fiona frowned. "Pre-scheduled or by his assistant?"

"Maybe," Cal said. "Wouldn't be the first celeb who batch-posts to look 'relatable'. But maybe someone else had his phone and posted it to mess with the timeline."

Ahead, Vance looked over his shoulder. Ryan suspected the head of security was listening to every word.

They entered a modern reception area with uncomfortable-looking leather and chrome furniture. Publicity photos from the show loomed down from the walls. Taking pride of place was a massive poster promoting the first season of *Crown of Shadows*. Surrounding it, artistic posters displayed the lead characters. Ryan recognised Cyrus Wilde's arrogant smirk in the Caspian Drest poster. He stood in leather and armour with a sword levelled at an unseen enemy, the backdrop a fortress illuminated by lightning. A tagline ran across the bottom:

EVERY KINGDOM NEEDS A TYRANT

"Subtle," Cal said.

Out of the corner of his eye, Ryan saw Sheri pause in front of the Caspian poster. Her wide-eyed gaze travelled over the character, then the tagline. Her hand moved as if to touch it, then dropped back to her side.

Off to one side of the lobby, a lanky man in a black turtleneck leaned on the reception counter, channelling Steve Jobs. His grey hair was swept back and styled with care, but it was the cobalt frames of his glasses that commanded instant attention, jutting from his face in rigid geometric angles. As they approached, Ryan wondered if the man needed the glasses for his vision or if they were more to make a statement. From the way Vance hurried them over, Ryan assumed he must be the showrunner. The head of security had called ahead from the hut.

"Detective Inspector Hale? Isaac J. Emerson, showrunner and executive producer," the man said. His handshake was firm but brief, as if any longer was an unnecessary nicety and a waste of his time.

Ryan nodded. "Mr Emerson. This is my team—"

"DS Bennett, DC Pine, and DC Dewan," Isaac finished as he pointed at each of them. "I've read your files."

Fiona raised an eyebrow. "Our files?"

"Superintendent Toddock did me a favour," Isaac said. He gave a thin smile. "It's important I know who's investigating our... situation. I thought DCI Lee would be with you?"

"She's coordinating the operation from the station," Ryan replied smoothly.

Isaac waved a hand at Vance. "That will be all."

The head of security gave a crisp nod and left.

Ryan studied the man before him. The expensive watch. The artfully casual clothes. Everything about Isaac J. Emerson looked carefully calculated.

"How can we help with your situation, Mr Emerson?"

"Call me Isaac." He glanced around the lobby. "Let's move this discussion to my office."

He beckoned to a young South Indian woman who hovered nearby. She approached with quick, nervous steps, her hands in the pockets of her baggy black hoodie.

"This is Advika, one of our production assistants. I believe you wanted your team to inspect Cyrus's trailer? She can escort them on set while we talk upstairs."

The woman, barely more than a teenager, gave them a shy smile. A neat plait held back her dark hair, and a lanyard with production credentials hung around her neck.

Ryan nodded to Fiona.

"Come on, Cal," Fiona said. "Let's give the DI a break from your charms."

Cal opened his mouth then wisely shut it again.

"I'll take good care of them, Mr Emerson," Advika said in a soft voice hinting at West Country origins.

Isaac gave a dismissive nod. "Detective Inspector, shall we?"

No mention of DC Dewan, Ryan noticed. He turned to Fiona.

"We'll catch up with you later," she told him. She followed Advika with Cal in tow.

Isaac led Ryan and Sheri to an industrial lift at the far end of the lobby.

"So Mr Emerson," Ryan said as they stepped inside. "How long has Cyrus Wilde been missing?"

Isaac scanned a key card and pressed the button for the top floor. "No one has seen him since Saturday evening. He should have been on set Monday morning for the blocking rehearsal of the season climax. When he didn't show, I sent someone to his trailer."

The lift doors opened, and Isaac brought them down a corridor lined with framed awards.

"And?" Sheri prompted.

"Everything his assistant left was still in place. Wardrobe laid out, coffee untouched. No Cyrus."

Without acknowledging his secretary, Isaac led them through the outer office. He stopped at a door with his name etched into a brass plate and pushed it open. "And before you ask, no, I don't think this is one of his usual escapades."

"What do you mean by usual escapades?" Ryan asked.

"This isn't the first time Cyrus has disappeared."

CHAPTER FIVE

Fiona and Cal followed Advika through a maze of production offices and into a tent filled with extras dressed as soldiers, who sat at plastic tables playing cards or scrolling on their phones. They weaved through a jumble of cables and crates. Someone had taped off the worst of the trip hazards, but the discarded piles still made Fiona's fingers itch to sort them into neat, labelled stacks. They emerged onto the backlot. The rain had stopped, and the half-built sets—a crumbling castle wall and the bare timber frames of a medieval village—glistened in the weak afternoon sun.

Advika's walkie-talkie crackled to life for the third time in as many minutes. The young production assistant winced as she listened to the garbled messages.

"Is everything all right?" Fiona asked.

Advika grimaced. "Yes, sorry. Just some weather effects drama. The special effects supervisor has misplaced the fake snow." She looked down as her walkie-talkie squeaked again.

"Oh, God! They can't find the ceremonial dagger for tonight's scene."

She sighed. "Look, if you wait here, I can be back in fifteen minutes tops."

Fiona shook her head. "Don't worry about us. We can find our way to Cyrus's trailer."

"Are you sure?" Advika chewed her lip. "Mr Emerson prefers visitors to be escorted."

"We'll be fine," Fiona assured her. "I'll make sure this one doesn't poke his nose anywhere he shouldn't."

Advika glanced between them, uncertainty etched on her face. "Okay. It's down that lane, last trailer on the left. Big blue one with a gold star on the door. You can't miss it."

"Thanks, love," Cal said.

They watched her jog back the way they'd come.

"Well, here we are, all unchaperoned like," Cal said, sliding his hands into his pockets. "Wanna snoop around before we head to the trailer?"

"Possibly," Fiona replied as her phone rang. She looked down at the name, and her chest tightened. "Just give me a minute."

She answered. "Hi, Nate."

"Hey." Nathan's tone was warm but held an edge she recognised. "Checking you're still on track. Max's teacher said he's been practising his breakfalls all day. Nearly put his foot through the alphabet wall."

The Aikido tournament. She'd written it on the kitchen calendar in red pen, circled it twice. "Nathan, I—"

"He wants you to sit in the front row so you can see his—"

"I'm not going to make it."

Silence stretched down the line.

"We caught a new case."

"Right," Nathan replied, his voice clipped. "And there's no one else who can handle it? For a few hours?"

"It's not that simple. We're over in Buxton..."

"You promised him, Fi. You looked him in the eye and promised."

Fiona turned away from Cal. "That's not fair," she said, her voice low. "You know what this job involves. You knew when you married me and when we agreed to have kids."

"What I know is your son's been counting down the days. He asked me in the car on the way to school if Mum was definitely coming, and I said yes because I believed you when you said you'd be there."

"I'm sorry." The words came out rougher than she intended. She pressed her fingers to her temple. "I am. I'll make it up to him."

"You always say that."

Movement caught her eye. A figure, bulky in what looked like costume armour, ducked behind a stack of metal crates twenty metres away. Her instincts sharpened.

"Nathan, I have to go. Can we talk about this when I get home?"

"Fi..."

"I promise. Tonight." She ended the call and slipped her phone back into her pocket. The guilt sat like a stone in her chest. She turned back to Cal.

"You hungry?" He nodded towards a food truck emblazoned with 'Dragon Bites', its windows steamed up from the heat inside. "Could use a bacon butty before we rummage through a missing actor's undie drawer."

Fiona checked her watch. It had been a long time since breakfast, and she'd skipped lunch because of the Peasley confrontation. "Five minutes. And coffee. They'd better have decent coffee."

As they approached the truck, Fiona felt the prickle of being watched again. She glanced back casually and spotted a head peeking out from behind a large wooden prop. She nudged Cal.

"We've got a tail. Three o'clock, behind the catapult."

Cal didn't look. "You mean the fat bloke dressed like a soldier who's been following us since we left the extras tent. Terrible at hiding. Subtle as a brick through a window."

Fiona's eyebrows shot up.

Cal huffed a small laugh. "You don't grow up on an estate and miss blokes lurking where they shouldn't be."

"Keep walking," Fiona murmured. "Let's see what he does."

They reached the food truck and placed their orders. Their shadow moved closer, now pretending to study a pile of silver shields.

Fiona collected her coffee and the bacon butty while Cal paid. "Let's sit on those chairs." She pointed to a row of plastic chairs under a white gazebo with no sides. "Give our friend a chance to make his move."

They didn't have to wait long. The soldier, dressed in aged leather and tarnished chain mail, entered the tent and sidled up behind them. He stopped nearby and hovered uncertainly.

Fiona whirled around. "What are you doing?"

The man recoiled, gloved hands raised in surrender. A scraggly beard covered his cheeks. "Ah..."

"Who are you?"

"I'm Max Steele, actor. Well, Colin Rogers officially, but I go by Max professionally." He stepped forward and extended his gloved hand.

Fiona ignored it while Cal chuckled into his coffee cup.

"Something funny?" Colin asked. His smile faltered.

Cal said. "Sounds like a male stripper's stage name, is all."

Colin's face fell before he rallied. "My agent thinks it has star quality. Memorable, you know?"

"Why are you following us, Mr Rogers?" Fiona interrupted, using the voice she reserved for lying witnesses and her twin children when they played up.

"You're the detectives investigating Cyrus's disappearance, right? It's all around the set." He leaned forward conspiratorially. "You see, I've got a part coming up. It's small, but pivotal, playing a suspect on Heartbeat."

"Show's been off air for years," Cal pointed out.

"It's a reboot. Anyway, I thought watching real detectives on the job could help with my notes."

"Notes?" Fiona asked.

"Yeah, I thought I could take notes when you found one."

"Found what?"

"A suspect."

Fiona took a deep breath. "Let me get this straight. You're sneaking around the studio following two police officers investigating the disappearance of one of your fellow cast members so you can take notes for your next part?"

"You called me a cast member," Colin said. He stood straighter. The leather of his costume strained over his potbelly.

"Well, Mr Rogers, we can do better than that. Nothing beats first-hand experience, right? DC Pine, please arrest Mr Rogers for suspicious behaviour and hindering a police investigation."

Colin backed away, eyes wide. "I was..." He threw Cal a desperate look.

"You should make yourself real useful, real quick," Cal told him.

"Wait! Maybe I could help with Cyrus? I hear things, you know. Been an extra on *Crown* for two seasons." He tapped his nose. "Got the inside track."

Cal nodded. "What things?"

"Oh, loads." Colin checked no one was in earshot. "Like

Blaise, he's head of costumes. Has a husband but, word is, he's secretly obsessed with Cyrus."

Fiona and Cal shared a look. Fiona noted how quickly Colin had connected Blaise's sexuality to the accusation, as if one explained the other.

"Go on," Fiona said.

Colin leaned closer, practically vibrating. "Rumour is, he's got this notebook filled with love poetry about Cyrus." He lowered his voice. "Maybe even... some photographs."

"And you know this how?" Fiona asked.

"Everyone ignores the extras, and the crew like to gossip. I overheard one of the wardrobe girls... Harriet I think?... she was talking about it. She said she saw it. Blaise thinks nobody knows, but it's the worst-kept secret in costuming." He paused dramatically. "If there's foul play involved, could be your motive right there."

Fiona considered the extra's tale. Bizarre as it was, they couldn't ignore a potential lead. Stalker obsessions sometimes escalated to violence or abduction. "Does this Blaise have access to the set after hours?"

"Oh yeah, all department heads have master keys." Colin nodded eagerly. "And get this, Blaise was working late Saturday. I saw him myself when I left, rolling this massive garment rack into the wardrobe department."

Fiona finished her coffee. "Consider this a warning, Mr Rogers. If I catch you following us again, I will report you to studio security."

"Vance probably gave her his direct line," Cal added with a straight face.

Fiona's eyes narrowed.

"Want me to show you where the costume department is?" Colin offered. "I know a shortcut through the caves."

"It won't be necessary," Fiona said. She stood.

Colin sighed. "Oh. Well, if you need anything, I'm usually hanging around the extras tent. Or you could give me your number? For professional reasons?"

"Pushed your luck far enough, don't you think?" Cal said.

Colin jerked his head, did a weird little bow to the two detectives, and scuttled off in the direction he'd come.

Grabbing Fiona's empty coffee cup, Cal threw it in the bin with his own. "Bad cop suits you."

Fiona rolled her eyes. "Let's find Blaise after we inspect Cyrus's trailer. In case there's more to this than made-up gossip from bored crew members."

CHAPTER SIX

Isaac ushered the two detectives into his office.

The room occupied the entire top corner of the building. Floor-to-ceiling windows offered a view of the quarry edge, where mist still clung to the limestone like a shroud.

A modernist desk of chrome and glass dominated the centre. Behind it, mounted on exposed brick, a neon sign glowed in vibrant blue: 'Genius at Work'. Awards lined a shelf beneath.

Isaac waved at the sign with false modesty. "A silly gift from the crew at the end of season one. I didn't want it, but they insisted."

No one had asked.

Shelves lined the opposite wall, bent under hardback books arranged by height and colour rather than subject or author. Ryan noted their pristine spines, not a crack among them. Kafka, Joyce, and several French titles.

He'd eat his warrant card if Isaac had read any of them.

Sheri caught his eye. A hint of mischief flashed across her face as she turned to Isaac.

"Après avoir lu L'Être et le néant, vous êtes-vous senti plus libéré par les idées de Sartre sur la liberté, ou plus accablé par la responsabilité dont il parle, Monsieur Emerson?" she asked.

Isaac blinked. "I'm sorry?"

"Sartre's famous work 'Being and Nothingness'." She gestured to the shelf. "I asked if, when you read it, you felt more liberated by Sartre's ideas about freedom, or more burdened by the responsibility he speaks of? Since you're such a fan of French philosophy, I figured you might have an opinion."

"Ah." Isaac recovered quickly. "It's been a while since I've delved into its depths. My leisure time is limited these days."

Ryan suppressed a grin. "Let's focus on Cyrus Wilde, shall we?"

Isaac sat in his leather chair and steepled his fingers. "Inspector Hale, Cyrus has form for this sort of thing. Disappearing acts usually involve a hotel penthouse, copious amounts of illegal substances and a bill that makes the studio accountants weep." His fingers curled into fists. "He calls it 'method acting immersion'. We call it being a pain in the arse."

"So why call us in this time?" Ryan planted his hands on the edge of the gleaming desk. Its surface felt cold beneath his palms.

Isaac's gaze flicked to Ryan's scars, then drifted to the misty quarry view. "Because this time feels different. His usual haunts have come up empty. No five-star hotels, no exclusive clubs. A crew member found his mobile yesterday afternoon. They gave it to Advika, who recognised it and passed it to me."

"Where was it found?" Sheri's pen hovered over her notebook.

"Jammed between two rocks down in the old quarry workings. Pure coincidence. The man had gone there to smoke, I believe. The screen's smashed." He paused. "And he left Duchess."

Ryan raised an eyebrow. "Duchess?"

"His cat. Horrible creature, but the man dotes on it. Gets more affection than his own child. Cyrus never goes anywhere without arranging a sitter, a specific feeding schedule, the works. This time? Nothing. The poor creature was locked in his trailer for twenty-four hours before anyone realised."

"Where's the phone now?"

Isaac opened a drawer in his desk and took out a smartphone with a cracked screen inside a clear plastic bag. He placed it on the glass surface.

Sheri stepped forward and produced a larger evidence bag from her satchel.

"Does anyone have a reason to want Mr Wilde out of the picture?" Ryan asked.

Isaac gave a humourless laugh. "Inspector, it would be a shorter list if you asked who doesn't want to see the back of him. Cyrus collects enemies like I collect first editions." He gestured to the bookshelves. "He's lucky his talent for antagonising people is surpassed by his acting abilities. Like it or not, Caspian Drest is the reason people tune in. You cannot have *Crown of Shadows* without its bastard prince. The audience will forgive a lot if the villain keeps them entertained."

Ryan leaned forward. "Should you be on my list? You're married to his ex-girlfriend. I hear there's a custody battle over their son."

Isaac's lips pulled back in what Ryan guessed was supposed to be a smile. "Astrid and me getting together is water under the bridge. Memories are short in this industry, and it's very incestuous. Besides," he spread his hands wide, radiating smug satisfaction, "I got the girl, didn't I? Cyrus lost. Why would I need him gone?"

"People hold grudges," Ryan observed.

"Perhaps." Isaac tapped a finger on his desk. "But if you're looking for more immediate conflict, Piper gave him quite the mouthful the afternoon before he disappeared. Very public spat on set."

"Piper Stone?" Sheri prompted.

"Our leading lady. Fiery temperament. They have a... complicated dynamic. Cyrus has been lobbying me to replace her, telling anyone who'll listen she's past her prime. Piper is less than impressed." He chuckled as if the drama amused him. "Then there's Margot Ellison. Set decorator. Talented girl, but sensitive."

Ryan sensed evasion. "Sensitive how?"

Isaac rubbed his temples. "She made a complaint against Cyrus last season."

"What type of complaint?" Ryan pushed.

Isaac sighed. "A sexual harassment allegation."

Sheri looked up from her notebook, eyes narrowed.

"And what happened?" Ryan pressed.

"We handled it internally," Isaac said. "A misunderstanding. HR mediated. Everyone moved on."

"Swept under the rug, you mean?" Ryan met Isaac's gaze.

Isaac shifted in his chair. "These productions are delicate ecosystems, Inspector. Sometimes, for the greater good, compromises are made. Time is money, and a scandal helps no one." He looked over at Sheri. "You understand the complexities in these types of situations, I'm sure, Constable?"

"It's Detective Constable Dewan," Ryan snapped before Sheri could lunge over the desk and throttle the man. She looked like she wanted to. "And these 'situations' have names and legal rights."

"Of course." Isaac raised his hands in surrender. "I'm merely explaining the process. The complaint was investigated thoroughly, and no disciplinary action was taken."

Ryan exchanged a glance with Sheri, trying to convey without words that they'd circle back to this after the investigation had concluded. "Any other incidents worth mentioning?"

Isaac shifted again. "There was a minor disagreement last week about Cyrus's stunt work. Just him being his normal prima donna self. But it was resolved. He understands we need to keep pushing to be bigger, better than the other one... you know, the one with the dragons."

"You mean—" Sheri began.

"Don't say it," Isaac interrupted. "It's a dirty word around here after Carlyn Gladding from Vanity Fair called us 'a pale imitation with all the charm of a Renaissance fair porta-potty.' The nerve of that parasite after I took her to Nobu." The smarmy smile returned. "But I digress."

"We'll need to speak with both Ms Stone and Ms Ellison," Ryan said.

"Of course." Isaac steepled his fingers again. "Unfortunately, most of the principal cast and key crew are filming on location today. Up on Chrome Hill. If Cyrus doesn't turn up in the meantime, I'll ensure Piper and Margot are available first thing tomorrow morning. Will this suffice?"

"It'll have to," Ryan said. "But delays cost you money, don't they, Mr Emerson? Every hour Cyrus is missing—"

The office door swung open. A slender blonde woman entered. A small, dark-haired boy clutched her hand.

Isaac's demeanour softened. He rose from his chair. "Ah, darling. Inspector Hale, Detective Constable Dewan, allow me to introduce my wife, Astrid Emerson. And this," he ruffled the boy's hair as the kid ducked away, "is Freddy."

Astrid held out her hand limply. Ryan gave it an awkward shake. "I still go by Astrid Belmont professionally," she told them.

Opening desk drawer again, Isaac pulled out a tablet. He handed it to the boy, who took it without a word then climbed onto the leather couch on the far wall. Their movements suggested it was a common occurrence.

Ryan watched the boy slump onto the expensive couch, the tablet already glowing in his hands. Dark hair, sharp cheekbones and a certain dismissive set to the mouth even at his tender age. The resemblance to the missing actor was striking.

Hmm... that one's going to be a handful in a few years. Ryan turned his attention back to the woman. Astrid Belmont. Poised, elegant, with a hint of fragility around her eyes that didn't quite match the calculating glint within. She arranged herself on the arm of Isaac's chair. Isaac's hand moved around her waist and pulled her closer. The woman leaned away unconsciously.

"Ms Belmont," Ryan said, "given your past relationship with Mr Wilde, we'd like to ask you a few questions when you have a moment."

Astrid waved a delicate hand. "Oh, Inspector, call me Astrid. Anything to help find Cyrus. Of course. We can talk right now if it's convenient?" All polite attentiveness as she looked from him to Sheri. A performer waiting for her cue. Ryan suspected the unfolding drama thrilled her.

She turned towards the office door. "Janet!"

Isaac's PA appeared a moment later. A harassed-looking woman with a tight bun and a long face. "Please take Freddy into your office. Find him some crayons or something. Sweetie, mummy needs to have a word with the detectives."

Janet looked from Astrid to Isaac. Her expression suggested she was unimpressed to play babysitter. Probably not the first time. Isaac gave a barely perceptible nod, and Janet sighed. "Come on then, Freddy." The boy slid off the couch without protest and followed her out with his eyes still glued to the screen. The door clicked shut behind them.

Astrid turned back, her face set in an expression of weary resilience. "Please ask whatever you need. Though I doubt I can tell you much. Cyrus and I... we haven't been close for a long time." She glanced at Isaac. "Isaac saved us, Freddy and me. After Cyrus left when I was eight months pregnant." She trailed off, letting the implication hang in the air. Cyrus, the abandoner. Isaac, the saviour.

"How were things between you and Mr Wilde recently?" Sheri asked. Her pen scratched across the page.

"Civil," Astrid replied. She smoothed down her floaty dress. "For Freddy's sake. Cyrus can be..." She paused, searching for the right word. "A shitty person. He was a terrible boyfriend. But he's still Freddy's father, and I want him to be a part of his life." Ryan caught the slight hesitation, the careful calibration of her words. Rehearsed, hollow. He wondered if she'd been cultivating Isaac even before Cyrus exited the picture.

"There's a custody hearing pending?" Ryan prompted.

Astrid's sculpted eyebrows drew together. "Yes. Cyrus decided he wanted more access. It's been very stressful." She sighed. "He couldn't stand seeing Freddy happy with Isaac. He's jealous, of course. My sweetie pie—sorry I mean Isaac—is everything Cyrus pretends to be. Successful, powerful, respected. Cyrus can't stand it."

Isaac preened at her words and stroked his wife's leg. Ryan fought the urge to roll his eyes.

Astrid placed a hand almost possessively on her lower abdomen, and the fabric of her dress fell over a gentle curve that hadn't been obvious. Her eyes met Ryan's, a triumphant glint replacing the earlier fragility. "And soon, we'll have a child of our own."

Ryan watched Isaac's chest puff out as the hand around Astrid's waist tightened. "We're so excited, but I'm sure the announcement was very triggering for Cyrus," the showrunner said.

The entire scene felt choreographed.

"Congratulations," Sheri said.

"And do you have any idea where Cyrus could be?" Ryan asked.

Astrid shook her head. "No, sorry."

"Right." Ryan stood. He doubted half of what he'd heard was true. He pulled two cards from his wallet and handed one to each. "If either of you thinks of anything that might help us locate Mr Wilde, please call."

Isaac took the card with a nod. "Of course, Inspector. Anything you need."

Astrid accepted hers with a faint, enigmatic smile. "We want him found safe, Inspector. For Freddy."

Outside in the corridor, Ryan waited until they were well out of earshot before turning to Sheri. "Thoughts?"

"On our picture-perfect couple? I counted at least three instances where her body language to her 'sweetie pie' contradicted her words."

They walked in silence down the metal staircase and back out into the grey afternoon.

The towering stage warehouses circled the yard like silent witnesses. Ryan glanced at Sheri. Her gaze fixed straight ahead.

"Didn't enjoy Emerson's take on workplace harassment?" he asked.

Her lips pressed together. "It's not..." She stopped. "I don't want to get into it, Sir." She took a deep breath and looked away towards the quarry walls, her gaze lost somewhere in the stark landscape. Or perhaps in memories Ryan knew nothing about.

Ryan snorted. "Genius at Work."

Sheri laughed. "It's so pretentious, but everything in the film industry is about cultivated personas. They only work if people buy into the myth."

He considered her words. "Let's scratch under the shiny surface and see what dirt we can uncover."

CHAPTER SEVEN

Fiona stepped inside Cyrus Wilde's trailer and stopped. Not a trailer, a mobile palace. Custom wood panelling trimmed in brass lined the walls, accented by recessed lighting. A television dominated one wall above a full bar and beyond it, a stainless-steel kitchen gleamed with expensive appliances. Through the bedroom door, silk sheets draped an unmade king-sized bed.

Cal whistled. "Blimey. Bit different from those." He thumbed his finger at the window.

Fiona glanced out at the crew's cramped white cabins lined up like Lego bricks.

"Bet you have silk sheets, though." Fiona pulled on a pair of latex gloves.

"Guilty." Cal laughed as he peered into the ensuite. "Bet the shower pressure is way better than the dribble at my flat."

"Right," Fiona said. "You take the bedroom, I'll start with the living area."

Everything screamed luxury, yet the space felt sterile.

Fiona's mantlepiece at home was crammed with family photos, while the trailer had no photos or personal items. Only a pile of magazines with Cyrus's face on the covers.

Five minutes of methodical searching yielded nothing but a stack of old yearbooks from Highfields School. There were no signs of a struggle or obvious clues about where Cyrus might have gone. No convenient diary left open to reveal his plans.

Cal opened a tall cupboard in the kitchenette. A blur of cream and brown fur launched itself out with a demonic hiss, claws extended.

"Bloody hell!" Cal stumbled back as the creature landed on his shoulder. He grabbed for it and earned a row of thin red scratches down his hand. The cat leapt down and darted under the bed frame.

Fiona stifled a laugh. "You found the cat."

Cal inspected the damage. "Can cats give you tetanus?"

They peered under the bed. Two startling blue eyes glared back from the shadows, followed by a hiss and a swipe of claws. Cal looked at Fiona.

"I'm more of a dog person," she said.

"All right, tiger," Cal said. "You stay there then."

Fiona turned to the kitchen. Unlike the pristine surfaces elsewhere, the fridge door was plastered with hand-scribbled Post-it notes. Most were reminders. *D's night shoot - alt takes, stunt rehearsal - contract, Duchess Food Millie,* but one note with rows of alphanumeric sequences stood out.

SSPD-234

SSPD-562

SSPD-621

SSPD-798

"Cal, come look at this."

He appeared at her shoulder, dabbing at his wounds with a tissue. "Wait, what am I looking at?"

"I'm not sure. Could be nothing, but..." She gestured at the note.

Cal pulled out his phone and snapped several photos of the fridge, then close-ups of the individual notes. "I'll send these to Digit. If anyone can make sense of random numbers and letters, it's him."

There was a knock at the trailer door. Advika Patel poked her head in, followed by a young woman Fiona hadn't seen before. The newcomer was plain, almost mousy, with no make-up and light brown hair pulled back in a simple clip. Yet something about her clothes demanded attention. She'd paired a stylish silk blouse in a vibrant floral print with tailored trousers that hung perfectly. Expensive, deliberate choices at odds with her bare face.

"Sorry to interrupt," Advika said, her professional smile in place. "Took longer than I thought. This is Millie Higgins, Mr Wilde's personal assistant."

Advika's walkie-talkie squawked. She sighed and pressed the side button. "Patel here... Missing troll head? Understood." She turned back to Fiona and Cal. "So sorry, I'll be outside if you need me. Millie knows everything about Mr Wilde's schedule." She gave Millie an encouraging look and disappeared.

Millie stood awkwardly just inside the door, hands clasped. Her eyes searched the trailer's interior.

"Miss Higgins," Fiona said gently. The girl looked like she was about to bolt. "I'm DS Bennett, this is DC Pine. Would you mind answering a few questions about Cyrus Wilde?"

Millie chewed her lip. "Okay, but could you help me get Duchess into her carrier first? I'm meant to take her to Cyrus's mum's house, but she hates me. The cat, I mean, not Mrs Brown. And I'm allergic."

Cal held out his scratched hand. "Tell me about it. Little git already had a go at me."

Horror crossed Millie's face. "Oh, God. I'm so sorry. Is that assaulting a police officer?"

"I'm not going to press charges against a cat."

"She does that to everyone. If you try to pet her or even look at her, really."

"Hopefully, she'll warm to me." Cal rolled up his sleeves. "Okay, Duchess. Round two."

Fiona watched as Cal coaxed the Siamese cat out from under the bed with soft words and a discarded pen lid as a lure. Millie stood well back, carrier open at arm's length. After a brief standoff and another near-miss swipe, Cal bundled the cat into the carrier. Millie snapped the door shut with relief.

"Nice," she said. She set the carrier near the door.

"Happy to help," Cal replied.

Fiona stepped back and let him take the lead. Millie still seemed wary, but Cal's easy charm and their shared battle with Duchess appeared to forge a connection.

"So, Millie..." Cal leaned against the counter. "How long have you worked for Mr Wilde?"

"Three months." Her voice was flat. "Feels like three years."

"Not enjoying the glamour of showbiz?"

A hollow laugh escaped her. "Glamour? It's fetching dry cleaning that costs more than my car and listening to him complain the Evian water isn't room temperature. I thought..." She hesitated and looked down at her hands. "I thought it would be exciting. A foot in the door. But it's abuse, mostly. So much shouting. He threw a script at my head last week because his almond milk latte wasn't frothy enough."

"That bad, eh?" Cal sympathised.

"When I started, I was over the moon. Working for a proper celebrity! My mum was so impressed." Millie's expression soured. "The worst is the stupid demands at all hours. He made me reorganise his entire wardrobe at 3:00 am because he couldn't sleep and decided his winter jumpers were giving him 'negative energy'. The man's psychotic."

"Did he ever make you feel uncomfortable? Any inappropriate remarks?" Fiona asked, remembering Sheri's comments at the briefing.

Millie snorted and gestured at her plain face. "Not his type, am I? He likes them gorgeous and curvy. The only upside to looking like me in this place."

Her matter-of-fact self-deprecation made Fiona wince. Working in this industry was bound to do a number on anyone's self-esteem.

"Lucky escape, if you ask me," Cal said with a frown. "Though that suggests others haven't been so fortunate?"

Millie nodded. "The pretty ones have to be careful."

"What do you mean?"

"The extras, the make-up girls, anyone young and hopeful." Millie shrugged. "But they stick together now. After the Margot thing."

"The Margot thing?" Cal echoed.

"Margot Ellison. She's a set decorator. Super tall and gorgeous." Millie picked at a loose thread on her blouse. "I shouldn't say anything, he's my boss."

Fiona smiled. "That's a beautiful blouse you're wearing, Millie. The colours really suit you."

The unexpected compliment transformed Millie's face. Her eyes lit up, and a genuine smile replaced the wary expression. "Oh! Thank you. I love fashion. It's vintage Dior. I found it at a charity shop in Matlock." She smoothed the fabric almost reverently.

The joy was fleeting. A weary sigh followed. "Anyway, I'm the third PA Mr Wilde's had this year. The last one, Chloe? She works at Costa Coffee in Chesterfield now. Cyrus got her blacklisted from the industry. Said she stole from him."

"Did she?" Cal asked.

"I doubt it. Cyrus destroys people for fun. Especially if they inconvenience him or forget to separate his whites and darks properly." She ran a hand over the granite worktop. "I just need to stick it out. Six months, maybe a year. Get a decent reference, then move on and get a proper job in the costume department or in production, like Advika."

Fiona exchanged a glance with Cal. Lasting six months sounded like a long shot.

Millie seemed to read her thoughts. "People think they're special, these celebrities." She pointed at a magazine with Cyrus's airbrushed face. "But underneath all the fakery and polish, they're just like us. Probably worse." She gestured to the stack of yearbooks. "His agent wanted an 'early days' pic of Cyrus for some puff piece. Sent me down to his mum's place to dig them out. I spent hours going through dusty boxes." She rolled her eyes. "Complete waste of time. I found some photos. Awkward teenage Cyrus, with dodgy hair and spots. When I showed them to him, he had a fit. Said they made him look 'unrelatable'. He made me use a gym selfie he took last month and claim it was from when he was a teenager. Can you believe it? Now I've got to get rid of these before someone splashes gawky Cyrus all over the internet." She picked up the yearbook at the top of the pile. She flicked through the pages and then tossed it back down.

"When was the last time you spoke to him?" Cal asked, returning to the matter at hand.

Millie frowned. "Saturday evening. About nine-thirty? He called because he wanted the remote for the telly. It was on the ledge, where it always is." She sighed. "That's the weirdest thing, actually. Him being so quiet."

"How so?" Fiona asked.

"He calls me constantly. Texts every five minutes. Needs this, needs that. Complaining about the scripts, the food, Piper Stone breathing too loud." She tapped her phone as if to check he hadn't messaged and tucked it into her back pocket. "And he lives on social media. Always posting. He rages if someone disses him in the comments."

"So you don't manage his social media?" Cal asked.

She shook her head. "Won't let anyone near it. For his phone to be off, or for him not to be calling me demanding something every five minutes... It's not like him. I'm starting to think something bad might have happened."

A sudden scrabbling noise came from the carrier as the trailer door opened and Advika reappeared, clipboard in hand. "Troll head located."

Duchess yowled through the mesh, her tail twitching.

"Coming, Duchess." Millie sighed. "Even the cat bosses me around." She gathered up the yearbooks and balanced them under one arm, then she picked up the vibrating cat carrier with her other hand.

"Millie," Fiona said, "if you think of anything else, call me." She pulled out her business card.

Hesitating, Millie looked down at her full hands, then back at Fiona's card.

Cal went to help, but Advika beat him to it. "Give those to me."

"Thanks, Advika." Millie handed over the yearbooks. "They just need to go in the skip."

"Sure."

Millie took the card Fiona offered. She gave a brief, uncertain smile before manoeuvring herself and the cat carrier out of the trailer.

———

RYAN SPOTTED Fiona and Cal emerge from between two equipment trucks and raised a hand. Sheri fell into step beside him as they crossed the backlot.

"Any luck?" he asked.

"Maybe," Fiona said. "A few codes on a Post-it. They might be something. And a lead on the head costume designer, who may have an unhealthy interest in Cyrus. We were about to go looking for him."

"He won't be here," Ryan replied. "All the people we need to talk to are on a location shoot until tomorrow. We'll head back to the station for now and regroup."

Fiona nodded.

Something was off. She looked distracted as her gaze flickered to her phone.

"Everything all right?" Ryan asked.

"I'm fine."

"Her kid's got something on," Cal said. "She's going to miss it."

Fiona shot him a look that could have curdled milk.

Cal shrugged. "What? You were standing two feet away. I can't turn my ears off."

Ryan glanced at his watch. "We can drop you off on the way. Where is it?"

"Sir, it's fine. I don't need special treat—"

"Cal can fill us in on what you found." Ryan kept his tone casual but left no room for argument. "Why miss it if you don't have to?"

Fiona hesitated. For a moment, he thought she might protest further. Then her shoulders dropped. "Thank you. I'd appreciate that."

As they walked back towards the car park, Ryan watched her pull out her phone and tap out a quick message. The relief on her face was obvious.

He wondered how long she could keep both plates spinning before one of them crashed.

CHAPTER EIGHT

RYAN SURVEYED THE LARGE WHITEBOARD. A BLOWN-UP photo of Cyrus Wilde dominated the centre, his name printed beneath in DC Cal Pine's tidy letters. The rest of the team slumped in their chairs with mugs of lukewarm tea or coffee clutched in their hands. Time to go through what they knew. Or, more accurately, what they didn't.

"Right," Ryan began. He gestured at the board. "Cal, you're on marker duty again."

Cal approached the whiteboard and popped the cap off a black marker with a flourish.

"Let's get the basics down first. Our missing person." Ryan pointed to the photo. "Cyrus Wilde. Age twenty-seven. Lead actor and nasty bastard from the sound of things."

Cal wrote it all under the name, leaving off Ryan's last statement. As he reached up, his shirt cuff slipped and flashed the small yellow-and-black worker bee inked on his wrist.

"Digit, what have you got for us?"

Adjusting his wire-rimmed glasses, Digit consulted his screen. "Cyrus Wilde is a stage name he adopted when he moved to London. He was born with the far more pedestrian appellation of Cyrus Brown in Matlock, Derbyshire, on 12 August 1998. According to an interview, his mother was a big fan of Billy Ray Cyrus and named him after the singer, though I couldn't confirm this."

Cal paused his writing. "Jesus, Billy was right there, and she went with Cyrus?"

"His birth date makes him a Leo. Interesting because Leos are overrepresented in the acting profession by approximately 12.7%. One could hypothesise it's due to their astrological traits of attention-seeking behaviour, a domineering nature, and excessive ego." Digit's leg bounced. A sure sign he was heading off on a mental tangent. "Multiple peer-reviewed studies have found no correlation between birth month and personality traits, despite the persistent cultural mythology suggesting otherwise."

Ryan cleared his throat.

"Ah yes, Cyrus. He's a Leo. No siblings. Which could also correlate with his tendency—"

"Digit. Highlights only."

"Right, moving on. His parents are Carol Brown, a part-time receptionist at a local welding company, and David Brown, a retired plumber. They still reside together in Matlock. He attended Highfields School. No significant juvenile record beyond a caution for shoplifting at age fifteen. Lead in the school plays, then a few commercials. Accepted into the London Academy of Music and Dramatic Art. After graduating, he headlined some plays to critical acclaim but no recognition outside of traditional acting circles. During this time, he had a couple of bit parts in various BBC dramas, including Northern Line, where he met Astrid Belmont. He didn't become famous until he landed the role of Caspian Drest on *Crown of Shadows* three years ago."

"Anything else relevant?" Ryan asked.

"He frequently features in magazines and gossip columns, often for his behaviour or excesses. His breakup with Astrid Belmont, who was heavily pregnant at the time, was tabloid fodder for weeks, with both camps leaking information to the papers." Digit pushed his glasses back up his nose. "Financially solvent, though online analysis suggests a high burn rate indicating potential future instability if his income decreases." He tapped his screen. "I also uncovered rumours online that he has disappeared without notice before. Four separate occasions over the last two years."

"Isaac Emerson also confirmed this," Ryan replied.

Sheri leaned forward. "So is this another tantrum?"

"Possibly," Ryan conceded. "But I think the hidden smashed phone changes things."

Cal nodded along. "Millie, his PA, confirmed he's glued to it. And then there's the abandoned cat."

"Leaving both behind feels... off," Sheri said. She retrieved the bagged phone from her bag and gave it to Digit. "It wouldn't power on. The battery's dead, on top of the physical damage."

"Can you get anything off it?" Ryan asked.

Digit took the bag and studied the shattered screen. "The physical damage is extensive, but the internal components might be operational. Data retrieval could be possible, dependent on the encryption protocols and the integrity of the memory storage."

"Have a go. Texts, calls, location data, anything you can salvage."

Digit nodded and placed the bagged phone on the desk beside him.

"Okay." Ryan turned back to the board. "Let's assume Cyrus hasn't wandered off."

The team worked through the list of suspects while Cal recorded it all on the whiteboard. The board filled up. Names, connections, potential motives. A convoluted web surrounded a missing actor who sounded like more trouble than he was worth.

Cal used the eraser to rub out the crooked line connecting Astrid to Cyrus and redrew it.

Ryan surveyed their work. Piper, the leading lady. Isaac, the showrunner. Astrid, Cyrus's ex and mother to his son. Margot, the set designer. Blaise, the head costumer. A collection of people tied to Cyrus Wilde through ambition, resentment, fear, or fractured love. Somewhere in the mix, Ryan hoped, lay the truth about Cyrus's whereabouts.

"All right." He rubbed his tired eyes. "It's getting late. Finish up what you're working on, and then we'll pick this up fresh in the morning. Cal, custody battle details. Digit, start background checks on everyone we've listed. The plan is to start formal interviews tomorrow. Sheri, schedule Piper Stone, Margot Ellison and Blaise Kerrington first thing. Coordinate with the production company regarding their availability. We'll meet back here at eight and see what tomorrow brings."

<hr>

RYAN SLIPPED his arms into his brown overcoat and winced as the movement pulled at his damaged shoulder. The day had begun with an aggressive MP, continued with a high-profile misper, and would likely end with a sleepless night as he stared at the ceiling and pondered how he'd royally stuffed up the first, and would probably stuff up the second.

Everyone but Digit had left. Lines of code scrolled up the screen as his fingers flew over the keyboard.

Ryan waved his hand between Digit and his screen. Digit pulled off his headphones.

"Don't stay too late, Digit. It can wait till tomorrow."

Digit nodded but went back to his work. Ryan doubted the detective constable would follow his instructions, but at least he'd tried.

As he closed the door of the incident room behind him, a familiar voice called out.

"Ryan? Got a minute?"

He turned as Dr Alexis Hope approached, her dark hair tied up in its usual no-nonsense bun and her caramel woollen coat cinched at the waist. A coffee stain marked the lapel. She clutched a worn leather messenger bag against her side, her face set in the pinched expression he recognised from back when she'd been Jaime's best friend. Her "bearer of bad news" look.

"Lexi. Bit late for you to still be in the building."

Alexis served as the department's consulting psychologist, her presence at the station more frequent as mental health concerns surrounding both suspects and witnesses mounted.

"A consult ran long. Can we talk?" Her gaze darted up and down the corridor. "Not here though."

Ryan checked his watch. He was intrigued, but there was a hungry corgi at home. "No problem, but can we keep it quick? Winston needs his dinner."

"Twenty minutes tops. Please, Ryan." The urgency in her voice gave him pause.

"The greasy spoon on Market Street?" he suggested. Between Peasley and Wilde, he hadn't eaten since breakfast.

She smiled, and her shoulders relaxed. "Sure."

They walked down the road and into the diner.

The Bell Diner smelled of fried onions and grease. Ryan slid into a vinyl booth with his back to the wall, an ingrained habit after fifteen years in the police. He shifted, and the cracked red seat squeaked in protest.

"Sausage and mash, extra gravy." The words were out of Ryan's mouth before the tired server had stopped at their table. "And tea strong enough to stand a spoon in."

Alexis ordered a green tea and waited for the server to shuffle away.

"There's something I need your help with," she said.

Ryan stretched his legs under the table. "Professional or personal?"

"Professional. And sensitive." She took a manila folder from her bag. "Do you remember a case from a decade ago? A boy named Matthew Benson, who was murdered by his mother? It's the ten-year anniversary this month, so there's been some news coverage."

"The one in Tansley?"

Alexis nodded.

"I remember hearing about it. Wasn't involved, though. I'd transferred to London by then."

The server returned with their drinks. Ryan wrapped his hands around the mug and let the warmth seep into his palms.

Alexis waited until she left. "Matthew was twelve. Stabbed multiple times with a pair of sewing scissors in their kitchen. The neighbour found her holding the boy, covered in blood. The husband called the police, and the boy's mother, Bee Benson, confessed."

Ryan added milk to his tea. "So what's the problem? Are the brass looking for a cold case review?"

"Not officially." Alexis dropped her voice. "Bee never gave a reason. Throughout the entire investigation, the trial, everything, her only response to why she'd done it was, 'I'd rather not say, dear.' That's all she's said in the last ten years."

That specific phrase triggered his memory. It had captured

the public's imagination, and the press had dined out on it for months. Ryan's old boss Lampton, a man who still considered Ryan the human equivalent of a persistent verruca, had been the Senior Investigating Officer. Any involvement in one of Lampton's old cases would be like poking a badger in its sett with a sharp stick.

"And?" Ryan asked, already sensing the inevitable undertow.

"I have a patient," Alexis continued. "Lynsey Cooper. She's been having sessions with me for years, but she never mentioned she was Bee Benson's next-door neighbour. Lynsey's dying of cancer and in hospice care. She came to me yesterday and said she couldn't die without clearing her conscience. Bee Benson was with her that morning. The timing for her to have killed Matthew doesn't line up."

Ryan's food arrived, a mountain of mash swimming in brown gravy with four fat sausages plonked on top. He considered Alexis's words as he dug in.

"She confessed," he said.

"Lynsey believes Bee's confession is impossible."

Ryan paused, fork halfway to his mouth. "Why?"

"She wouldn't tell me the specifics. Said she'd only talk to someone from the police who was prepared to listen. To someone who could free Bee." Alexis leaned forward. "Ryan, I've treated this woman for years. She isn't prone to flights of fancy, and she doesn't have much time left. Weeks at most, possibly days."

Ryan knew firsthand how quickly those last days could disappear. "So based on this you think Bee Benson is innocent?"

"I think there's a strong possibility she was protecting someone. Lynsey's testimony, if it's credible, could blow apart the official narrative." Alexis's gaze was steady. "Lampton closed the case fast. Maybe too fast? Bee's quiet refusal to elaborate was all he needed."

Ryan ran a hand over his face. Cyrus Wilde's disappearance was already a high-wire act over a pit of vipers. Reviewing a decade-old murder without official sanction, especially one Lampton had signed off, was close to professional suicide. Lee would have his guts on a plate.

"Lexi, I'm neck-deep in a high-profile missing persons case right now. The media are sniffing about, the brass are twitchy, and I accused a sitting MP of domestic violence to his face this morning. I'm not sure this is the time for me to stick my neck out."

"Lee briefed me. I know about Cyrus Wilde. It's possible he could just turn up, right?"

Ryan nodded.

"I wouldn't ask you to look into it now if Lynsey had more time." Her expression softened, but not her resolve. "This was a twelve-year-old boy, Ryan. Who was stabbed to death. And the woman convicted of his murder might have taken the fall for the actual killer." She paused. "If it were Jaime... if there was even a whisper of fresh evidence, a reliable testimony that was missed?"

She didn't know about Jaime's horseshoe necklace delivered to Fiona at the station and the lab report that had told him sod all he didn't already know. Epithelial cells on the clasp and a DNA profile matching his still missing wife. No foreign profile and no prints. The padded envelope had been dropped in a suburban Chesterfield post office box a few days before it landed on Goody's desk, sorted and scanned like any other bit of post.

Whoever sent it had waited twelve years, then been careful enough to leave him nothing but confirmation of what he already knew in his heart. His wife hadn't walked out on him, and someone out there knew what had happened.

He opened his mouth to tell her, then shut it again when Alexis pulled out an A4 photo of a young boy with an impish grin and placed it in front of him.

He sighed. She knew which buttons to press. The raw, unhealed wound of Jaime's absence or any case involving a child.

"Bee Benson has served ten years of a twenty-year sentence. If she's innocent, every extra day she spends in prison is an injustice. If Lynsey's story dies with her..."

He pushed his plate away, appetite gone. "Lampton will see this as a personal attack."

"Since when has that stopped you from doing what's right? Just talk to Lynsey. That's all I ask. If you think there's nothing to it, you can walk away."

Ryan let out a slow breath. She had him, and they both knew it. The ghost of Matthew Benson grinned up at him from the photo with bright blue eyes.

He stood, took a handful of banknotes from his wallet, and dropped them on the table. "Give me Lynsey's details. And Bee Benson's. Where she's serving?"

Alexis exhaled, then smiled. "New Hall." She put the photo of Matthew back in the folder and passed it to him. "It's all in there. Thank you, Ryan. I knew I could count on you."

"Don't thank me yet. This could get messy."

CHAPTER NINE

RYAN FOLDED THE MANILA FOLDER AND SHOVED IT INTO the pocket of his overcoat as he approached the station. His mind raced through what investigating such an old case might entail. He'd need access to evidence, witness statements, court transcripts, all without alerting DCI Lee or anybody who might report back to her.

Cold cases were hard enough with full departmental support. Going at this alone, with Cyrus Wilde's disappearance hanging over him, was impossible.

Ryan found the incident room still lit. He pushed open the door. The scent of Digit's peculiar matcha tea hung in the air. As he'd predicted, DC Asare remained hunched over his bank of monitors, his fingers a blur across the keyboard. Rows of social media feeds scrolled on one screen. Instagram, TikTok, X, a waterfall of digital noise, all related to Cyrus Wilde. On the other screen, CCTV footage from the studio scrubbed past.

Ryan leaned against the doorjamb and watched Digit for a moment. He should go home. Feed Winston and try to get some sleep before another day wrestling with slippery celebrities and their even slipperier secrets.

But the folder Alexis had given him sat heavy in his pocket, and the image of that bright-eyed boy staring up from the photograph had already lodged itself in his brain.

"Thought I told you not to stay late," Ryan said.

Digit nearly jumped out of his skin. He yanked his headphones off. "Technically, you told me not to stay 'too' late, which is a subjective temporal designation. It's only 20:13, which for me is merely moderately late."

Ryan removed his coat and hung it over the back of a chair, then stood behind Digit. "Okay. What are you doing with the footage?"

The detective constable's fingers resumed their lightning-fast dance on the keys. "I've created a piece of software that identifies the human form or anything out of place in the footage. It alerts me if someone enters the frame."

As if to illustrate his point, the computer beeped and the footage slowed to real time. A pair of crew pushed a trolley loaded with cables into the frame, then out the other side.

"There is data corruption in the footage from the only surveillance camera with an unobstructed sightline to the entrance of Mr Wilde's trailer. The entire file exhibits uniform white noise interference with zero recoverable visual information. My program is analysing the studio's six primary feeds operational between twenty-one hundred hours and zero-three hundred hours on the night in question."

Ryan's shoulders tightened. He'd heard a version of that story before. Twelve years ago, the one traffic camera that might have caught Jaime's car had suffered a "data corruption event". An hour of footage gone, sandwiched between hours of clear morning traffic. Forensics had blamed it on a damaged SD card. Lampton had shrugged and moved on.

Ryan slid into the chair beside Digit. He weighed his next words carefully.

"Digit, can you do me a favour?" He paused, still unsure whether he should involve anyone else in this. "Off the books?"

The young detective's fingers stilled, his eyes locked on his screen. "What kind of favour?"

"The kind I need to stay between us," Ryan replied, lowering his voice despite the empty room. "At least for now."

Ryan felt an unfamiliar prickle of discomfort. He preferred to carry his own burdens. Asking for help, especially from a junior officer on a case that had the potential to detonate careers, went against his instincts.

But he couldn't find what he needed without help.

Digit turned his chair to look Ryan in the eyes, a rare gesture showing he understood the gravity of the request. "I'm listening."

Ryan pulled the folder from his coat pocket and placed it on the desk between them. "Matthew Benson. Twelve years old. Murdered in Tansley ten years ago. His mother, Bee, confessed to killing him with a pair of scissors. Never gave a reason."

Digit's eyes widened. "The 'I'd rather not say, dear' case." At Ryan's surprised look, he added, "I listened to a podcast episode about it recently. The psychological aspects of her refusal to provide a motive make it a notable case study."

"Right. Well, Dr Hope approached me with new information. A neighbour claims she saw something that day that contradicts Bee's confession. Something that might exonerate her."

"Ten years after the fact?" Digit's brow furrowed. "Statistically unusual. Witness recollections degrade by fifty percent after one year."

"The witness is dying. Terminal cancer. She claimed to

Alexis she couldn't take the information to her grave." Ryan ran a hand through his hair. "Look, I need to be straight with you. It was Lampton's case. He closed it fast, and going after it now will be... politically sensitive."

Digit nodded, already processing. "DCI Lampton maintains significant influence within the station and local judiciary. Current Chief Operating Superintendent Harris was Lampton's mentee. Reopening the case officially would require substantial new evidence and likely face significant administrative obstacles."

"Which is why I'd like to keep it quiet." Ryan opened the folder. "Could you analyse the case files for me? And maybe track down if any of the remaining family still live locally?"

Digit stared at the folder. Ryan could practically see the calculations running behind his eyes as he weighed the risks, estimated the time commitments and considered all potential outcomes.

"I'm already running data analysis on seventeen distinct factors related to the Wilde case," he replied. "Adding this would reduce my efficiency on our primary investigation by twenty-two percent or two point three hours."

Ryan sighed. "You're right. Forget I asked. I shouldn't have put you in this position."

"I didn't say I wouldn't do it." Digit dragged the folder over. "I was merely calculating resource allocation. I can adjust my sleep pattern to accommodate both tasks."

"Don't do that. Your brain needs rest."

"Studies show polyphasic sleep can be quite efficient if properly structured." Digit flipped through the folder, scanning each page. "I'll need to access historical case files. The police database architecture from the period utilised a different indexing system. I'll need to write a script to extract the relevant—"

"Digit," Ryan cut him off gently. "I... ah... thank you."

The young detective looked up. "You're welcome, DI Hale. It's a fascinating challenge. Besides, the statistical probability of false confessions in cases involving family members is surprisingly high. Approximately twelve percent of maternal filicide confessions contain significant contradictions or impossibilities when compared with forensic evidence, so there's a chance the answer lies there."

Ryan stood and grabbed his coat off the chair. He hesitated. "We should keep this between the two of us. Until we know whether there's anything worth pursuing. I'll talk to Lynsey first thing tomorrow."

Digit nodded solemnly. "Understood. Information compartmentalisation maintains operational security and prevents premature judgments from compromising the investigation."

"If that means let's try to stop it reaching Lampton's ears, then yes." Ryan walked to the door, then paused. "And Digit?"

"Yes, Sir?"

"Don't stay too late. For real this time."

Digit's lips quirked. "Statistically speaking, Sir, that's unlikely."

CHAPTER TEN

Ryan found Lynsey in a private room at the Matlock hospice. The air was thick with the scent of lilies and antiseptic. He rapped softly on the door frame, the sound loud in the hushed corridor.

The woman in the bed looked up, her hollow eyes brightening.

"Mrs Cooper? I'm DI Hale."

"Call me Lynsey, please." Her voice was a dry whisper, like autumn leaves rustling in a soft breeze. "Thank you for coming, Detective."

The man beside her bed rose stiffly. He was tall and weathered, with kind eyes and a cardigan that had seen better days.

"This is my husband, Greg," Lynsey said.

Greg tucked a crocheted blanket around her thin frame and then patted her hand. "I'll just be outside, love." He turned to Ryan. "You'll not tire her out?"

"I'll keep it brief."

Nodding, Greg closed the door behind him.

A small vase of bright, defiant daisies sat on the bedside

table next to a stack of well-thumbed paperbacks. Framed photographs of a smiling, healthier Lynsey dotted the nearby surfaces. Now, her skin stretched taut over sharp cheekbones and possessed a translucent, papery quality. Her grey hair was sparse but combed. The room was nicer than his mother's had been.

Ryan took Greg's chair next to the bed. "Thank you for agreeing to see me so early. I understand this is difficult."

"Difficult doesn't quite cover it, not after all this time." She gestured with a trembling hand. "But I had to... I couldn't..." She took a shallow breath. "I believe Bee couldn't have killed Matthew."

Ryan leaned forward. "I reviewed the files, but tell me what you remember about that day."

Lynsey's gaze drifted to the window, as if replaying the events in her mind. "It was a bright morning. Warm for early spring. Bee and I had been friends for years, neighbours. We'd had tea out in my garden, just like we did most Saturday mornings. Just our usual natter. We were planning a garden swap later that month. Sharing cuttings, that sort of thing. Bee left mine around half ten. Said she wanted to finish a few bits in the garden before Amos got her started on some chore or another."

Lynsey paused and gathered her strength. "I went back inside to make myself another tea, and I watched Bee in the backyard while the kettle boiled. She was pottering about, tidying up a couple of stray toys the kids had left out, straightening a plant pot. Nothing out of the ordinary. Then she went into her kitchen through the back door, and I heard it."

Her voice cracked. "A scream filled with pure terror. It was Bee."

"What did you do?"

"I dropped my mug on the bench and ran. Didn't even think to knock. I barged straight in through her back door. And there Bee was." Lynsey's eyes filled with tears. "On the floor, clutching Matthew in her arms. Blood everywhere."

She swallowed and winced. "Bee was rocking him and wailing. Then my nurse's training kicked in. I pulled her away and checked Matthew for a pulse, but he was gone. I told Bee I was going to get Amos and call the police."

Her breath hitched. "She grabbed my arm. I remember she left a bloody handprint on the sleeve. She begged me not to say anything for the sake of our friendship. Then she picked up the scissors. I didn't understand what she meant, but she looked so... broken. I agreed. At the time, I put her reaction down to shock. When you've worked in A&E, you see all sorts of responses to trauma."

"What happened next?"

"I shouted for Amos, and eventually he came thundering downstairs from his study."

"He didn't hear her scream?"

"He said later he hadn't."

Ryan made a note. "And how did Amos Benson react when he got to the kitchen?"

"He was bellowing at me about the shouting. Then he saw us and stopped. His face went a sort of mottled purple colour as he looked from Matthew to Bee and then at the bloody scissors in her hand. He didn't rush to comfort her. He just stood there, looking down at his dead son, and then he said, 'What have you done, Beatrice?'"

Lynsey's expression soured. "No yelling, which was very unlike him. Just this calm accusation. Like he was talking about a broken vase, not their child. Looking back, I wondered in the moment if he was coaching her."

"Was anyone else there?"

"Jacob, Bee's brother. He'd been staying with them for a few weeks. Recovering from a work injury, if my memory serves me. He'd been sleeping in the TV room at the front of the house. I remember his face crumpling when he saw Matthew. He rushed to Bee and tried to put his arms around her, but Amos shoved him away. Yelled at him to get out of his house, but my main concern was the children. Hannah and Peter."

"I thought there were only two children?" Ryan asked.

"Peter is Bee's nephew. He was the same age as Matty. Bee's sister Michelle had died suddenly the year before, and the father was a drunk. Peter practically lived at the Bensons, he was there so much." She shook her head. "Then this happened. The poor child."

She paused and took a sip from the glass of water beside the bed.

"When Hannah and Peter appeared in the hallway, I herded them into the front room before they could see inside the kitchen, and put on the telly. Hannah wanted to watch a show called Skins. I don't know why I remember that." She stared into the distance, lost in the memories. "Then the police arrived and Bee confessed straight away. I was too stunned to say anything different in the moment."

"But you tried to tell DI Lampton later?"

A bitter laugh escaped her. "DI Lampton, yes. Despite my promise to Bee, I couldn't keep quiet. The next day I went to the station and told him Bee couldn't have gone into the kitchen, found Matthew, killed him, and then screamed in the time she was out of my sight. He barely looked up from his paperwork."

Ryan nodded. Lampton had always prioritised solve rates over inconvenient truths.

Lynsey's eyes narrowed. "He told me I must be confused. The shock of seeing Matthew's body, the trauma, it must have made me misremember the timing. I was shaking with rage.

The patronising git. But I didn't push it. I felt guilty, you see. For breaking my word to Bee."

Trembling, Lynsey continued. "They had Bee's fingerprints on the scissors, Matthew's blood on her dress, and a confession. Case closed. They searched the rest of the house and took statements from Amos and Jacob. But it felt... cursory. Like they'd already made up their minds." Lynsey met Ryan's gaze, a fierce light in her bloodshot eyes. "But I know what happened. I wasn't confused."

Ryan let the silence sit for a moment. "Did you ever visit Bee in prison? Ask her about it?"

"Yes." The word was a sigh. "Once. About a year after. I had to know. I asked her, 'Bee, why? Why did you say you did it when I know you couldn't have?' And do you know what she said to me?" Lynsey's voice was laced with a fresh wave of hurt. "She said, 'I'd rather not say, dear.' That stupid, infuriating line she kept parroting to the press. To me. Her best friend of fifteen years. I walked out and never went back." Fresh tears traced glistening paths down her gaunt cheeks.

"My one wish is I'd fought harder for her. Made a fuss or gone to the media. I let my best friend go to prison when I knew she was innocent."

He gave her a moment. "The rest of the family, do they still live in the house in Tansley?"

"No, Amos died in a car crash about three years after Bee went to prison. Good riddance, if you ask me, though I shouldn't speak ill of the dead. Hannah had just turned eighteen. She sold the house almost immediately, not that I blame her. After Bee was arrested... I didn't see Jacob or Peter again. Amos was a petty man. I assume he kicked Jacob out. And Peter... well, with Matthew gone and Bee in prison, there was no reason for him to be there anymore." She patted his hand. "So will you look into the case for me, Detective?"

Ryan stood. For a heartbeat, it wasn't Lynsey lying there. It was his mother, her hand reaching for his, asking him to do better, to measure up to her exacting standards.

"One last thing. If it wasn't Bee, who do you think killed Matthew?"

She looked down at her hands and twisted the edge of the crocheted blanket. "Amos used to fly off the handle over the smallest thing. He ruled that house with an iron fist and a Bible. But to kill his own son?" She hesitated. "I struggle to believe it, even though I think he was capable. But Bee... she would only take the fall for family."

Ryan bit back a groan. He couldn't get a confession out of a dead man.

CHAPTER ELEVEN

Ryan and Cal crossed Silverheath's backlot towards the cluster of trailers reserved for the show's stars. The previous day's rain had given way to a crisp, bright morning, the limestone quarry walls lit up by the sun.

"This is massive, you know?" Cal's voice trembled with excitement. "Piper Stone. I mean, did you see her in *Black Tide Rising*? The scene where she—"

"Jesus, next you'll be asking her to autograph your chest." Ryan frowned. He should have brought Sheri. "Keep it professional. We're investigating a disappearance."

"Course, boss." Cal straightened his shoulders.

Last night, Ryan had forced his way through the first episode of *Crown of Shadows* to see what all the fuss was about. What a load of bollocks. He'd switched over to the darts.

They approached a sleek silver trailer with 'SHADOW QUEEN' emblazoned on the door in gothic lettering. A harried woman with a headset and clipboard intercepted them before they could knock.

"You must be the detectives." Her gaze flicked between them, then lingered a beat longer on Cal in his well-fitted suit. "Ms Stone has thirteen minutes before she's due in makeup. Not a minute more."

"That will do," Ryan replied.

The PA punched in a code and swung the trailer door open. A waft of sandalwood incense drifted out and clogged Ryan's nostrils.

Inside, the space was a riot of contrasting colours. Plush ivory carpets and purple cushions embroidered with arcane symbols. Fantasy-themed props scattered among Buddha statues and collections of crystals.

Piper Stone reclined on a red velvet chaise, one leg extended like in a Renaissance painting. She wore ornate shoulder pauldrons and an intricate laced corset over what appeared to be yoga pants. Her auburn hair cascaded over her shoulders in styled waves. She didn't glance up from the script in her hand.

A wardrobe assistant materialised from the bathroom, a tape measure looped around her neck and an armful of leather straps over one elbow.

"Sorry, Pip, the director wants the bodice tighter for the close-ups." The assistant stepped behind the chaise.

"Of course he does," Piper muttered. She lifted her arms and glanced up at Ryan and Cal. Her gaze sharpened.

The assistant gave a brisk tug on the corset laces. The whalebone creaked.

Piper's breath hissed. "Easy," she snapped. "I'd prefer not to black out mid-soliloquy."

"Mr Lionell's orders," the woman said with a grimace. She knotted the laces then wrapped a strap of leather over the top. "He likes the silhouette."

Piper sighed. "Men always do."

The assistant vanished out of the trailer as quickly as she'd appeared, leaving the scent of hairspray in her wake.

"Gentlemen. I hope this won't take long," Piper said, her voice carrying the seductive vowels of her on-screen persona. "I'm preparing for a rather intense scene."

Ryan pulled out his warrant card. "I'm Detective Inspector Ryan Hale, and this is Detective Constable Cal Pine."

Cal almost tripped over his own feet as he hurried forward. "Big fan," he blurted out. A red flush crept up his face. "Of the show, I mean. Not in a weird... I mean, you're very good at your job."

Piper's lips curled. "I'll try not to let it go to my head, Constable."

Ryan shot him a look that said, *steady,* and Cal stepped back. "We need to ask you some questions about Cyrus Wilde."

"Of course you do." Piper set her script aside with a dramatic sigh. "Everyone's obsessed with Cyrus and his little adventures. It's very tiresome." She gestured to the sofa opposite. "Sit, if it pleases you."

Ryan took his seat while Cal perched on the edge like an eager schoolboy with his notes app open.

"When did you last see Cyrus Wilde?" Ryan asked.

Piper crossed her long legs and adjusted a crystal pendant at her throat. "Saturday afternoon, I believe. We had a rather spirited discussion about creative differences. I'm sure you've heard about it."

"Creative differences," Ryan repeated. He consulted his notes. "That's not what witnesses described. They called it a blazing row, heard halfway across half the backlot, where you threw a plastic skull at his head."

A flicker of annoyance crossed her face. "The acoustics in

this place are dreadful. Honestly, you can't have a private conversation anywhere."

"What was the argument about?"

Piper flipped back her hair and looked up at him through her long lashes. "Didn't your little spies tell you?"

Ryan crossed his arms.

"Fine. Cyrus felt my character should have fewer lines in the finale. I disagreed. Creative tension is the lifeblood of art, detectives." She waved a hand. "Because of his insufferable method acting, people think he is Caspian—scheming, cruel—but he's not all the time. He can be kind when it suits him."

Cal jumped in. "Like when Caspian rescues the boy from the gallows in season two."

Piper's mouth twisted. "Exactly. He likes people to owe him." She reached out and stroked Cal's leg. "Tell me, Detective. Do they make them all this handsome at the station?"

Cal nearly dropped his phone. He cleared his throat. "Uh..."

"Cut the crap, Ms Stone," Ryan said. "Right now, you're our lead suspect in Cyrus's disappearance, and you're not saying anything to convince me otherwise."

Piper blinked and dropped her hand back to her lap. Her shoulders sagged. "Fine, Cyrus and I argued," she said in her normal speaking voice. "He was lobbying for my character to be killed off in the season finale or for me to be replaced with another actress in season four."

"Why would he do that? You're brilliant," Cal said.

Ryan sighed.

Piper preened. "Thank you, sweetie. Because he's a jealous, petty little man-child who can't stand sharing the spotlight." Genuine venom laced her words. "He's been sabotaging me since the moment he joined the show and pushing for someone else to take my part."

"Astrid Belmont? She's Mr Emerson's new 'muse', right?" Cal said.

Ryan couldn't tell if the constable's comment was innocent or calculated.

"Muse!" Piper spat the word at Cal. He leaned back. "I paved the way for Isaac to even direct this series, and now I'm an afterthought."

"You say 'muse,' but Astrid is pregnant with Isaac's child," Ryan said. "Mother of his child is a bigger role. Does it bother you?"

She barked out a laugh. "Me? Have a child? No, thank you. I was Isaac's muse long before that wannabe stumbled on set and latched onto anyone with power. I starred in all of Isaac's early indie films. I put my name and face on the line to help him break into the industry. Now he's rewriting all the storylines for her." She straightened her corset. "Villains can wear the pretty masks in this place, Detective. I don't forget that."

"Back to Cyrus," Ryan said. "You had a public row. He's out in the open, lobbying for you to be replaced, and I've been told your character wears prosthetics, so a replacement isn't impossible. Next thing, Cyrus vanishes."

Piper rose from the chaise and adjusted her half-laced corset. The stays barely shifted under her fingers.

"I've worked too damn hard to let some pompous so-called star overshadow me. But I wouldn't risk my career by harming him." Her fists clenched at her sides. "I know how these rumours spread. 'Diva actress freaks out, kills co-star.' It's cheap drama. I wouldn't give the tabloids or Isaac the satisfaction."

Ryan's gaze flicked to a cluster of well-worn scripts near her vanity.

"Where were you Saturday night?"

"Here," she said. She gestured around the trailer. "Learning lines. Sleeping. Alone for a change." She gave Cal a wink, and the detective flushed.

"Convenient," Ryan said.

"Not really. I'd much rather have had witnesses." She locked eyes with Cal. "Maybe I should make sure I have an alibi until Cyrus turns back up."

Cal flushed a deep shade of red but wisely ignored the comment. "Ah... Is there anyone who might have seen you enter or leave your trailer?"

She sighed. "No."

Ryan studied her. "You've been on set with Cyrus for how long now?"

"Two and a half insufferable years." Piper moved to her make-up table and trailed her fingers over perfume bottles. "Long enough to know where all the bodies are buried, so to speak."

"Interesting choice of words," Ryan remarked.

"If you're looking for suspects, talk to Isaac. He's been asking the principal actors to do dangerous stunts. I've refused, but Cyrus lapped it up. He's compared himself to Tom Cruise in interviews." She rolled her eyes.

"Why would Isaac want that?"

"He says it improves the realism of the scenes." Piper's mouth curved into a knowing smile. "But I actually read my contract. Buried in the legalese was a clause letting the production take out serious injury and life insurance on me if it wants. On any of us."

Ryan frowned. "You're suggesting Isaac's endangering his cast in the hopes there's a serious accident and an insurance payout?"

"He might play the tortured creative genius, but he's a ruthless businessman. There are whispers on set that the production is deep in the red, and Cyrus has been causing more problems for Isaac than I have." She lowered her voice. "I also heard Cyrus had backed out of doing this season's stunts last minute. Maybe Isaac took matters into his own hands?"

"That's a pretty bold accusation," Ryan replied.

Piper shrugged.

"Is there anyone on set Cyrus is close to? A new girlfriend or a poker buddy?" Cal asked.

"All Cyrus has are sycophants and people riding his coat-tails. Sad, isn't it? I heard he has a little side project with Jasper, but I try to spend as little time thinking about Cyrus as possible."

"Jasper?"

Piper waved her hand dismissively. "The Props Master. Stout fellow with shifty eyes. Beautiful work though. Look at this." She held out a sheathed dagger with an ornate jewelled handle.

A sharp rap at the door interrupted them. The PA stuck her head in. "Five minutes, Ms Stone."

Piper nodded, then turned back to Ryan. "Are we finished? I have a kingdom to rule."

"For now. We might need to speak again."

She looked Cal up and down. "Anytime." With a dismissive wave, she picked her script back up.

As they stepped back outside, Cal exhaled. "Bloody hell. She's something else."

"She's something, all right." Ryan squinted against the sun. "If we ever need a suspect list read aloud with dramatic flair, we know who to call."

"I've done screaming girls in the footie stands, boss, but that was... different. Hard to remember your line of questioning when the poster from your teenage bedroom wall flirts with you."

"She's a convincing actress."

Cal thought for a second. "Hey, wait a min—"

"She's also got motive and no alibi. Call Digit and ask him to dig into the insurance policies. She might be trying to deflect suspicions, but it's worth looking into." He stretched his stiff fingers.

"There are more rumours on this backlot than extras. Sorting fact from fiction's going to be half the bloody job."

———

A SCREAM SLICED through the air from further down the row of trailers.

Ryan exchanged a glance with Cal, then both broke into a run towards the source of the sound. The screaming continued, punctuated by sobs.

They skidded to a halt outside a trailer identical in appearance to Piper's. The door hung open. Inside, a young woman knelt on the floor and clutched her bleeding arm. Ryan followed Cal inside. Drawers were yanked out and upended, and someone had emptied the contents of the wardrobe onto the floor. Papers littered every surface, and an empty file box lay discarded on the kitchen counter.

"Millie, what happened?" Cal crouched beside the girl.

Ryan grabbed a clean tea towel hanging from the oven handle and gave it to Cal.

"I... I came to get Cyrus's dry cleaning." Millie sobbed as Cal applied the cloth to her wound. She winced. "The door was cracked open. I thought maybe I'd forgotten to lock it? When I opened the door, it was dark, so I stepped inside, and someone... someone shoved past me. I fell and cut my arm." She pointed to the shards of mirror scattered across the floor.

"Did you see who it was?" Ryan asked.

"They wore black. That's all I saw."

Ryan fought the urge to roll his eyes. Half of the crew wore black. He turned as a nervous PA peered in from the doorway, clearly drawn by the commotion.

"Did you see anyone running from here?"

The short woman shook her head. "No."

"Find the studio doctor and tell Vance we need security here. Now."

The PA scurried off. Ryan flicked on the trailer lights and studied Millie. Despite her tears and the blood seeping through the towel, there was something almost eager about her expression. Like she was finally part of the drama instead of outside looking in.

Ryan fished his phone out of his pocket and dialled forensics, then snapped several photos of the destruction.

Leaving Cal to nurse Millie, Ryan stepped out of the trailer. Next to the bottom step, pressed deep into the clay-like earth, was a large footprint.

A size eleven or twelve with thick lugs for grip.

"Not Italian leather loafers," Ryan murmured. *A work boot made this.*

Footsteps approached from the direction of the security office. Ryan straightened to see Vance Mitchell march towards him, flanked by a man carrying a green plastic case with a white cross on the side.

"What's going on, Hale?" Vance demanded, his face flushed pink. "My radio's going mental. You're disrupting the shooting schedule."

"Nice to see you too, Vance." Ryan pointed to the trailer. "You've had a break-in and an assault. Your doctor needs to treat a young woman with a serious cut. She's inside."

The man didn't wait for Vance's permission. He nodded to Ryan and hurried up the steps into the trailer.

Vance stopped next to Ryan, hands on his hips. His security badge gleamed in the sun. "A break-in? In broad daylight? Come on. We have patrols."

"Evidently not effective ones." Ryan pointed at the footprint. "Watch where you walk. That's evidence."

Vance looked down and sneered at the mud. "A boot print? On a studio that's basically a building site? Groundbreaking detective work, Hale. The print could belong to any of the crew."

"Which is why I'll have forensics cast it." Ryan stepped into Vance's personal space just enough to make the other man flinch, then instantly regretted it. As much as he disliked the man and the way he'd treated Fiona back in the day, now wasn't the time to let his personal feelings interfere with the job. He retreated. "I need you to lock down this immediate area. No one goes in or out until forensics are done."

Vance blustered. "I can't prevent the cast and crew from accessing their trailers. Mr Emerson will have my hide."

"Then let him yell at me. Unless you want to explain to the chief constable why you contaminated a crime scene connected to a high-profile missing person case?"

Vance's jaw worked silently, and his eyes narrowed. "Fine. I'll put a cordon up. But if this turns out to be nothing, just the girl tripping over her own feet and making a scene, I'm filing a report with the station about wasted resources."

"Understood," Ryan replied.

"Boss?" Cal appeared in the trailer doorway. "Millie needs stitches. The doctor wants to take her to the medical bay."

Ryan protected the footprint as the doctor led the shaking young woman down the stairs.

"Go with them," Ryan told Cal. "Take a full statement once she's stitched up. Ask her about anyone she's seen hanging around the trailer in the last few days. And find out who else has a key."

Cal nodded.

Ryan looked into the trailer at the chaotic mess inside, then back at the heavy boot print. What had the person been looking for?

And did they find it?

CHAPTER TWELVE

Ryan's phone buzzed against his hip when they were halfway across the backlot. Cal had filled him in on what Millie had told him, which added up to bugger all.

"DI Hale," Ryan answered, tucking the mobile closer to his ear as an icy breeze cut across the trailers.

All he got was a mix of crackle and static.

"... n't hear..." The voice, which sounded like Vance, broke up, mangled by the terrible signal around the stages. "... gate... for you... won't... in—"

Ryan moved into the centre of the backlot, as if three steps might gift him an extra bar of reception. It didn't.

"Try that again," he said.

More static. Something that might have been 'supporter' or possibly 'potato'.

"Vance, I caught nothing except 'gate'. Do I need to come to you?"

"... yeah, gate... now."

The line went dead.

Ryan stared at the phone for a beat. "Brilliant."

Cal hovered a few feet away with his hands jammed in his pockets. He lifted his eyebrows. "Problem?"

"Security wants me at the front gate. At least I think they do."

Cal brightened. "Sweet. When you're done, I'll be at the Dragon's Bite." He jabbed a thumb at the catering truck on the other side of the lot. "Best bacon butty I've ever had. And I've done the full tour of greasy spoons from here to Newcastle."

Ryan snorted. "You live a rich life, Pine."

"Rich in saturated fat," Cal said cheerfully, already striding away. "Text me if we need to leg it anywhere, yeah?"

Ryan shook his head and headed for the entrance gate. By the time he reached the security hut, the wind had worked its way through his coat and his temper. Vance stood inside the open door, his radio clipped to his shoulder and his expression set to his usual default of inconvenienced by everyone's existence.

"You called," Ryan said. "Or whatever that was."

Vance jerked his head towards the road. "Got a visitor asking for you. I'm not letting her in."

"Why not?"

"Smells like a reporter," Vance said, with the same tone most people reserved for finding gum on their shoe. "And I don't like her attitude."

"Right." A reporter with an attitude. Normally, that wouldn't narrow down the options, but he knew who it would be. "Did she leave?"

"No." Vance lifted a hand and pointed past the gate. "She's over there. Been parked up for the last fifteen minutes."

Ryan followed the line of his finger. A black Corolla sat against the fence on the far side of the gate, nose pointed to the road and engine off. He slipped around the barrier gate and walked over to the car.

The driver's door opened, and Sophie Ryder emerged. His steps faltered as she leaned against the bonnet, her blonde bob tucked behind her ears and her phone clutched in her gloved hands.

Her resemblance to Jaime always struck him like a physical blow. Same sharp chin, same determined set of the shoulders. Only the mole on her left cheek distinguished them at a distance.

Sophie straightened and pocketed her phone. "Morning, Ryan."

"What do you want, Sophie?"

"Can't I want to see my brother-in-law?" She pressed a hand to her chest in mock hurt.

Ryan slipped his hands under his armpits in a futile attempt to warm his fingers. "I don't know how you knew I was here, but I'm busy, Sophie. If this is about yesterday—"

"Cyrus Wilde." She stepped closer. "Word is your team's investigating his disappearance."

"No comment."

"Come on, Ryan. I'm not asking for quotes. I'm offering information. Why else would I be sitting around in the cold waiting for you instead of enjoying a cup of coffee in the office?"

He studied her face. Sophie never offered something for nothing, especially not to him. "What kind of information?"

She smiled, the predatory glint in her eye uncomfortably familiar. "The exclusive kind. But I want something in return."

"Of course you do."

"Full access to your investigation. I'll be your shadow, but nothing gets published until you give the green light."

Ryan laughed. "Not a bloody chance."

"Fine. Plan B, then. First interview with you after the case closes. Either way, my information's good."

Ryan wasn't surprised she'd led with an offer she knew he'd turn down. Jaime had always done the same thing. "You seem confident this missing person case is newsworthy. Famous actor goes on another bender, hardly headline material."

She tilted her head. "We both know he would have turned up by now. I could have published my information. Let your department find out with everybody else."

"Then why didn't you?" Ryan asked, curious.

Sophie looked away.

"You can't verify it," he guessed.

"No," Sophie conceded, "but it's from a reliable source, and I wouldn't have published it, anyway. Do we have a deal?" She looked up at him through her blunt fringe, and Ryan had to remind himself it wasn't Jaime asking him for a favour. This was her sister, the unscrupulous journalist. To be fair to his sister-in-law, she kept their personal connection out of their business dealings. She might be a pain in his professional arse, but unlike some journalists Ryan had dealt with over the years, she had a moral code. A warped one he often disagreed with, but he could just about make it out if he squinted.

"Fine. First interview after the case concludes, if we solve it. Exclusive. Ten minutes of my time."

"Thirty."

"Twenty, and you buy the coffee."

"Done." Sophie pulled out her phone, swiped past several screens, then held it up. "Cyrus Wilde filed for full custody of Freddy three months ago. Revenge for Astrid getting engaged to Isaac and pregnant with his child."

"We know that, Sophie."

Sophie handed him her phone. "Yes, but what you don't know, because the court records are sealed, is he's using Astrid's past drug addiction against her. No one knew she used drugs back when they first got together. Somehow, it never got out.

My source says this is true, but Cyrus's testimony claiming she's back using since she started attending industry parties with Isaac, is false. He produced evidence she snorted coke at the BAFTAs while pregnant."

Ryan scanned the message chain on her screen, saved as 'Cyrus Source'. "Without the court records, this is hearsay."

"The source is deep in Cyrus's camp." Sophie smiled. "They say the case is going Wilde's way. The judge has been sympathetic to his argument about providing stability. But the evidence he supplied to the judge was doctored, and he blackmailed a witness to back up his story."

Ryan's mind raced. Astrid had painted herself as the responsible parent and implied Cyrus had little interest in Freddy beyond a power play. But if Cyrus was winning the custody battle, how far would a desperate mother go? "Why is the source telling you this?" Any betrayal was suspect.

"I think they hoped I could expose Cyrus's lies before the hearing's decided. They care about Freddy's future. But if I publish these accusations against Cyrus without proof, I risk the newspaper being sued for libel. Then it might harm Astrid's position more than help."

"If the public finds out about her drug use, even if it was in the past, she could be hung out online as an unfit mother," he murmured.

"Exactly. Opinion counts for more than facts to a lot of people these days. I can't take the risk when a child is involved. The final ruling is next week. If Wilde doesn't show up..."

"The case gets thrown out or delayed." Ryan handed back the phone. "Your source...?"

"Absolutely not." She put her phone away. "That wasn't our deal."

"Worth a try." He went to step past her, but she blocked his way. "Your current team, they're good? I heard—"

"My team's none of your business, Sophie. And don't think I've forgotten about your mysterious inside source on the Mathers case."

"Just making conversation," she replied, sounding wounded. "Mum's been asking about you, you know."

His stomach dropped. "How is Ruth?"

"Same as always. Waiting by the phone. She's convinced now you're back you'll find Jaime." Sophie's face twisted. "The rest of us have let it go, but she has this unwavering and unwarranted faith in you, Ryan. God knows why."

He closed his eyes briefly. "Don't."

"Fine." She glanced at her watch. "I'll text you about the interview. Don't forget our deal."

CHAPTER THIRTEEN

Advika led Sheri across the backlot with Fiona a step behind. The production assistant's brisk pace suggested she'd walked these paths countless times as she dodged stacks of equipment and crew members who didn't glance up from their tasks.

"Margot should be at High Tor." Advika pointed to the largest of the soundstages looming ahead. "They're prepping a tavern scene this afternoon. The set is her baby. She likes to make the final adjustments before the lighting team arrives."

"This industry you work in is quite something," Sheri said as she watched a pair of crew weave their cart of props around a huddle of extras enjoying a rare moment of sunshine. "It's so exciting."

Advika flashed her a smile. "It has its moments. Beats a desk job, for me anyway. I started as an unpaid intern, then got hired full time after uni."

"Film studies?"

Advika laughed. "Media and Communications at

Manchester. My parents wanted business or medicine, but they came around when they saw how passionate I was."

Sheri raised an eyebrow. "They were supportive?"

"Surprisingly, yes. Dad was sceptical at first. What Indian father isn't about creative careers? But Mum convinced him. They even watch the show despite it not being their cup of tea. They prefer the energy and melodrama of Bollywood. But it's nice they make the effort."

A twinge of something like jealousy twisted in Sheri's stomach. "That's great."

"Your parents weren't on board with police work?" Advika asked, no doubt catching the note of bitterness Sheri couldn't keep out of her voice.

"Not exactly. They had a very specific plan. Business school, marriage, motherhood. In that order."

Advika slowed her pace and studied her face. "Yet here you are, Detective Constable Dewan."

"Here I am." Sheri stroked the ruby pendant at her neck. "Though every family gathering still includes at least one relative asking when I'll come to my senses."

Advika laughed. "My aunts say the same about film. 'Nice hobby, beta, but when will you get a proper job?'" She nudged Sheri's elbow. "We should compare family horror stories over a drink when this is all over."

Sheri smiled. "I'd like that."

They reached a colossal sliding door with "HIGH TOR" stencilled in faded grey paint across the front. Advika swiped her card and held the smaller side door open. The air inside smelled of sawdust and fresh paint. Dim work lights hung from distant rafters and illuminated a partially constructed medieval pub.

"Is that the *'Drunken Dragon'*?" Sheri flushed. "Where

Niamh kissed Lyrian and then knocked him out? It looks the same. As on the show, I mean."

"You're a fan then? Yeah, I still get a buzz seeing it in real life," Advika replied.

A woman, tall and curvy with dark hair escaping a messy bun, directed two crew members as they positioned a heavy oak-topped bar. She had to be Margot Ellison.

"Margot!" Advika called out when they reached the edge of the set.

The woman turned and assessed them. A smudge of brown paint streaked her cheekbone. "Advika, hey."

Fiona stepped forward. "I'm DS Fiona Bennett, and this is DC Sheri Dewan. We're investigating Cyrus Wilde's disappearance. We'd like to ask you a few questions."

Margot's expression hardened.

"I hope the bastard's dead." The words, raw and devoid of artifice, sliced through the cavernous quiet of the soundstage. "I hope he's rotting somewhere, so I never have to feel his slimy hands on me again."

Sheri exchanged a glance with Fiona. The statement was damning, but Sheri recognised the emotion behind it. She'd felt the same helpless rage years ago. She forced herself to focus on the interview, not her own memories, and pulled out her notebook. "You filed a formal harassment complaint against him with the production team?" she asked.

Margot snorted and wiped her hands on a rag tucked into the waistband of her paint-splattered jeans. "A lot of good that did. They gave him a 'stern talking to' and told me to avoid being alone with him. As if I was the problem." Her lips flattened.

"Then why stay?" Fiona asked gently.

Margot's gaze swept around the half-finished set. From the intricate details of the mock-timbered walls and the distressed barrels to the pewter tankards ready for their close-up. Her face softened.

"Because this," her gesture encompassed the stage, "is *Crown of Shadows*. The biggest bloody production in the country. The kind of job that makes a career. I wasn't going to let that narcissistic prick brand me as a troublemaker and chase me away from the best opportunity I'll ever get." She gave the barstool an aggressive wipe. "He got me to meet him at the ritual pit stage after hours. Said production wanted me to assess how his costume contrasted with the set design. But it was just a sick ploy to get me alone. He backed me up against the pit, grabbed my tit, and then in that bloody Caspian voice, said..." Her voice switched to a high-pitched singsong. "'You know how this works. Don't fight it. You give a little, you get a little.' Like I was part of a scene he was rehearsing. I kneed him in the balls and ran." She shuddered.

The weight of Margot's words settled on Sheri's shoulders. Should she mention her own experience at university? Would it help her build rapport with Margot or compromise her professionalism? Before she could decide, Fiona spoke.

"Ms Ellison, I understand this is painful for you, but I have to ask. Where were you on Saturday night? The night Cyrus Wilde was last seen."

Margot turned to the bar and ran a hand over its polished surface. "Thor's Cave, mostly. Stage Three. I was prepping the Shadow Queen's throne room set. Alone. I left around eleven and then I went back to my crew cabin."

"Anyone see you?"

"I doubt it. It was late."

"So you don't have an alibi," Fiona stated.

Margot's eyes narrowed. "Do I need one?"

"It depends," Fiona replied. "Did you have anything to do with Cyrus Wilde's disappearing?"

"No." Margot's response was immediate. She picked up a pewter tankard and gazed at her reflection distorted in its dull surface. "But if he never reappears, I won't pretend to be heartbroken about it either."

Sheri's pen hovered over her notebook. Margot had motive, opportunity and no alibi. Her psychology training suggested the woman's anger was healthy. Trauma victims often expressed rage when they felt safe to do so. But did that make Margot less likely to have acted on it, or more? Sheri wished she felt more confident in her assessment.

CHAPTER FOURTEEN

"MR EMERSON IS OFF-SITE DEALING WITH A CRISIS, DI Hale," Janet, the showrunner's secretary, said as she juggled their conversation and her perpetually ringing phone.

Convenient timing. He'd circle back to Emerson later.

"Right then." Ryan turned to Cal, who stood nearby waving his phone in the air with a frown. "Plan B. Let's pay a visit to the head costumer."

The wardrobe department occupied a vast, hangar-like building. Wool, hot irons and a faint floral perfume from a struggling diffuser combined to create a distinct smell. Labelled racks burst with clothes. Everything from mud-caked peasant smocks to gleaming armour lined up in neat aisles. In a corner surrounded by sketch boards and swathes of fabric stood the only person in sight. A young woman in a brocaded green velvet jacket with electric blue hair cut into a jagged bob. She didn't notice the detectives, her attention focused on stitching gold braid onto the cuff of a charcoal soldier's jacket. She froze mid-stitch and sneezed.

"Hi, we're looking for Mr Kerrington," Ryan called out, his voice echoing.

The woman looked up. Her eyes, already wide thanks to dramatic false eyelashes, widened further before a professional smile clicked into place. "You're after Blaise?" Another sneeze escaped, more forcefully this time. "Sorry. I'm allergic to dust. It's a curse working here." She picked up a pair of sharp-looking shears and snipped the ends of the golden thread.

"I'm DI Hale, and this is DC Pine." Ryan showed the woman his warrant card.

Her fingers stilled on the jacket. "Oh, you're the detectives. Blaise isn't here at the moment. His Persian, Coco, had a bit of an emergency. She ate Harriet's chocolate bar. Turns out chocolate's poisonous for cats as well as dogs, so he's taken her to the vet in Bakewell."

"Will he be back today?" Cal leaned against a rack of chain mail, then straightened abruptly when it started to roll.

"He should be back for the night battle shoot. Around seven, maybe? Pirate Queen Niamh will need some last-minute adjustments to her costume." She gestured towards a mannequin draped in an elaborate lacy shirt covered by a burgundy leather jacket. Blood-red pantaloons and a jewelled belt finished the outfit.

Ryan nodded. "Can I ask you a few questions, Ms...?"

"Grace. Grace Bonnes. I'm the associate costume designer. Blaise's right-hand gal." She gave a short laugh, as if she'd said something funny.

Nerves. People often got anxious speaking to the police, even if they had no reason to be. "We've heard some talk about Mr Kerrington. That he might have taken a keen interest in the actor who's gone missing? Cyrus Wilde."

Grace cut along a frayed edge, then yelped. A bright bead of blood welled from her finger.

"Shit." She reached for the box of tissues on the table. "Occupational hazard. We all bleed for the show round here. Sorry, you were saying?"

"Your boss and Cyrus Wilde," Ryan replied.

Grace's smile thinned. "Mr Kerrington is a great admirer of talent, and Cyrus is undeniably charismatic on screen. A lot of the team are fans." Another sniffle.

"Are you a fan?" Ryan asked, remembering the conversation with Isaac about the sexual harassment allegations. "I hear he can be difficult for female crew members to work with."

Grace shrugged. "I've never had much to do with him. Luckily, from the sounds of things. Blaise handles his costumes, and I'm glad to let him."

Ryan pressed on. "Blaise's interest in Cyrus sounds like more than admiration. Have you seen any inappropriate behaviour? During fittings, that sort of thing? Maybe a notebook dedicated to Cyrus or intimate photographs?"

Her gaze flicked up to meet Ryan's, then away.

"Honestly, detectives, people around here love to gossip. Blaise collects memorabilia from all the shows he's worked on. It's professional interest. He's an artist. He sees beauty in many forms." She laughed a little too brightly. "He's hardly Norman Bates."

"So you've never seen this notebook?"

"No." She paused. "Blaise did tear apart the department this morning looking for something, but I don't know what it was. He didn't say, and I've learned not to ask."

"What kind of boss is he?" Ryan said.

"He's a perfectionist, and he demands a lot from me and the team, but he's a hard worker. He lives nearby in Buxton, but he's in here so much after hours he often sleeps here." She waved her hand at a velvet chaise lounge with puffy cushions tucked into the corner of the room.

Her pager, lying beside a pot of pins, beeped. She glanced at it and frowned. "Excuse me. They need me on set. It's the extras. If I don't hold their hands, they'll turn up for the medieval village battle scene dressed as Roman legionaries, whining the armour rubs or their boots pinch." She snipped a piece of loose braid off the cuff, then gathered up a measuring tape and her shears and put them in the work-belt slung low on her hips. "Look, I have to go, sorry. Can I help you find your way out?"

Ryan ignored her obvious attempt to get them out of there. "We know the way."

She gave a tentative nod. "Please don't touch anything. Blaise notices if even a button is out of place." She gathered a few more items and hurried out, casting one last glance at the detectives as she closed the door behind her.

"Did you clock those boots?" Cal asked once she'd left. "Alexander McQueen. Four hundred quid at least."

"I don't even want to know how you can recognise women's designer boots."

Ryan's attention was on the benches and cupboards as he moved around the room. He paused in front of a pinboard crowded with ripped-out pages from glossy fashion magazines pinned between costume sketches, then took out a pair of plastic gloves from his pocket and snapped them on. He opened a nearby cupboard. The top shelf contained neatly labelled boxes of buttons, ribbons, and lace. The bottom held rolls of fabric. Nothing out of the ordinary. A nearby set of drawers labelled 'KEEP OUT' drew him over. He rattled the handle, but the drawer was locked. He tugged it harder, and the flimsy lock gave. "Oh... look, it's unlocked."

"It is now," Cal replied with a smirk.

Ryan ignored him and pulled the drawer open. It was filled with sketchbooks. He lifted the top one and flicked through it.

There were detailed sketches of costumes for the Shadow Queen and Cyrus's character, Caspian Drest, but nothing inside that would be considered obsessive. At the bottom of each design was a swirling mark. Ryan could make out a B. Blaise's signature?

Cal looked over his shoulder. "These are amazing."

Ryan nodded in agreement and put the sketchbook back in place. "But not evidence of an obsession with Cyrus."

He closed the drawer and hoped Blaise would think he'd forgotten to lock it.

CHAPTER FIFTEEN

RYAN LEANED AGAINST THE BREAK ROOM DOORWAY WHILE the kettle boiled. The whiteboard held a lot of names, but none had been cleared. Vance had reluctantly given them Blaise Kerrington's contact details. The mobile had rung through to voicemail, and officers had found no one at Blaise's home in Buxton. The head of security had assured Ryan he'd call as soon as the head costume designer appeared.

Ryan had just brewed himself a mug of tea when Digit appeared in the doorway, clutching a tablet.

"The studio's gate visitor logs show three hundred and forty-seven individual entries during the forty-eight hours surrounding Mr Wilde's disappearance," he said. "Suppliers, contractors and authorised visitors. Cross-referencing and conducting verification interviews with each would require one hundred and seventy-three personnel hours, assuming an average interview duration of thirty minutes per person. I've also completed my review of the perimeter CCTV footage for the same period. Mr Wilde doesn't appear in any frames. The only plausible explanations for his departure would be concealment within a vehicle or scaling the 2.4-metre razor wire fence. Neither seem probable. Therefore, the evidence suggests Mr Wilde remained on the premises throughout this period."

"We might have to do a full search of the studio grounds."

"Sir." Digit's voice dropped to a conspiratorial whisper that probably carried further than his normal tone. He beckoned Ryan into the break room, away from the open door.

Ryan raised an eyebrow but followed.

Digit leaned in. He smelled faintly of matcha tea. "Regarding the other matter."

Sighing, Ryan added a dollop of milk to his mug. When he'd recruited Digit to help with the Benson case, he'd known the DC was the least subtle member of the team.

Or at least tied with Cal.

"I've confirmed Amos Benson is deceased." Digit's whisper remained loud. "Killed in a single-vehicle road accident three years after Beatrice Benson's incarceration. The pathologist confirmed no alcohol or narcotics."

"Being dead doesn't exonerate him as a suspect in Matthew's murder," Ryan muttered into his mug. "What about the daughter, Hannah?"

"It's peculiar. I located the Land Registry records for the sale of the family home in Tansley three months after Amos's death. However, I found no trace of her afterwards. No current address, no tax records, no employment information, no social media footprint under her name. She's vanished, well enough that my bots can't find her."

"And the others who were in the house that day?" Ryan asked.

"The uncle, Jacob Long, still receives a disability pension and lives locally on Cindermere Estate. The nephew, Peter York, is pursuing a Master's in Molecular Biology at the

University of Sheffield." Digit tapped his tablet. "Beatrice Benson remains at HMP New Hall, Flockton."

"Right. Can you reach out to Jacob Long? See if he's amenable to a chat tomorrow afternoon. Informal, for now."

Digit nodded. He glanced left and right before he answered in an exaggerated whisper. "Consider it done."

They emerged from the break room together. Fiona, handbag on her shoulder, gave Ryan a questioning look as she passed them on her way to the door. She'd obviously heard them whispering. Ryan offered her a bland smile and pretended to study the dregs of tea in his mug. Fiona wouldn't forgive being sidelined. He'd need to deal with that later.

———

THE COLD HIT Ryan the moment he headed outside. He walked towards his car through pools of streetlight, in and out of the dark. Winston would be bouncing off the walls of his flat by now, desperate for his dinner and his evening walk.

He'd had to park his Range Rover on the street when they'd returned from the studio. The station's car park had been filled with the cars of officers attending a seminar upstairs. As he approached the driver's door, he spotted something brown beneath the windscreen wiper. Another parking ticket? He'd paid for three hours.

Ryan plucked the folded paper from under the wiper and unfolded it beneath the glow of a nearby street lamp. No official letterhead or council stamp. Just eight words scrawled in black marker:

STOP DIGGING, OR ELSE SOMEONE WILL GET HURT.

His pulse quickened as he turned the paper over. Nothing on the back. No signature, no identifying marks.

Ryan's heart thumped as he glanced around the empty street, aware of how exposed he was. The problem was, which investigation did the note refer to? Cyrus Wilde's disappearance? Matthew Benson's decade-old murder? Or his private investigation into Jaime's case? The fact he didn't know made him question his life choices.

He fished an evidence bag out of his pocket, folded the note, and slipped it in. After eight years leading the Met's murder squad, a threat was nothing new. The only problem was when the person would act on it and from what direction it would come. Ryan flexed his damaged fingers, pushing back the buried memory of his finger bones snapping that rose to the surface. He checked the back seat before he slid behind the wheel and mulled over the possibilities as he drove home.

Ryan's key scraped against the lock three times before he found the keyhole. Fatigue blurred his vision as he pushed the door open and stepped into the darkened flat.

"Winston," he called, expecting the familiar click of nails against the laminate flooring and excited corgi whines.

Silence answered him.

"Winston?" Ryan flipped the switch. Light illuminated the sparse living room. No wiggling corgi bum, no excited barks.

He went into the kitchen. Winston's food bowl was empty, his water lower than this morning. Ryan's throat tightened as he moved through the flat. He even looked under the bed where Winston hid during thunderstorms.

Nothing.

The cat flap in the kitchen door that led to the small, enclosed backyard was ajar. Winston preferred the warmth of the flat during the evenings, but he might be out there. Ryan unlocked the back door. The outside sensor light flooded the small garden.

"Winston!"

The yard was empty. Ryan checked the gate. Still latched. The threatening note burned in his pocket.

Stop digging, or else someone will get hurt.

What if they meant Winston?

CHAPTER SIXTEEN

Ryan marched through the glass entrance of Silverheath Studios with Winston at his side. The corgi's stubby legs worked double-time to keep pace as they approached the security desk, where Vance Mitchell stood with his arms crossed and a clipboard tucked under his elbow.

"Er, boss? I still don't understand why you brought Winston," Cal said. He eyed the corgi nervously.

Winston hadn't been dognapped. He'd broken out. Once Ryan had calmed down, he'd remembered the GPS chip on the corgi's collar and found him sniffing letter boxes three blocks away.

"He escaped last night," Ryan said. "I can't afford the time to go and to collect him if he gets out again and someone calls me. Better to keep him with me."

Cal looked sceptical.

Ryan knew it was a flimsy excuse, but had no intention of telling his team about the threatening note left on his windscreen. The last thing he needed was Cal spiralling into conspiracy theories or Fiona insisting he report it up the chain.

This afternoon he'd arrange doggy daycare for the rest of the week, but with the note, he didn't want to risk leaving Winston at home by himself today.

"He'll probably lead us straight to Cyrus. Winston's got exceptional instincts," Ryan added.

Cal cocked his head. "For finding missing celebrities?"

"For finding trouble," Ryan muttered, which was true. If Cyrus was anywhere on the premises with a strip of bacon, Winston would find him in minutes.

"Not happening." Vance stepped forward and blocked their path. "No animals except trained performance animals are allowed on set."

Winston sat at Ryan's feet and stared up at Vance with his most innocent expression.

"He's not a pet," Ryan said, his face neutral. "He's a working police dog."

Cal choked back a laugh and turned it into an unconvincing cough.

Vance's eyes narrowed. "That's a corgi."

"Well spotted."

"The police don't use corgis. He's also wearing a tartan collar with little ducks on it."

"He's highly specialised." Ryan knelt and unclipped Winston's regular collar, then replaced it with an official-looking one he'd borrowed from the dog unit.

The startled corgi looked up at him with curious eyes.

"Now he knows it's time to work. He's a drug detection canine. We believe Wilde's disappearance may be connected to narcotics."

Vance studied Winston, who chose that moment to sit and scratch behind his ear. He almost toppled over in the process. "That's a drug dog?"

"New programme," Ryan said without missing a beat.

"Smaller dogs can access tight spaces. Lower maintenance costs. Very efficient."

The head of security rolled his eyes.

Ryan leaned closer. "Look, Vance. This is going one of two ways. Either the dog comes in with us now, or I get a warrant mentioning you by name and the words obstruction of justice."

Vance's jaw tightened. After a long moment, he stepped aside and jabbed his pen at the clipboard. "Sign the dog in. If it pisses on any sets or costumes, we'll be sending the Derbyshire Constabulary the bill."

"Understood."

"And keep it under control."

"Him," Ryan corrected. "And he's better behaved than most of your cast and crew." He scribbled his signature. "Has Blaise Kerrington come in today?"

"No. Never showed up last night either. Called in sick. Something about his cat."

Ryan nodded. "Let's find Jasper Fenn," he said to Cal.

They stepped out into the light drizzle and made their way across the backlot, dodging puddles, while Winston tugged against the lead to stop and sniff at interesting corners. The complex was quieter than yesterday. Crew members hurried between buildings with hoods pulled over their heads.

Cal consulted the sitemap on his phone. "Props department should be through here. Digit says Fenn's been here since day one. OG crew. So if Piper's right about their little side hustle, this bloke'll have the inside track on Cyrus."

They pushed through a set of double doors into the props department. The space stood empty, workbenches cluttered with half-finished chain mail. The walls were lined with bins full of medieval weapons. Everything from basic swords to ornate golden spears with delicate gold filigree.

"Not here," Cal muttered. "Would've thought someone would be around."

"Let's try the green room we passed. Someone there might know where he is."

The extras' green room buzzed with activity. Soldiers in medieval costume lounged on mismatched sofas while make-up artists touched up faces. Winston's arrival caused a stir as several extras pointed at the corgi and smiled.

Ryan spotted Grace Bonnes in the corner, her blue hair unmistakable as she knelt beside a tubby soldier and made last-minute adjustments to the greaves of his armour. Winston pulled him over to her, or rather, towards the open packet of crisps on the table beside her.

"Miss Bonnes."

She looked up, and her hands stilled on the soldier's ankle. "Good morning, detectives. Back so soon?" Her gaze dropped to Winston. "With reinforcements?"

"Drug detection specialist," Cal said with such conviction Ryan almost believed him.

Grace's eyes widened. "You think that's necessary?" She covered her mouth with her elbow and sneezed. "Sorry."

"We're exploring all avenues," Ryan replied. "Are you expecting Mr Kerrington to come in this morning?"

"Not for a couple of hours. He's still at a hotel near the vet. He called me last night in a real state. Coco didn't respond well to the treatment. Who knew a block of dark chocolate could be so lethal?" She tugged on a leather strap, struggling to get the hole to line up with the buckle. "But he just texted to say she's stabilised, so I imagine he'll come straight here."

She gave the strap a hard yank.

The soldier yelped. "It's pressing on my calf."

"Hold still, you big baby. It's the only size I've got left. You're an actor, so pretend you've marched for days. It'll look great on camera. Maybe you'll get featured." Grace stood and brushed the wrinkles from her skirt, then shifted over to the next guy.

Ryan followed. "Have you seen Jasper Fenn, the props master? He wasn't in the props department."

"No, sorry." She tucked the new soldier's sleeve into his glove, then sneezed again.

"He was here," the soldier said. "Looking for Dominic. Dom's the stunt coordinator." The extra grinned. Only his teeth were visible through the bushy beard as he bobbed his head. "Detective Pine."

"Boss, this is Colin," Cal said, then caught himself with an exaggerated wink. "Sorry, Max Steele."

"DI Hale, pleasure to meet you," Colin said. "I've played one of the boys in blue before, you know. An episode of Midlands Murders as 'Officer Who Finds Body.' Very intense scene work." He held out his gloved hand.

Grace rolled her eyes behind the extra's back, then moved on to the next soldier.

Ryan shook Colin's hand. "Did you see which way Jasper went?"

"He and Dom headed out to the backlot maybe half an hour ago. Sorry, at oh-eight-hundred hours," Colin confirmed. "Something about rigging the trebuchet for today's scene. I could show you?"

"No, you should, ah... stay at your post," Ryan replied.

"Heard anything interesting, Columbo?" Cal asked.

Colin's face lit up. He glanced around conspiratorially, then leaned closer. "Actually, there's a rumour going around about Astrid's baby."

"What about it?"

"Well," Colin lowered his voice, "word is it might not be Isaac's at all. According to a reliable source, Astrid was seen leaving Cyrus's trailer looking dishevelled, but in the best possible way." He wiggled his bushy eyebrows. "You know what I mean?"

"Yeah, mate, we get it. They weren't playing Scrabble," Cal replied.

Ryan exchanged a glance with Cal. "And when was this supposed to have happened?"

"Four months ago when Isaac was in Iceland, scouting locations. Gone for two weeks, he was." Colin nodded knowingly. "Makes you wonder, doesn't it?"

"And who was this reliable source?" Ryan asked.

Colin drew back. "I can't reveal my sources."

"You're not a journalist or a lawyer, Colin."

The tubby extra thrust his hands out. "You'll have to arrest me." His eyes flicked behind Ryan. "Hey, that's him! That's Jasper!"

Ryan turned as a stocky man in cargo pants strode through the green room. He carried a tablet and wore a utility belt laden with tools.

"Right, Colin, we'll leave this for now," Ryan said. He followed the props master, with Cal and Winston at his heels.

Ryan tied Winston's lead to a rail in the corridor and followed Cal into the props warehouse.

Jasper was already busy with an array of medieval weaponry laid out on a worktable.

"Mr Fenn? DI Ryan Hale, Derbyshire Police. This is my colleague DC Pine." Ryan flashed his warrant card. "We've got a few questions about Cyrus Wilde."

Jasper continued to inspect a battleaxe. "Everyone does lately. I've got a trebuchet to rig and about forty weapons to check before the battle scene. Is this going to take long?"

"We heard you and Cyrus are close," Cal said.

The props master's fingers froze on the axe handle. "Who told you that?"

"Does it matter?"

Something flickered across Jasper's face. He set the axe down. "I get on with him better than most of the crew, but I wouldn't call us close."

Ryan studied the man as he fidgeted with the tools on his belt.

"Not what we've heard," he said. "Piper Stone mentioned you're buddies. That Cyrus and you have a little project together."

"Piper talks a lot of crap." Jasper grabbed a sword from the table and ran a polishing cloth down the blade, but he couldn't meet the detective's gaze. "She's trying to point fingers in any direction but her own." The man was a terrible liar. Truly horrendous.

Ryan, distracted by the sound of a dog growling from further away than it should be, took a step towards the door.

"Did you notice anything unusual last Saturday night?" he heard Cal ask, stepping into the spot he'd vacated.

"Unusual how?" Jasper replied.

"Any unfamiliar people on set, noises, anything out of place?"

Ryan spied the empty K9 collar, the dog lead still tied to the rail. He unclipped it and swore under his breath.

"Help!" a woman shrieked from down the corridor.

Winston barked in response.

"Bollocks," Ryan grumbled.

CHAPTER SEVENTEEN

Sheri followed Fiona towards the production offices.

"Detective Bennett!"

They turned. A slight figure hurried over, arms wrapped around something clasped to her chest. The young woman's eyes were wide and her cheeks flushed.

"Sorry to bother you." She glanced around. "Could I have a word? In private? I don't want to get anyone in trouble."

Sheri studied the girl. Her plain features were twisted with anxiety, but Sheri's attention caught on her jeans. Vintage-cut denim with intricate wildflower embroidery running up both legs. Exceptional craftsmanship that looked hand done.

Fiona guided them to an empty dressing room. "What's happened, Millie?"

The girl was Cyrus's personal assistant, Sheri realised.

Millie shut the door behind them, still clutching whatever she held like a shield. "I found something this morning. On the front seat of Cyrus's Porsche." Her words tumbled out. "The MOT certificate was about to run out, so I—"

"What did you find?" Fiona asked.

Millie's grip relaxed and revealed a red notebook. She bit her lip. "I'm not sure I should give it to you. Perhaps I ought to have just returned this to the owner? It seems rather personal."

Sheri leaned against a make-up counter. "But you brought it to us instead."

"With Cyrus missing, I thought..." Millie's fingers drummed on the notebook's cover. "It's probably harmless." Her face suggested otherwise.

"Why don't you let us decide?" Fiona pulled on a pair of gloves and held out her hand.

Millie hesitated, then thrust the notebook forward. "Here."

Fiona took it. A simple notebook with a worn elastic band holding it closed. The corners were frayed, and the cover scratched from frequent handling.

Well used, Sheri thought.

Fiona flipped it open, and her eyebrows rose as she scanned the first page. They widened further when she turned to the next page. Sheri fought the urge to look over her shoulder.

"You said you found this inside Cyrus's car?" Sheri asked as Fiona read. "Was it locked?"

"No. Everyone knows that Porsche is Cyrus's. Who'd steal it?"

Fiona turned several more pages, her face screwing up the more she read.

"Christ, how would that even work?" She muttered under her breath, then looked up. "Can you bag this for me, DC Dewan?"

Sheri removed an evidence bag and plastic gloves from her satchel. Once she'd pulled them on, Fiona passed her the notebook. "Look at your own risk."

Sheri couldn't help herself. She flipped the notebook open to a random page and glanced at the cramped, looping handwriting. The prose appeared to be an amateurish poem about Cyrus Wilde. What it lacked in craft, it made up for in graphic detail. The next page held another explicit fantasy involving Cyrus and Blaise.

Sheri stopped there. "This is not a good day to have eyes."

"There's more," Millie said, barely above a whisper. "At the back."

Sheri flipped to the last page, and several folded photographs slipped out. She opened one. It showed a crudely photoshopped image of Blaise and Cyrus embracing on a beach like a couple on holiday. The edges were worn, white creases crisscrossing the image as if it had been folded and unfolded countless times. The other photos were more of the same.

"Wow," Sheri murmured. She returned the photos to the notebook and sealed it in the evidence bag. She filled in the label before removing her gloves.

"Thank you for bringing this to us, Millie," Fiona said. "You did the right thing."

Millie frowned. "I hope so." She rubbed at a spot on her embroidered jeans. "I'd appreciate if you didn't mention who found it. Cyrus will kill me if any of the contents get out."

"We'll be discreet," Fiona assured her. "But it would be helpful if you could keep this to yourself. Don't discuss it with anyone else on set."

A flash of guilt crossed Millie's face.

Colin had mentioned Blaise's notebook yesterday, and now less than twenty-four hours later, it appeared? Had Millie actually found it, Sheri wondered, or had she known where to look?

"Did Cyrus ever mention anything about Blaise that concerned him?" Fiona asked.

"No, he barely acknowledged Mr Kerrington's existence during fittings." Millie twisted her hands together. "Cyrus treats all the crew like furniture."

"And you've never seen this notebook before?" Sheri pressed.

"Never." Millie's answer came quickly.

Fiona nodded. "Thank you again, Millie. We might have more questions later."

Once Millie had left, Sheri turned to Fiona. "Bit convenient, isn't it? We hear rumours about this notebook, and today it magically turns up?"

"This level of obsession would be difficult to fake at short notice, but you're right. We'll need to verify its authenticity. And the best way to do it is to track down Mr Kerrington."

CHAPTER EIGHTEEN

RYAN SWORE AGAIN AS HE SPRINTED DOWN THE HALLWAY
with Cal beside him. The short corridor opened into a wider,
gloomier space lined with closed roll-up doors. The barking
changed to growls, mingled with sobs.

A familiar cloying scent thickened the air.

Ryan skidded to a halt before an open doorway. Inside the
cramped storage space, mannequins in various states of undress
leaned against the walls. A heap of realistic dummies, smoth-
ered in blood and dressed as fallen soldiers, lay piled in one
corner. Among the homespun wool, a patch of midnight blue
velvet and gold stood out. The signature costume of Caspian
Drest. The grey face, partially obscured by the pile of
dummies, belonged to Cyrus Wilde. It could have been a still
from the show if it weren't for the unmistakable smell of death.

Winston, tail wagging, tugged on one of the actor's knee-
high leather boots.

"Looks like we've found Cyrus," Ryan said.

Cal exhaled. "Well, shit."

A young woman in her mid-twenties, headset askew, crouched inside the door with her hand pressed to her mouth as if it could contain her sobs. Cal placed a gentle hand on her shoulder.

"You all right there? Come on, look at me," he coaxed. "Easy now. We're the police. Breathe, yeah?" He flashed her his warrant card.

The crew member rocked, her breathing shallow. "I... I opened up to get more spears... and the dog, he ran through my legs. I tried to grab him, and I bumped into the dummies, and then—" She broke off as her eyes drew back to the corpse.

Cal guided her out the door. "Let's step outside, get you some air."

"Winston, leave it," Ryan commanded. The corgi backed away from the boot. Ryan slipped the collar around the dog's neck and held him on a short lead.

Cyrus's hand emerged from the dummies at a strange angle, as if he were calling for help. Ryan figured the pose was random, created when the woman and Winston had disturbed the pile, but he couldn't shake the creepy feeling Cyrus was performing, even in death.

Ryan pulled out his phone and dialled Lee's number. She picked up on the third ring.

"Hale? What is it?" Her voice crackled through the poor reception.

"We've found Wilde." Ryan moved away from the body. "In a storage space. He's dead. Been here for days, by the look of it."

"What? You're breaking up. Did you say dead?"

"Yes, dead. In a props storage room."

A burst of static. "... coming through... say again?"

Ryan walked to the door, dragging Winston behind him as

he searched for better reception. "We need Dr Yates and the forensics team out here."

More crackling, then Lee's voice came through clearer. "...sending them now. Secure the scene." The line went dead.

Ryan tried to phone Fiona next, but the call wouldn't connect. He pocketed his phone with a frustrated sigh.

"DI Hale?"

Ryan glanced up. Advika Patel stood in the doorway, her eyes wide as she took in the scene. To her credit, she didn't scream or faint.

"Ms Patel." He gestured to the space outside the storage room. "I need to cordon this area off. No one can come in here until forensics arrives. Can you track down Fiona and Sheri? I'll need their help here, and my phone hasn't got reception."

Advika nodded, her gaze rested on Cyrus's blank eyes before she composed herself. "I'll take care of it." She unclipped the walkie-talkie from her belt. "Jess, I need you to track down DS Bennett and DC Dewan for me. Direct them to the props department, storage room C, immediately." She paused and listened to the response. "Yes, it's urgent."

She clipped the radio back onto her belt and pointed to Winston, who now sat obediently by Ryan's feet. "Do you want me to take your dog to the production office? Keep him out of the way and give him some water?"

Ryan hesitated, then nodded. "Thank you. That would be helpful. His name is Winston. Also Advika?"

"Yes?"

"Please keep this discovery to yourself for now."

She nodded. "I will. Come on, boy."

Winston trotted off beside her without a backwards glance.

Ryan examined the scene. The room was cluttered, but nothing seemed disturbed beyond the jumble of dummies the production assistant had knocked into. That suggested Cyrus had been hidden, stashed among props designed to look like dead bodies.

A few minutes later, footsteps sounded outside. Fiona appeared in the doorway, breathless, with Sheri close behind.

"Ryan? What's—" Fiona's question died as she spotted the body. "Is that?"

"Cyrus Wilde," Ryan confirmed. "Winston found him. Though I imagine the smell would have caught someone's attention in the next day or so."

Fiona pulled a pair of gloves from her pocket and crouched beside the body. "No obvious defensive wounds on his hands. Single injury to the stomach from what we can see of him." She pointed to the dark stain on the front of Wilde's costume.

"Stabbed or shot, it's hard to tell through the fabric," Ryan agreed. "Odd Bod should be able to tell us more."

Sheri remained at the threshold, her notebook already out. "Should I collect statements from the crew?"

Ryan shook his head. "I need you to go to Vance and organise for his team to secure the area until officers from Buxton arrive. Then see if there's any CCTV footage of this corridor from the past five days."

The detective constable hurried off.

"Based on the smell, I'd say he could have been here since Saturday night," Fiona said. "Exactly when he disappeared."

"Dumped among the fake dead," Ryan murmured. "Someone has a sick sense of humour."

Ryan stepped back from the corpse, but his eyes lingered on Cyrus's lifeless face. His thoughts drifted to Freddy, Cyrus's young son, who would grow up without his father. He wondered if, given Cyrus's manipulative personality, that would end up being a positive thing for the lad.

At least he had been found. Cyrus Wilde might have been a questionable character in life, but in death, his family would have something Ryan couldn't give to Jaime's family or himself. Closure.

Ryan turned away from Cyrus's body. "Let's get this processed. Someone out there thought they were being clever. Let's prove them wrong."

CHAPTER NINETEEN

RYAN MUTTERED A CURSE AS HE EYED THE CONGREGATION of curious crew members at the corridor's end. The production assistant who'd found Cyrus must have talked. He pulled out his phone to take preliminary photos, but without proper lighting, they'd be useless beyond basic documentation.

The phone rang in his hand. Five bars where minutes before he'd had none. He'd never understand the mobile signal. Digit's name flashed on the screen.

"Hold the fort until Odd Bod arrives," Ryan said to Fiona. "And keep that lot back." He jerked his head towards the onlookers.

Ryan slipped through the throng, ignoring questions from the bolder crew members, and pushed through a side exit into the crisp morning air.

"Digit, what have you got for me?" He leaned against the exterior wall. The corrugated metal chilled his back.

"Sir, I've cloned Cyrus Wilde's phone data. The screen was shattered, but the internal memory remained intact," Digit explained. "I used a technique involving—"

"Great work, Digit, but keep to the facts. What did you find?"

"Message exchanges. Cyrus used information or blackmail to threaten or manipulate cast and crew members."

Classic Wilde, from the sound of things. Right until he pressed someone too far. "I'll need a list of names."

"Yes, Sir. There was also a text exchange right before his disappearance, from a burner phone since I can't trace the number in the studio database. The conversation took place on Saturday evening at 8:47 pm."

Ryan straightened. "Read it to me."

"The unknown party wrote: 'I'm not doing this anymore. I'm done'."

"And Wilde's response?"

"'We had a deal. It continues, or you know what happens'."

"Go on."

"The last message from the unknown sender reads: 'Fine. Meet me at your usual spot at eleven. I've got an idea that will benefit both of us'."

"His usual spot," Ryan repeated. The message came from someone who hadn't been intimidated by Cyrus. Had the actor's murder been premeditated, or a decision made in the heat of the moment? "Good work, Digit. That gives us a better timeframe and a potential second crime scene." Though how they would figure out where Cyrus's usual spot was, he didn't know. He filled Digit in on the discovery of Cyrus's body.

"There's something else," Digit said. "I've arranged for you to speak with Jacob Long, Bee Benson's brother. He's expecting you this afternoon."

Ryan closed his eyes. "I can't. With Wilde's body found, this is now a murder inquiry. I'm going to be tied up here for hours, maybe days." He rubbed his temples. His promise to

Alexis echoed in his head. If there was one person he didn't want to disappoint, it was her.

"Ah." Digit sounded deflated. "Shall I cancel?"

An idea—unwelcome but necessary—took root. "No. Don't cancel." Ryan took a breath. "How far is Long's place from the station?"

"1.2 miles. A short bus ride or a twenty-minute walk, depending on pace and traffic conditions."

"Digit," Ryan began, choosing his words with care. "How would you feel about conducting the interview yourself?"

Silence. Ryan could almost hear the cogs turning.

"Me, Sir? Conduct a witness interview? In person?"

"You know the basics of the Benson case, and you've read the file. Talk to him. See what he knows, what his impressions were."

"Interpersonal communication skills are not my strongest attribute. My ability to interpret non-verbal cues is below average. What if I misread the situation? Or offend him?"

Ryan suppressed a sigh. He knew Digit's limitations. But he also knew the young DC was brilliant and, beneath the awkward exterior, dedicated. "You'll be fine, Digit. Be yourself. Listen more than you talk. Ask open questions. You're good at spotting patterns and finding inconsistencies. Think of it as analysing a live data stream." He mentally crossed his fingers. This could go spectacularly wrong. Or Digit might uncover something vital.

"A live data stream..." Digit repeated, as if trying the words out. "I suppose human interaction could be modelled as a complex system with unpredictable variables."

"Exactly," Ryan said, not understanding what that meant. "Observe. Note down anything that stands out. You don't need to solve the case in one conversation."

"I... I would like to attempt the interview, Sir. It will be... a novel experience." A spark of something, enthusiasm, or perhaps intellectual curiosity, entered Digit's voice.

"Good man. Let me know how it goes. And Digit?"

"Sir?"

"No need to mention where you've been to Lee unless she asks."

"Understood. Discretion assured."

Ryan disconnected the call, his mind already shifting back to the studio case. Where was Cyrus's usual spot? He walked back to the door. The chatter of the crew members grew louder as he pulled it open. Someone muttered, "Got what he deserved," as Ryan stepped through, but it was impossible to tell who in the small crowd had said it.

Vance stood near the entrance to the props storage room, arms crossed, his expression a mixture of officiousness and concern as one of his uniformed security personnel established a cordon with bright yellow tape. He hovered near Fiona, who briefed the other guard.

"If you need to take a break, Fi, I understand," Ryan heard Vance say as he drew closer. "Perhaps you could help DC Dewan with the footage collection? Dead bodies can be quite shocking for people who aren't used to them."

Fiona's smile looked painted on. "And how many dead bodies do you come across in your line of work, Vance?"

"I'm just saying, if you feel faint—"

"I don't feel faint." The words came out close to a growl.

"No one would think less of you for stepping outside," Vance continued, oblivious. "It's only natural for a woman to be squeamish about these things."

Ryan watched Fiona's fingers flex, like she was imagining them around Vance's throat.

"Everything under control?" he asked loudly, making Vance jump.

"DI Hale." Vance straightened and puffed out his chest. "We've secured the perimeter and cleared nonessential personnel from the immediate vicinity." He gestured to the yellow tape strung down the corridor with all the pride of a child showing off a crayon drawing.

"And I suppose you're essential personnel?" Fiona asked sweetly.

Before Vance could respond, a familiar voice echoed down the corridor. "Right, where's our unfortunate fellow? Let's have a look-see."

Cal appeared first, his usual bounce subdued. He offered Ryan a grim nod. Close behind, Dr Edmund Yates, the pathologist known as Odd Bod, bustled into view, his battered leather medical bag swinging at his side. The doctor's brightly patterned waistcoat and candy-cane-striped jacket stood out against the subdued palette of the crew members he walked through.

Behind Odd Bod, the forensics team followed. Paul Smith, head of EMSOU forensics, led the way. The collar of his checked shirt peeked from the top of his white Tyvek suit, and his camera bumped against his chest as he walked. Beside him, Eloise Durrant, his senior crime scene officer, moved with a dancer's grace despite the heavy evidence cases in her hands, her dark skin stark against the white suit zipped to her throat.

"Ryan, my boy," Odd Bod chirped, his eyes already fixed on the storage room. "I believe we have a celebrity demise? Most irregular for this neck of the woods."

Paul directed a pair of newly arrived techs to establish a more formal perimeter. Eloise acknowledged Ryan with a curt nod, her eyes already scanning the environment, taking in the makeshift cordon, the dim lights, and the crew members Vance's security guards tried to usher away.

Odd Bod rubbed his hands together. "Well, let's not keep him waiting, shall we? Poor form."

Paul paused at the threshold, his gaze landing on the body. "I was a bit of a thespian in high school; no time for it now of course. Lily's going to be devastated. She's a huge Caspian Drest fan."

His wife? Ryan thought. Then he remembered. *No, his sister.* She had a chronic illness, and Paul was her primary carer.

"We'll work the perimeter first until Dr Yates has finished," Paul said, "then move to the interior." His gloved hand sketched an invisible grid across the floor. "No one crosses into the storage room without a suit and booties on. I want every dummy logged before we move Wilde. Eloise, I need you to process the weapons." He looked around at the bins filled with spears, swords, and axes. "Pull in some help. It's going to be a big job." He turned to Ryan and Fiona and held out a pair of bags with white suits inside. "You know the drill, detectives."

Once they were all suited and booted, they followed the pathologist inside.

Ryan watched as Odd Bod knelt beside Cyrus's body. The pathologist hummed a tuneless melody, his examination swift but thorough. Paul, meanwhile, conducted a methodical sweep of the room with his camera, the flash creating a strobe effect.

After a few minutes, Odd Bod stood and pulled off his gloves. "Yes, yes. One rather decisive puncture wound to the abdomen. Nasty bit of business." He pursed his lips. "There is relatively little blood here for such an injury. Which suggests Mr Wilde met his end elsewhere and was transported here."

"Can you tell what kind of weapon?" Ryan asked.

Odd Bod gestured to the bins of weapons. "Well, my dear Ryan, you're rather spoilt for choice around here, aren't you? We'll know more once I get him on my table, but a sharp, narrow blade, certainly." He peered at an ornate prop sword nearby. "Sharper than what you'd normally find on a set. The edges are clean."

"Any idea of the time of death?"

"Time stops for no man. Especially the impatient DI Hale... ah? The low ambient temperature in this room has likely slowed decomposition to some extent, but based on initial observations, the lack of rigor mortis, and the degree of putrefaction visible, I'd say he's been here three to five days at a minimum. I can give you a definitive timeline after I've conducted the autopsy."

Ryan nodded. "That fits. He received a text, a summons, to meet someone late Saturday night. No one's seen him since."

"Give it to me," Cal said from the door.

Ryan turned to find the detective holding a scruffy crew member by the arm.

"Come on. I know someone filming for their socials when I see it. Takes one to know one, mate. Unlock it and hand it over."

The man pulled out his phone and used his face to unlock the screen. He gave it to Cal, who deleted the video and sent the man on his way. No doubt a tabloid would have paid the opportunist a fortune for the clip.

Ryan excused Fiona and himself, and then gathered with Cal in the corridor.

"Sorry, boss. He snuck in behind me from one of the far corridors."

"No harm done," Ryan replied. All the nooks and crannies made the place a nightmare to lock down. He filled Fiona and Cal in on the text messages Digit had uncovered.

"His usual spot," Fiona said, tapping her chin.

"We need to find out where that is," Ryan replied.

"Margot, the set designer, mentioned something about him tricking her into meeting him at the pit?"

"Season two, right?" Cal bounced on his toes. "The dungeon at Ravendeep had a massive pit. They sacrificed some of Niamh's pirates they captured. Proper dark stuff. Still living in my head rent-free."

Ryan called over a security guard. "Is there still a set with a pit in it?"

The man nodded. "Yeah, Stage Five."

"Right," Ryan said as the man went back to his task. "Fiona, can you find Isaac Emerson and break the news about Cyrus? Get his initial reaction. Then see if you can track down Astrid. Despite their estrangement, Cyrus was still Freddy's father."

Fiona nodded, her expression composed. "Understood." She glanced over at where Vance still lingered. "I'll handle Mitchell as well."

"I'll head over to Stage Five now," Ryan said. "Have a poke around."

"Can come with you, boss?" Cal asked.

Ryan waved him off. "This isn't the Phantom of the Opera. It's not like the killer's still going to be lurking around in there. If I find anything to process, I'll call in the cavalry. In the meantime, I need you to give Eloise a hand cataloguing these weapons. Liaise with Jasper and see if he has a props list. Find out if anyone knows what's supposed to be here and what might be missing or used."

Cal's face underwent a rapid series of transformations. Initial disappointment warred with a sudden, dawning awareness. His gaze flicked to the beautiful, but also intimidating French SOCO, who discussed something in low tones with one of her team members holding a set of lights. A flush crept up Cal's neck, and his Adam's apple bobbed.

"Right, guv," Cal managed, his voice a little higher than usual. "Help with the props. Got it."

CHAPTER TWENTY

Ryan left Cal stammering at Eloise about the inventory and navigated the winding corridors. A props assistant with a buzz cut had given him directions to Stage Five but told him there was no filming scheduled there today, her blue eyes filled with curiosity.

The further he ventured from the hub of activity around Cyrus's body, the quieter the complex became. The distant murmur of voices faded until all that remained was the echo of his footsteps and the hum of ventilation.

He passed a series of numbered storage rooms and arrived at Stage Five's heavy steel door. The small red light above it was off, showing the set wasn't in use. The door stood ajar. Ryan pushed it open, and the hinges groaned.

"Hello?" His voice echoed through the vast space. Only a few auxiliary fittings cast a weak yellow glow across the stage.

Beside the door was a panel of switches. He flicked a few, hoping they were the main lights. Nothing happened.

"Brilliant," he muttered, pulling a small penlight from his

pocket. The beam cut a narrow tunnel of white light. The concrete floor leading to the set was scuffed and marked with coloured tape for camera positions.

As his eyes adjusted, the industrial room transformed. The set designers had created a ritual chamber straight out of a demonic nightmare. Rough-hewn balconies and walkways crisscrossed the upper levels, leading to shadowy alcoves carved into false rock walls.

He moved onto the set, and his footsteps echoed off the distant corrugated iron walls. The air tasted stale and metallic, laced with an astringent chemical smell. At the centre of the stage gaped a deep pit, its rim surrounded by artfully blood-stained stones carved with arcane runes.

"Bit over the top, isn't it?" Ryan said to himself, then felt foolish. Fantasy wasn't his thing. Give him a gritty crime drama like Breaking Bad or Line of Duty any day of the week. It didn't hurt to find out what the criminals were up to, even the fictional ones.

He shook his head. Talking to himself on an abandoned film set was either the beginning of a bad horror film or a sign the stress of the job was getting to him.

A faint creak sounded from above.

Ryan looked up and raised the torch. The beam sliced through the gloom and lit up a steel gantry with safety railings, lined with heavy weights fastened with chains.

For a moment, he thought he saw a shadow shift across an alcove on the upper level.

"Anyone there?" His voice was firm despite the sudden tightness in his chest. "Police. Identify yourself."

The darkness swallowed his words. Only the hum of the ventilation system answered.

Ryan swept the beam again, but the shadows remained

motionless. As he stared, the hair on his arms lifted. He tapped his phone screen. The signal bars stayed stubbornly empty. Of course. With masses of steel overhead and the thick quarry walls outside, the room was a perfect Faraday cage. He lowered the device.

He should walk out, find a signal and bring the team in, or at least someone who knew where the bloody light switch was. But if there was someone up there, leaving now would give them the chance to slip away. He'd lose them and any way of finding out the reason they were here.

If there was anyone lurking at all. The noise might have been a loose cable shifting. He pushed aside his unease as a familiar stubbornness settled in. It was nothing. His mind, already primed by the discovery of Cyrus's body, was reacting to the unnerving surroundings, however artificial they might be.

He moved onto the stage and spotted a collection of plastic containers and cleaning cloths near the far side of the pit, then his brain caught up with his nose. The chemical smell was bleach. Someone had attempted to clean up, but had they finished?

He crouched beside the pit and shone the torch beam inside. His attention snagged on the bloodstains. They weren't confined to the prop stones. Splatter extended onto the vibrant green fabric at the bottom. Ryan was no expert on the magic of filmmaking, but he was certain a green screen needed to be, well, green. The production wouldn't deliberately stain its expensive visual effects surface. Could this be Cyrus's blood? Was this set the actual scene of the attack?

He swung the torch in a circular pattern. Jammed against the inside of the pit, something metallic glinted. A dagger, just out of reach. It looked different from the props he'd seen in the storage room. Less ornate and a hell of a lot sharper.

A scrape. On steel. Loud. From directly above.

His head snapped up along with the torch beam.

For an instant, a pale face stared back at him from within the shadows of a black hood. Beyond it, something large and dark detached from the ceiling and plummeted towards him. He raised his arms and leapt, but it was too late.

The world went black.

CHAPTER TWENTY-ONE

JACOB LONG'S FLAT SAT TUCKED AWAY OFF CINDERMERE Road, in one of the squat concrete blocks of the Windermere Housing Estate. Digit counted four separate security cameras on his journey through the estate to Jacob's door. One functioning, three with cables detached or damaged. According to the latest reporting, the statistical probability of solving crimes on estates with non-functioning CCTV was 22.4% lower than those with fully operational systems. He set himself a voice reminder to contact Chesterfield Borough Council.

Digit knocked three times, then stepped back one metre from the door to maintain optimal personal space. From inside came shuffling, a muffled curse and then the rattle of locks disengaging.

Jacob Long filled the doorframe. Smaller than Digit had anticipated based on his physical statistics, though this was likely due to his hunched posture. He wore jeans and a faded grey hoodie with the hood pulled up despite being indoors. Weighted for increased age and girth, the face that scowled out of the hood matched the driver's licence image on file with enough accuracy for Digit to feel comfortable identifying him as Jacob Long.

"Mr Long," Digit said.

"You the copper?" Jacob squinted. His brows knitted together as he took in Digit's appearance.

"I am not DI Ryan Hale as originally specified. A concurrent investigation required his presence. DI Hale sends his apologies for not attending." He held up his warrant card. "I'm Detective Constable Mathias Asare, Jr. from the East Midlands Special Operations Unit Major Crimes. Although colleagues refer to me as 'Digit', which is a contracted form of 'digital' referencing my specialisation in computational—"

"You coming in or what?" Jacob interrupted, already turning away.

Digit followed him through a narrow hallway lined with peeling wallpaper and catalogued the details available to him. Three-day-old takeaway containers on the kitchen counter and the television tuned to a horse racing channel. The ambient temperature was cooler than outside. Insufficient heating for a man of his age.

Jacob nudged aside a pile of newspapers on the sofa. "Kettle's busted, but I've got beer." He held out an unopened can.

"No, thank you. I'm on duty, which prohibits alcohol consumption. Perhaps you could also abstain? Alcohol impairs cognitive function even at low doses, and we should both strive for optimal neural processing for this interview."

Jacob stared at him, then cracked open the can. "Right. You're a weird one."

Since it was a statement rather than a question, Digit ignored the remark and took his digital recorder from his pocket. "May I record our conversation? It allows for perfect accuracy compared to manual note-taking."

"Whatever. Just get on with it." Jacob dropped onto the

sofa while Digit perched opposite him on a rickety kitchen chair.

"I'm investigating the circumstances surrounding Matthew Benson's death," Digit began. He activated the recorder and moved aside an empty beer can so he could place the microphone at the optimum distance to pick up Mr Long's voice. "According to the case files, you resided with the Benson family at the time of Matthew Benson's murder?"

Jacob's eyes narrowed. "I thought that was all wrapped up. Bee confessed, didn't she?"

"Recent witness statements have introduced statistical anomalies that warrant re-examination. How long had you been staying with the Bensons when Matthew was killed?"

Jacob rubbed his stubbled chin. "About a month. Came down from Hull after the factory accident. Broke my back trying to fix a jammed conveyor belt." He leaned forward, and his voice rose. "Fell over six metres onto concrete, but did those bloody greedy robbers care? No, got a week's pay and a see-you-later. Doctor said I wouldn't be fit for heavy work again."

The workplace accident was irrelevant to the investigation, so Digit moved on. "And your observations of the family dynamic during cohabitation?"

Jacob frowned. "My what now?"

Digit mentally recalibrated his linguistic approach. "How did the Benson family get along?"

"They didn't." Jacob shifted on the sofa. "Matthew was a good kid, but Christ, he loved winding people up. Proper prankster. He'd be the one rigging the bucket of water over the door, but Peter'd be the one standing there dripping wet when Amos found them." He chuckled. "Whiny kid, Peter. Needed to grow a backbone and stand up to his cousin, but a harmless sort."

"Peter's your nephew?" Digit asked.

Jacob nodded.

"Did he live with the Bensons?"

"Nah, just hung around like a bad smell. Bee encouraged it. Michelle, our sister, up and died of kidney failure when the boy was ten. She was the baby of the family, so it was an enormous shock for all of us. Bob, the boy's dad, is a wicked drunk. Forgot to feed the kid half the time and smacked him round some. Even that arsehole Amos was more appealing than Bob."

"And Hannah Benson?"

"She could be sweet when she wanted to, but snarkier than the girls in my day. Always butting heads with Amos about his rules. But that's teenagers, innit? She was what? Fourteen?"

"I believe Miss Benson was fifteen when Matthew was killed."

"Whatever."

"Could you elaborate on Amos? Perhaps provide specific examples of his behaviour."

Jacob let out a harsh laugh. "Specific? Right. He was a holier-than-thou, fire-and-brimstone arsehole. Specific enough for you?" He leaned forward, elbows on knees. "Fear and manipulation in the name of God, that was his game. If the kids so much as breathed wrong, it was hellfire and damnation sermons for hours."

Digit nodded. "You seem to harbour strong negative sentiments towards Mr Benson."

"You're damn right I do." Jacob huffed. "Kicked me out. Soon as Bee was taken away. Realised my compensation claim from the factory wouldn't be the queen's ransom he'd imagined. Next thing, I was surplus to requirements. A parasite, he called me."

Digit tilted his head. "So the environment was characterised by rigid authority structures and significant interpersonal tension. Did you observe patterns of conflict between Amos and Matthew?"

"Conflict? Between Amos and everyone else. Amos was a controlling bastard who made everyone in the house miserable." Jacob took a gulp of beer. "Because deep down he knew he wasn't as important as he made out."

Small-community gossip often contained kernels of relevant information. Digit maintained eye contact and waited seven seconds, the optimal pause length according to interrogation studies to encourage an interviewee to fill the silence.

Jacob took the bait. "Never met a bloke with a bigger chip on his shoulder than Amos. His family had money. Owned an engineering firm. They backed Amos for the church, but the church wouldn't have him. Said he lacked compassion. Bee was the only true Christian in that house. So he pretended to work at the family firm."

Digit nodded along in what he hoped was an encouraging fashion.

"His brothers, they were the brains. Kept him away from anything important. Gave him a fancy title and let him swan about, but everyone knew he was about as much use as tits on a bull."

"Why did Bee marry him then?"

Jacob paused. "She was the prettiest girl in the village and very devout. He flashed his faith and supposed inheritance and reeled her in, I guess. He wasn't a bad-looking lad back in the day. Once they were married though, treated her like a skivvy. Worse sometimes."

"How did Mrs Benson respond to this treatment?"

"Bee?" Jacob's gaze focused on a stain on the far wall. "She was real loyal. Fiercely loyal. But you could see it ate at her. The disappointment. She spent her whole life shielding them kids from his rages and his never-ending bloody lectures. I remember the morning before it all happened. Matty was on at them for a pet. Begging, he was. Proper little terrier himself. But Hannah, she was allergic to cats and dogs. Bee was trying to explain it gently like, while Amos just banged on about how irresponsible Matty was and the cost of pet food."

"And you maintained no visual or auditory awareness of events preceding the discovery of Matthew's body?"

"What?"

"Where were you when the murder occurred?"

"Asleep in the TV room, wasn't I?"

Digit frowned. "I wasn't present, so I can't comment on the validity of that statement."

"Fine," Jacob grumbled as if Digit had forced him into a confession. "I'd taken painkillers for my back. Knocked me out. Needed the little buggers regularly back in those days. Didn't hear a thing until Bee screamed, and even then it took me a minute to come round."

Digit observed the pulse visible at Jacob's temple had increased. The memory was painful for him. A man with Jacob's working-class background might blame himself for failing to protect both his sister and his nephew. "Did you attempt communication with Bee post-incarceration?"

"Tried visiting her for the first few years. She refused to see me. Wouldn't even take my letters." Jacob's voice cracked. "My own sister."

"Did you see any unusual behaviour from strangers in the vicinity of the Benson residence? Do you deem it likely someone could have slipped on and off the property that day?"

"Nah, the neighbour would have noticed anyone hanging about. As for the house, you could check it out yourself, get a tour. It's up for sale again. The third owner just went bankrupt. The locals are saying it's cursed."

"Curses are statistically improbable and lack empirical

evidence," Digit replied. "Your consistent belief in Bee's innocence seems at odds with her confession."

Jacob's shoulders tensed. "Because there's no way my sister did it."

"What is the basis for your certainty? A confession has a high correlation with guilt in homicide cases."

"You didn't know Bee." Jacob's eyes locked with Digit's. "She loved those kids more than anything. She'd die for them, not kill one of them."

Digit looked away. "If statistical probability suggests Bee's confession shows guilt, yet your familial knowledge contradicts this data point, one variable must be incorrect."

"She didn't do it," Jacob whispered.

Digit's fingers tapped the side of the chair. "In most false confession cases, the subject is shielding another individual or covering up a larger crime. Here, the former is the most probable. Was there anyone else with a motive or opportunity to harm Matthew?"

Jacob seemed about to speak, then his expression closed off. "Look, I've said enough. This was all dragged out years ago."

"But the statistical analysis doesn't—"

"Not everything's about your bloody statistics, mate." Jacob stood abruptly. "Interview's over."

Digit remained seated as he processed the inconsistency. "Your emotional response suggests additional knowledge you're unwilling to share. This creates a data gap that—"

"Out. Now." Jacob moved towards the door. "I've got nothing else to say."

Digit collected his recorder. Jacob's reaction likely contained valuable information despite the interview's premature termination. But by his calculations, Jacob had revealed at least thirty percent more than he'd intended to.

Precisely as Digit had predicted.

CHAPTER TWENTY-TWO

Ryan tried to open his eyes then squeezed them shut against the bright light. The metallic tang of blood filled his mouth, competing with the acrid bite of bleach that burned his nostrils. Something coarse and heavy pressed into his back. His head throbbed, and a dull ache radiated from his temple.

For a heartbeat, he wasn't on a soundstage at all. He was tied to a steel chair, shoulders pinned. His fingers spasmed, bracing for restraints that weren't there. Panic flashed white-hot through his body before the present snapped back into place.

"Ryan? Can you hear me?" A hand shook his shoulder.

A soft voice nearby. "Security, this is PA Patel, requesting the studio doctor to Stage Five. We have a police officer down."

"What...?" Ryan's voice sounded distant. He sat up, disoriented as he looked around the set now bathed in light.

Fiona's face swam into focus. "Easy. Don't move too fast."

"What happened?" He blinked, trying to push past the fog in his brain.

"I couldn't track down Isaac, so I came back to the crime

scene. You'd been gone a while, and I got worried, so Advika showed me the way here." Fiona's hand steadied his arm.

"Here?"

Fragments surfaced. The yellow glow of the set. The glint of something sharp. A sudden rush of air. He remembered twisting out of the way on instinct. Then other memories muscled in. A chair, a voice he'd never put a name to, and the slow realisation he wasn't getting out of that room in one piece. He shoved them down.

"Something dropped on me."

"A sandbag, by the looks of it." Fiona gestured to a torn canvas sack spilling sand across the floor. She leaned down and examined the cut on his left cheek. "Not deep enough to add to your collection, I think. You're lucky it wasn't a direct hit, or we'd be scraping your brains off the polystyrene rocks."

"Always the optimist, Fi." Ryan's vision cleared and brought the set into sharp focus. "There was someone up there." He gestured upwards to the gantry. "Black hood, pale face. I think they'd been cleaning up."

"Well, they did a proper job of it." Fiona pointed to the dagger, now lying a few feet away on the stage. Its blade gleamed under the lights. "Everything within a two-metre radius is doused in bleach."

Ryan followed her gaze to the ritual pit. The bleach had eaten into the fake rune carvings and splashed down onto the green screen below, covering it in white splotches.

"They stayed to clean," he said. The realisation cleared his head further. "Even after they dropped a sandbag on my head. They didn't run; they stepped around me and carried on."

"Ballsy," Fiona agreed. "I guess us finding Cyrus's body must've spooked them into cleaning up."

Jesus, I'm lucky they didn't take the time to slit my throat.

Advika moved closer to the pit. "The stains... anyone

walking onto this set would have assumed they were part of the dressing. We use so much fake blood here." Her voice shook. "This set was scheduled for filming this past Monday, but production pushed the scene back at the last minute."

Ryan nodded as understanding dawned. "That's why they chose this location. The blood would blend in with the set design." Pain shot through his shoulder as he shifted position. "If filming had gone ahead before anyone took Cyrus's disappearance seriously, any evidence would've been trampled before we even knew to look."

"The old 'hide the crime in plain sight' trick," Fiona said. "Clever."

Fiona and Advika helped him to his feet. The room tilted. They guided him to a canvas-backed deck chair tucked in a shadowy corner.

The young doctor jogged through the stage door and knelt beside him. "We meet again, Detective. Name's Shaun. Took a tumble, did you?"

"More of a strategic dive."

Shaun chuckled. "Let's have a look at that head." He noticed the scars on Ryan's face and hands. "You're obviously no stranger to going three rounds."

Ryan winced as the doctor palpated the swelling on his temple, cleaned the cut on his cheek and applied butterfly strips to hold the wound closed. "You'll have a nasty bruise there. Maybe a mild concussion. Best get you to the hospital for a once-over."

"No." Ryan pushed Shaun's hand away. "I'm fine."

Yeah, right. Flat on his back under bright lights with people he didn't know prodding at him as the surgeon talked about cutting his wedding ring from his mangled finger like he wasn't even there.

This time he was more angry than injured. Angry at

himself. He should have brought Cal, and he should have anticipated that the person who'd killed Cyrus could be monitoring their every move. He'd let the killer get away. Let them destroy evidence right under his nose.

Fiona came to his side. "You need time to recover. Enough of this macho bullshit."

"Is that how you address a superior officer, DS Bennett?" He tried for stern, but suspected the blood drying on the front of his coat ruined the effect.

"It is when said superior officer is being a stubborn arse." Fiona smiled. "*Sir.*"

Advika's eyes widened at the exchange.

Ryan sighed. "Fine. But no hospital."

Fiona gave him a long, searching look, then nodded. "Okay. And for God's sake, don't wander off alone again. Christ, this isn't a Nancy Drew novel."

"Yes, Mum," Ryan muttered.

Fiona ignored him, then asked Advika and Shaun if they could give them a moment.

The PA nodded and moved away. Shaun handed Fiona an icepack, then followed.

"I'll ring Paul, get his team to treat this as a secondary scene and cordon it off," Fiona said. "There's also been another development I haven't had time to share with all the excitement."

She filled Ryan in on the notebook Millie had discovered.

"Sheri and I will pay Mr Kerrington a visit. See what he knows about bleach and inappropriate workplace behaviour."

"I should be..." Ryan tried to lever himself out of the chair. However the world spun. He sat back down, the chair scraping across the concrete.

"Have some faith in your team to deliver the goods." Fiona handed him the icepack. "Now put this on your enormous *block* head."

Ryan grimaced as he pressed the icepack to the lump. "Make sure someone from security comes here with the techs." Fiona had a point about wandering around alone. The last thing he needed was to endanger anyone else. There was a killer on set, and the attempt on his life was proof they weren't afraid to kill again.

CHAPTER TWENTY-THREE

Sheri followed Fiona through the workshop complex towards the costume department. The corridors narrowed, lined with racks of medieval garments and homespun tunics in muted colours.

"I'm letting you take the lead," Fiona told her.

Sheri nodded, trying to project confidence despite the knot in her stomach.

Fiona patted her arm. "Don't worry, you'll be great. Now, first rule of detective work," she said, her voice quiet enough it wouldn't carry beyond them. "Never believe the first thing a suspect tells you, but don't dismiss it either."

They rounded a corner and stepped into a packed room. Two assistants hunched over a workbench, dipping metal buckles into a chemical solution that made Sheri's eyes water. Three more worked at sewing machines, the mechanical whirr providing a steady backbeat to the chaos.

In the centre of it all stood Blaise Kerrington, his pouting face a match to his LinkedIn profile. He wore black from head to toe.

Sheri's pulse quickened. Pale face, black woollen jacket with a hood. A match to DI Hale's description. Stage Five wasn't far from here. He could have navigated the route without being seen.

"No, no, NO!" Blaise shouted at a terrified-looking young man holding a measuring tape. "How many times must I tell you? The neckline must be asymmetrical. The Queen of Shadows isn't some suburban housewife in a Marks and Spencer cardigan!" He snatched the tape away.

Fiona cleared her throat. "Mr Kerrington?"

The man turned, and irritation flashed across his face. "Oh, for God's sake." He gestured dramatically at the elaborate robe spread across the cutting table. "Can't you see I'm in the middle of something? This needs to be fitted in an hour, and we are inches... inches," he yelled, holding up his fingers for emphasis, "away from my entire artistic vision being ruined."

"I'm DC Dewan, and this is DS Bennett. We need to ask you some questions."

Blaise rolled his eyes. "Everyone needs a piece of me. The actors need alterations. Mr Emerson pulled forward the Pirate Queen's scenes, so I had to work all weekend. My sweet Coco is at the vet, so I had a second night of broken sleep." He sighed and then waved a dismissive hand at the measuring tape boy. "Go help Grace with the extras' uniforms. Get out of my sight."

Sheri stepped closer to the costume, unable to resist the allure of being near one of the show's iconic pieces. The robe's fabric shimmered under the lights, a deep indigo with silver thread woven into an intricate pattern of intertwining wyverns. The motif of the Queen of Shadows.

"This is stunning," she said, with genuine admiration in her voice. "Is this for Piper Stone's character?"

Blaise's posture shifted as professional pride overrode his irritation. "Part of the Queen's wedding gown." He leaned forward. "Though you didn't hear anything about a wedding from me."

Sheri's heart did a little skip. Fans had been arguing on Reddit for months about whether the Shadow Queen would ever marry the Storm Knight. "Right. Of course," she said, schooling her face back to neutral. She studied the wyvern motif again. "The beadwork is exquisite." She moved closer, using her admiration as cover to determine with a subtle sniff if Blaise smelled of bleach. Unfortunately, the chemical solution from the metal ageing process at the nearby table made it impossible to tell.

"Grace's work," Blaise admitted. "Can't design her way out of a paper bag, which is why she manages the extras' costumes. But she's a hard worker and a goddess at beadwork, bless her. She's so good at..." He paused, searching for the right word. "Assisting."

Sheri stiffened at his dismissive tone. Interesting how quick he was to downplay his assistant's contribution while still taking credit for the overall design.

Fiona caught her eye and gave a subtle nod.

Sheri straightened her shoulders. "Mr Kerrington, we need to talk about your relationship with Cyrus Wilde."

"Our relationship?" Blaise scoffed. "I dress him. He wears the clothes. Sometimes, if the planets align and the wardrobe gods are smiling, he manages not to spill his kale smoothie down a priceless silk jerkin."

"We know about your personal interest in Cyrus, Mr Kerrington," Sheri said, her gaze steady.

Blaise's eyes widened, then narrowed. He turned to the wider room and raised his voice. "Everybody out."

The assistants and machinists froze.

"Stop what you're doing and take a break. Now!"

An assistant dipping buckles looked like she might say

something but wisely chose not to. As the door swung shut behind the last machinist, Blaise turned back to the detectives with flattened lips.

"I'm not sure what you're trying to insinuate. I'm a happily married man."

Fiona stepped forward. "It's easy to see how it happens. Proximity leads to admiration, admiration deepens into something more, until you find yourself manipulating questionable images on your computer at midnight. Are you obsessed with Cyrus Wilde, Mr Kerrington?"

"Please." Blaise snorted. "Cyrus might be easy on the eyes, but anyone with a brain who's spent over fifteen minutes in the man's company can tell he's a viper who'd sell his grandmother for a five-minute chat with Christopher Nolan."

"We found your notebook and the photos," Sheri said.

"My what?"

"Your notebook containing explicit poetry about what you'd like to do to Cyrus... ah... sexually. It also contains manipulated photos of you both as a couple in the back."

"That's preposterous!" He dropped the robe in his hands. "What notebook? I haven't written a poem since juniors."

Sheri reached into her satchel and pulled out a handful of photocopied pages. "This is the notebook." She placed a photo of the red notebook on the table. "And this is a sample of the poetry." She laid down a few more pages.

Blaise's face went slack. "I've never seen this notebook before in my life." His voice climbed higher. "Someone's playing a sick joke."

Fiona picked up a handwritten note lying beside the robe. Instructions for the beadwork. "At a glance, the handwriting looks the same."

"No!" Blaise's composure crumbled. Tears welled as he

clutched the edge of the worktable. "It's not true. You don't understand."

"Then help us to," Sheri said.

"Do you know what it's like?" His voice cracked. "Every day, every single day, I fight assumptions. That I must be predatory. Dangerous." Tears tracked down his pale cheeks. "I've had to be twice as professional as everyone else just to be taken half as seriously. I would never risk my position or the relationship with the man I love for something so stupid." He swiped angrily at his tears. "My entire career, my relationship, everything I've worked for."

Fiona remained unmoved. "The evidence suggests otherwise."

"Then the evidence is fake!" Blaise shouted. "I'm being framed."

His raw emotion seemed genuine to Sheri. His distress emanated from a place of deep, personal pain. She recognised it, having felt similar frustration when her own background led people to make assumptions about her capabilities. But Fiona's scepticism of his story was obvious, and Sheri was the newest member of the team. Would telling Blaise she believed him make her look naive? Would it weaken the prosecution's case if they decided to charge him?

Fiona spoke before Sheri could respond. "Mr Kerrington, Cyrus Wilde has been found dead."

The colour drained from Blaise's face. "Dead?"

"His body was discovered an hour ago. Your interest in the victim makes you our prime suspect."

Blaise swayed. His lips moved, forming words that didn't emerge. Then his eyes rolled back, and he collapsed to the floor with a heavy thud, cracking his head on the concrete.

"Bloody hell," Fiona muttered.

Sheri knelt beside him and checked his pulse. Strong, but

he was out cold. A small part of her sympathy dissolved when she thought about the mountain of paperwork this would generate. She'd seen hardened officers go down the same way when stress and shock collided. The body had its own logic, but Blaise injuring himself during questioning meant they'd need to document everything and triple-check it to prevent a potential lawsuit.

Fiona marched to the door and yanked it open. "You," she said to the assistant loitering outside. "Go to Stage Five and see if Shaun, the doctor, is still there. Tell him we've got someone unconscious in the costume department."

The young woman nodded and hurried away.

Sheri placed her folded jacket under Blaise's head and stared down at his pale face.

He'd seemed confused by the notebook, and his shock when he'd heard Cyrus was dead appeared real. If he was lying, he was one hell of an actor. Then again, he'd spent his career surrounded by them. He must have picked up a trick or two.

When she looked up, she saw Fiona slip Blaise's scissors into an evidence bag.

CHAPTER TWENTY-FOUR

DIGIT ARRANGED THE PAGES WITH PRECISION AND aligned the stack with the edges of the binding machine. He'd calculated the optimal framework for maximum readability. Forty-seven lines of text per page, with consistent 1.25-inch margins and ideal leading between paragraphs. He'd just inserted the plastic binding comb when the copy room door swung open.

His boss, DCI Olivia Lee stood in the doorway. Her sharp gaze fixed on the document beneath Digit's hands as he pressed the handle and locked the binding in place.

"DCI Lee," he stammered. "I didn't anticipate anyone requiring the copy room."

"Is that the preliminary on Wilde, DC Asare?" She held out a hand. "Let's have a look."

Digit pulled the document off the binder and held it to his chest. He angled his body to shift the report away from Lee's line of sight. "It's still in draft phase, Ma'am. I haven't optimised it for external review."

"You think I can't read a draft, Digit?" The corner of her

mouth twitched. "Or that I'm not intelligent enough to keep that in mind?" She extended her hand again, palm up.

He clutched the report tighter. "The data requires further cross-referencing to achieve optimal accuracy. The current margin of error is unacceptable for dissemination to superior officers."

Lee sighed. "How do you fancy a spell on traffic duty, Asare? Monitoring the A617 roundabout."

Digit blinked. "Traffic duty? In what capacity? As an observer, data analyst or active participant in vehicle monitoring and citation issuance?"

"In the capacity of standing at a junction for eight hours wearing a fluorescent jacket, directing buses in the rain in February. I imagine you'll be able to collate lots of lovely data on driver incompetence."

"My expertise is in data collection and analysis for major crimes. Reassignment to traffic would be a significant misallocation of resources."

Lee folded her arms. "Digit."

Digit recognised the DCI's posture. His nervous behaviour had likely triggered Lee's investigative instincts. He calculated further resistance was futile and handed over the bound report. He winced as Lee read the title on the cover aloud.

"'Jacob Long Interview Analysis: Benson, M. - Historical Case File Addendum'."

Lee flicked through pages dense with text, charts and highlighted sections. She paused, then looked up, one eyebrow arched. "Funny, I don't see Cyrus Wilde's name in here?"

"I can provide a full contextual explanation, DCI Lee." The words tumbled out. "A trusted acquaintance, a medical professional exhibiting high veracity indicators, approached me. She possessed information regarding the potential innocence of Beatrice Benson, convicted of the murder of her son,

Matthew. The informant, a former neighbour of Mrs Benson, is in palliative care. The recent publicity surrounding the ten-year anniversary brought up repressed feelings, and the neighbour wished to disclose her observations prior to her impending demise."

Lee held up a hand. "Hold on. A friend asked you?"

"Ah... affirmative. Well, more of an acquaintance—"

"Who was this friend?"

Digit's fingers drummed on the counter. "Ah... Dr Alexis Hope." He gestured towards the report in Lee's hands. "This document contains a comprehensive breakdown of the case so far." He leaned forward. "I've highlighted the most statistically significant portions in yellow. The red tabs indicate contradictions within Mr Long's testimony or established case files, while blue represents areas requiring further data acquisition for conclusive analysis—"

"Whoa, back up a bit." Her eyes narrowed. "You're telling me you, DC Mathias Asare, decided to unofficially reopen a ten-year-old murder case? A very high-profile one Chief Inspector Lampton himself put to bed, without so much as a by-your-leave to me or DI Hale?"

Digit paused, his brow furrowed. "Autonomous action outside the chain of command does present as an outlier in my documented behavioural profile, Ma'am."

"Damn right it does." Lee tapped the report. "Sounds more like something DI Hale would pull, doesn't it? Especially given DI Hale and Dr Hope have a long personal history."

She held his gaze, and Digit felt himself squirm. He adjusted his glasses as a distraction. "DI Hale utilises a different operational methodology, Ma'am. His approach often incorporates intuitive leaps, whereas my process is data driven and adheres to established protocols where feasible."

"A very diplomatic way of saying DI Hale thinks rules and

procedures are for other people." She kept staring. "I'm only going to ask this once, DC Asare. Did DI Hale recruit you to assist with this unauthorised investigation?"

"Unauthorised is a subjective term. Many groundbreaking investigations were initially considered unauthorised before—"

"Traffic duty, Asare. For a month."

Digit's shoulders slumped. "Yes. DI Hale requested my assistance. But I concur with his assessment that the case warrants further scrutiny. The statistical anomalies alone..."

"Has this side project interfered with your work on the Cyrus Wilde investigation?" Lee cut in.

Digit straightened. "Absolutely not. I performed all research and analysis during breaks and non-work hours, maintaining strict temporal boundaries between official and unofficial investigative activities. My commitment to the primary investigation remains at one hundred percent efficacy."

"So you're saying you did it in your own time?"

"Yes, that's what I said." Digit tilted his head.

Lee surveyed him for a long moment. "Does DS Bennett know about this little side project?"

"Negative. DI Hale requested informational compartmentalisation to avoid compromising the integrity of either investigation."

"So he told you to keep it secret?"

"Not secret. Compartmentalised." Digit frowned. "Compartmentalisation is a valid information management strategy."

Lee took a deep breath. "DC Asare, when you see DI Hale, tell him I'd like a word."

"A single word? Which word would you prefer me to communicate? Context would suggest something forceful like 'immediately' or 'explain,' but without additional parameters—"

"Tell him I want to see him in my office upon his return to the station, and please keep this conversation between you and me. I'd like to inform DI Hale myself I am now across this investigation."

Digit's shoulders hunched as his finger taps on the counter increased in velocity. Keeping secrets was difficult for him. "Maintaining information silos can impede operational efficiency and inter-team synergy."

"Understood, Asare?"

Digit sighed. "Yes, Ma'am."

The door closed behind Lee, and Digit let out the breath he'd been holding. At least she hadn't directed him not to provide his report to DI Hale. He turned back to the copy machine and extracted the backup copy he'd wisely prepared.

CHAPTER TWENTY-FIVE

RYAN FOUND FIONA IN A CORRIDOR, FROWNING AS SHE typed on her phone.

"That bad?" he asked.

"Worse. Blaise keeled over when I told him about Cyrus."

"What, dead?"

"Fainted. Dropped like a sack of potatoes and cracked his head on the floor." A few curls had escaped Fiona's bun and bounced as she navigated them towards the main production area. "Sheri's gone with him in the ambulance. To make sure our prime suspect doesn't scarper when he's discharged."

She filled him in on the interview.

Ryan sighed. "Let's collect Winston from Advika's office, then." He looked around and realised he had no idea where the production offices were located.

"I know the way," Fiona said.

They reached a wide, glass-fronted office labelled 'PRO-DUCTION ASSISTANTS'. Inside, fluorescent tubes buzzed over desks stacked with scripts and half-empty coffee cups. Winston lay with his head on his paws beside Advika's desk.

The corgi sat up when he spotted them, and his tail thumped on the carpet.

Advika noticed them and rose. A pile of high school yearbooks sat on her desk. She followed Ryan's gaze.

"They're Cyrus's. He wanted them dumped, but now he's... gone, I wonder if I should send them back to his mum?"

"I think she'd like that," Fiona replied.

Advika untied Winston's lead from the desk leg as the corgi gazed up at her like she was the goddess of sausages.

"He's a sweetheart," Advika said with a bright smile. "I had to keep him occupied with leftover salami from craft services. I hope it's okay?"

At the word 'salami', Winston glanced up eagerly as Ryan took his lead. The corgi had an extensive vocabulary, but only when it came to food.

"That's fine. Thanks for looking after him."

Before they could leave, Isaac Emerson appeared in the doorway with an older man at his side. The man wore a crisp navy suit and what Ryan recognised as the smug face of a man eager to overcharge by the hour.

"Detectives," Isaac said. "A moment?"

Ryan exchanged a look with Fiona before he let Isaac usher them to the lift leading to his office. Winston padded along, sniffing at the suited newcomer's polished shoes during the journey up. Ryan didn't stop him.

The man in the suit set his briefcase on Isaac's desk. "Christopher Barnaby," he said as he looked Ryan and Fiona up and down. "I'm the studio's legal counsel. Mr Emerson sought my advice after the unfortunate discovery this morning." His voice dripped with the rehearsed sincerity of someone billing by the minute.

Isaac cleared his throat. "We asked Christopher to advise

on the best course of action, given the seriousness of the... ah... recent events."

"Can we call it a body on your property?" Ryan replied as Winston tried to pull him over to a bar cart against the wall. Knowing his luck, the corgi would piss on it, and Vance would send him the bill.

Barnaby's nostrils flared as if Ryan's blunt statement carried a certain odour. "I regret to inform you that, effective immediately, the studio will cease any cooperation beyond what's required by law. No more interviews with cast or crew without an attorney present. And as for any intended searches on site, drug-related or otherwise," his gaze flicked to Winston, then back to Ryan's face, "we'll require a court warrant and the appropriate documentation."

Ryan attempted to appear innocent as Winston flopped to the ground and rolled over, begging for a belly rub.

Fuck it.

He bent down and gave the corgi a quick scratch.

"You can't obstruct a murder investigation," Fiona said.

Barnaby gave her a smarmy smile. "Hardly obstruction, Detective Sergeant. We are merely protecting our clients' interests."

Ryan stood. "A man is dead."

"And it's regrettable," Barnaby replied smoothly. "However, we have a responsibility to our investors, our cast and our crew."

"Your responsibility is to help us catch Cyrus's killer."

"Going forward," Barnaby continued as if Ryan hadn't spoken, "all interviews must be scheduled through me or my office. The board also wants daily briefings from your team on the investigation's progress."

"Would you like us to bring you tea and cake while we're at

it?" Ryan levelled his gaze at Isaac. "Hampering our investigation isn't a brilliant look."

Barnaby's thin smile returned. "We look forward to continuing our cooperation within the legal framework."

"I bet you do." Ryan whistled for Winston to follow and turned to leave.

"One more thing, Detective." Isaac's voice stopped him at the door. "I'd appreciate it if you could keep disruption to filming at a minimum. We're already behind schedule."

Ryan didn't trust himself to respond. Instead, he nodded curtly and stepped into the corridor. Fiona closed the door behind them.

Ryan exhaled. "I should have let Winston piss in his whisky."

———

THEY FOUND Cal in the backlot leaning against an abandoned cart as he typed on his phone. A cluster of wardrobe staff hurried past, arms full of armour. Grace marched in front, electric-blue bob unmistakable as she barked something about mud continuity.

Winston recognised Cal and tugged Ryan over.

Cal looked up. "Boss, there you are. Been looking all over."

The corgi sniffed at Cal's leg, and the detective yelped. He yanked his leg away and dropped his phone.

"Shit, Winston. You can't sneak up on me like that," Cal said. "You know we're a work in progress." He leaned down to collect his phone and tentatively patted the straining corgi on the head.

"Please tell me you've got something, anything, that makes this miserable day worthwhile," Ryan said.

"Odd Bod's finished with Cyrus's body on site. They've

taken him to the morgue." He consulted the notes on his phone. "The doc did a quick comparison of the dagger and the wound; says it's likely a match but not definitive yet."

"Good. What about the storage room?"

Cal grimaced. "The techs are still processing the scene. Eloise insisted they catalogue all the weapons, in case the dagger from Stage Five was a plant. Backup has arrived from Buxton, so she told me I'm surplus to requirements. The post-mortem is scheduled for tomorrow morning."

"Any surprise findings?"

"Not with the body, but..." Cal's expression brightened as he produced an evidence bag containing a piece of paper. "I found this when I was poking around the props department." He held it out to Fiona. "See anything familiar?"

Fiona scrutinised the document, an invoice from the Props Department. Her eyes widened as they fixed on a string of characters at the top.

"The invoice number..." she said.

Cal grinned. "Matches the alphanumeric codes on the Post-it from Cyrus's fridge."

Ryan leaned in to look. "Nice catch, Cal."

"That's not all," Cal continued, vibrating with excitement. "When I confronted Jasper about the Post-it and the invoices, he crumbled faster than the Spurs in the final. Turns out he and Cyrus were falsifying inventory records, invoicing the production for non-existent swords. He's the one who trashed Cyrus's trailer. He was searching for the evidence Cyrus kept on him."

"So fraud," Fiona murmured.

Cal nodded. "Started during the first season after Jasper lost big to Cyrus in a poker game. He couldn't pay up, so Cyrus suggested the scheme as a payment plan."

"But he's denying murder?"

"Says he's only guilty of fraud and vandalism."

Ryan clapped a hand on Cal's shoulder. "Good work today."

Cal's chest puffed out. "Thanks, boss. Best buzz I've had since match day." He glanced away. "You know. Before."

"Don't let it go to your head. We've still got work to do," Ryan warned, but his tone was light. "Right, let's get back to the station. I've had enough of television people for one day."

CHAPTER TWENTY-SIX

D IGIT APPEARED AT HIS ELBOW THE MOMENT RYAN stepped off the lift onto the second floor. The DC must have been waiting for him.

"Sir." Digit held out a bound document. "My analysis of the Jacob Long interview."

Ryan stared at it. At least thirty pages, complete with colour-coded tabs. "Christ, Digit. I asked for a summary, not a dissertation."

"I find summaries reductive. This includes a comprehensive breakdown of non-verbal cues, statistical analysis of truth probability based on micro-expressions, and three potential scenarios with corresponding likelihood percentages."

Ryan took the tome and headed down the corridor. "Thanks. I'll look at it later."

"I've highlighted the most relevant portions in yellow," Digit added. "The red tabs indicate contradictions, while blue represents—"

"I'm sure it's thorough." Ryan interrupted. "We'll discuss it once I've reviewed it."

"Also, Sir, I need to tell—"

"It'll have to wait, Digit. I've got to brief Lee on where we're at with the Cyrus case."

"But I—"

"Later, Digit." Ryan waved the document and hurried into the incident room. He almost collided with Fiona.

She cleared her throat. "What interview?" Her gaze dropped to the report in his hands.

"It's a side enquiry."

"A side enquiry you're running without informing me?" Hurt edged her voice.

"It's barely taking any time," Digit volunteered from the doorway. "I spent only four point five hours on the interview and analysis, which represents a mere eight percent of my working week."

Great. The rest of the team couldn't have failed to hear that.

"Five hours." Fiona's voice remained even, but Ryan knew the signs. The slight flush at her neck. The way her fingers drummed against her arm. "On something that's not related to a murder investigation we're all working flat out on?"

"It's unofficial. I didn't want to involve the whole team until there's something solid."

"We're a team, Ryan. You shouldn't keep us in the dark." She glanced towards Digit. "Especially not when you're involving a junior officer without briefing me."

Ryan rubbed the back of his neck. "I was going to fill you in once I had more to share."

She studied him, then shook her head. "You can't do everything on your own."

"I'm not trying t—"

"You are," she interrupted. "And if you're not careful, it's going to backfire."

He opened his mouth to reply, but the words stuck.

She isn't wrong.

"Look," she said more softly, "just trust us, okay? We're here to help."

He met her gaze and nodded. "I'll brief you and the team once I'm back from Lee's office."

———

Ryan tucked Digit's report into his belt at the small of his back and tugged his jacket down to cover the bulge. He should have left it in the incident room, but he'd been too busy running away from Fiona's disappointed face to realise he still held it. The thick document stuck out awkwardly, but his options were limited. He'd have to hope Lee wouldn't notice the rectangular protrusion making him look like he'd grown a third buttock.

DCI Lee's office door stood ajar. Ryan knocked twice and pushed it open without waiting for a response. Lee sat behind her desk, silver-framed reading glasses perched on her nose as she reviewed a file. She glanced up.

"Hale. Take a seat."

Ryan lowered himself into the chair and suppressed a grimace as the report dug into his back.

Lee took off her glasses and placed them on the desk. "How's the head?"

"Fine. Thank you, Ma'am." The throbbing had intensified, but he wasn't about to admit that.

"Good. Update me on Wilde."

Ryan outlined their progress and the discovery of the notebook.

"So Kerrington's our prime suspect."

"Looks that way. I'd like to bring him in under caution as soon as he's discharged from hospital."

"Under caution? Why not under arrest?"

Ryan shifted in his seat. "Gut instinct. I'm not sure we have enough yet."

"Your gut instinct." Lee's voice was flat. "The same gut instinct that had you explore Stage Five alone and nearly get your head caved in with a sandbag?"

Ryan winced. "Point taken. There's something else I need to discuss with you."

Lee waited.

Ryan closed his eyes and took a deep breath. "I've reopened a cold case. The Benson case. Matthew Benson, the twelve-year-old murdered—"

"I know the case, Hale. What I don't know is why you've been investigating it without authorisation or why you failed to bring it to me first." She reached into her desk drawer and pulled out a document identical to the one shoved in his trousers. Lee dropped the report on her desk with a soft *thud*.

Ryan recognised Digit's meticulous tabbing system visible along the edges. His stomach dropped.

"Care to explain why you've got DC Asare conducting interviews for an unofficial investigation into a decade-old case while we're in the middle of a high-profile murder?"

"How did you..."

"I found Asare in the copy room binding this doorstop of a report."

Ryan's jaw clenched. He'd have words with Digit later about keeping his mouth shut. Though to be fair, the lad couldn't lie to save his life.

"I planned to come to you once I had something concrete."

She tapped on Digit's report. "Thirty-two pages of analysis isn't concrete enough?"

"It was a preliminary enquiry. Dr Hope approached me

with new information from a dying witness contradicting the mother's confession."

"And you couldn't spare two minutes to run it by me?"

"I'd be wasting your time if it turned out to be nothing."

Lee leaned back in her chair. "That's bullshit, and we both know it. This was Lampton's case, wasn't it?"

Ryan nodded. He knew where this was going.

"I imagine you didn't fancy asking me if you could pick apart one of his convictions."

"It wasn't—"

"It is exactly that." Lee cut him off. "Listen to me, Hale. I'm not Lampton. I don't give a damn about protecting anyone's reputation if we got it wrong. What I do care about is being blindsided by one of my officers conducting a rogue investigation."

"Do you want me to drop it?"

"No, I've skimmed Asare's report, and it included a detailed summary of your interview with Lynsey Cooper. There's enough in her story to warrant further investigation." She leaned forward. "But I don't want to be blindsided again. You clear anything related to this case with me first, understood?"

"Yes, Ma'am."

"And remember, your primary focus is the Wilde murder. The studio's already obstructing us, and the political pressure's growing. We need to build a solid case against Kerrington."

"What about Lampton?"

"We both know he'll throw a fit when he finds out. Be prepared for the storm when it comes." She pointed a finger at him. "But if there's evidence Beatrice Benson didn't kill her son, I want to know about it."

A weight lifted from Ryan's shoulders. "I'll keep you informed."

"See that you do." Lee slipped her glasses back on. "Now, get out of my office."

Ryan stood, careful not to let Digit's report slip from his waistband. As he reached the door, Lee spoke again.

"And Hale?"

He turned back.

"I know you see me as one of the brass, but next time, remember I'm a police officer too."

Ryan dipped his head in acknowledgement. He should have trusted her from the start. Unlike Lampton, Lee hadn't given him any reason to believe she'd let institutional politics stand in the way of justice.

They were more alike than he cared to admit.

CHAPTER TWENTY-SEVEN

RYAN CLEARED HIS THROAT. THE TEAM'S ATTENTION shifted from their screens. Even Cal paused mid-attempt to balance a pen on his nose.

"Right, gather round. There's something outside the Cyrus case I need to bring you all up to speed on."

He pulled an A4 photo of Matthew Benson from a folder and taped it to an empty whiteboard.

"A few days ago, Dr Hope approached me about an old case." Ryan's gaze flicked to Digit, then away. "The murder of this twelve-year-old boy, Matthew Benson, ten years ago. The boy's mother, Beatrice, confessed when police arrived at the scene. Now her neighbour has offered information suggesting the confession was false. DCI Lee is now aware I've been looking into it." Ryan could hear the frustration in his voice.

Digit sank into his chair. The constable might miss some social cues, but he was far from an idiot.

Cal sensed the undercurrent. "So, this Benson case, anything we can do, guv? I mean, Sir?" He glanced at Digit, then back at Ryan, a protective glint in his eyes. "Digit's a whizz with old files, you know. Proper digital archaeologist."

"Indeed," Ryan said. "Though his findings have a habit of ending up on the wrong desks."

He regretted the words the moment they left his mouth.

Fiona stepped forward. "If you need bodies on the ground or someone to run down leads, I can make time after-hours."

Sheri nodded. "I can too, Sir. Whatever you need."

"I appreciate that, but you all have lives and families," Ryan said. "For now, just be aware it's on the back burner." He clapped his hands together. "Right, Wilde case. Anything from forensics yet?"

Digit sat up straighter. "Affirmative. Senior Crime Scene Officer Durrant's preliminary report just arrived. Her team lifted a viable thumbprint from the top of the hilt of the dagger recovered from Stage Five. The killer wiped down the handle before dousing it in bleach, but forensics think they might have missed it due to the location."

Fiona paused in her note-taking. "And?"

"The print matches one of the latent prints from Mr Kerrington's scissors."

The significance rippled through the group.

"Christ. So Blaise handled the murder weapon." Ryan ran a hand through his hair.

"There's more." Digit's fingers tapped an invisible keyboard on his desk. "Most of the fingerprints pulled off the cover of the notebook were a match for Blaise Kerrington or Millie Higgins, but two partial fingerprints weren't. They were a match for Cyrus."

Ryan glanced at Fiona. "If Cyrus handled the notebook, he knew about Blaise's obsession."

"Maybe Cyrus got all up in the costume guy's grill about it and things got nasty?" Cal guessed.

Fiona nodded. "Things are looking bad for Mr Kerrington."

"What about the CCTV?" Ryan asked.

"I'm still working on the warrant after Barnaby's little performance," Fiona replied. "But when I was poking around earlier, the maintenance staff confirmed the back entrance to Stage Five could be accessed from several departments and the backlot without passing any cameras."

Cal let out a low whistle, marker pen hovering over Blaise's name. "Our obsessed fanboy handled the dagger, and the victim's thumbprint is on his naughty notebook. Opportunity. Motive. Looks like we've got our man."

"Maybe," Ryan replied. "But there are still some loose threads we need to tie up."

———

Later, Ryan found himself in the small break room, wrestling with the temperamental espresso machine. The aroma of burnt coffee filled the air.

Fiona leaned against the doorframe. "He was cut up about it, you know."

Ryan didn't turn around. "Who?"

"Digit." Fiona pushed off the frame and joined him at the counter. She flicked the kettle on. "He told me about his 'debrief' with Lee. I think he tried to take the full force of her displeasure for the Benson thing."

Ryan coaxed a sputtering stream of dark liquid from the machine. "Is that so?"

"He even asked me for advice," Fiona continued as she dropped a tea bag in her mug. "Wanted to know if there were any 'tactical prevarication techniques' he could employ next time, to avoid, and I quote, 'inadvertently implicating a superior officer conducting unsanctioned investigative activities'."

Ryan winced. The image of Digit earnestly seeking lessons in deceit hit a nerve. He scrubbed a hand over his face. "Bloody hell."

Abandoning his coffee, Ryan walked back into the main incident room where Digit was engrossed in a complex diagram on one of his monitors.

"Digit."

The detective constable swivelled in his chair and blinked at him. "Sir?"

Ryan walked over to his desk, the rest of the team now listening. "About the Benson case and your chat with DCI Lee." He took a breath. "I owe you an apology. I put you in an unfair position by asking you to keep my investigation quiet. It wasn't right."

Digit's brow furrowed. "DI Hale, the request from a superior to a subordinate to exercise discretion is a common occurrence in hierarchical organisations. My failure to manage the DCI's enquiries was perhaps a deficiency in my strategic communication skills."

Cal snorted. "Means he gets it, guv. You're off the hook."

Ryan managed a small smile. "Thanks, Digit. But to be clear," he addressed the room, "none of you should ever feel you have to hide anything from DCI Lee or any other officer on my account. If I ask you to do something that puts you in that position, I'm the one in the wrong, and that's on me."

He thought of Jaime, his need to find answers, and the temptation to pull Digit into it. With his skills... but he couldn't. The kid was too honest. It would be like asking a compass to point south.

Unfair.

And dangerous.

It was the one case Lee had expressly forbidden him from

investigating. If she found out, he'd be fired, and he couldn't take any of his team down with him.

CHAPTER TWENTY-EIGHT

Kerrington was still in the hospital. The warrants for the head costume designer's residence and studio financials would take hours. Days, knowing the glacial pace of the courts.

So Ryan ignored the voice in his head telling him not to be a damn idiot and drove to Sheffield. Peter York's current location.

Digit occupied the passenger seat, vibrating with the same eager energy Winston displayed when he heard the word 'park'.

"Sheffield University's Department of Molecular Biology ranks fourth in the UK for research impact," Digit announced. "Their work on protein crystallography alone resulted in forty-three peer-reviewed papers in the last academic year."

Ryan tightened his grip on the steering wheel. His residual guilt from earlier had driven him to invite Digit along. After an hour of nonstop trivia about Sheffield's academic standing, the history of molecular biology, and a detailed explanation of microscope evolution since the seventeenth century, the guilt had evaporated.

"Universities operate on a feudal system," Digit said, continuing the verbal diarrhoea as Ryan pulled into the university car park. "Professors are essentially lords with their graduate students as serfs, labouring in their name for the glory of the academic realm." He unbuckled his seatbelt. "Not dissimilar to film studios, though with considerably smaller budgets and more metaphorical swords." He chuckled at his own joke as he shut the door.

Ryan locked the Range Rover. "Let's just hope no one else gets stabbed."

"We're like Sherlock Holmes and Doctor Watson," Digit said as they walked through the glass doors.

"Ah... okay."

"Elementary, my dear Watson."

Ryan paused. "Wait. You're Sherlock and I'm Watson?"

"When you have eliminated the impossible, whatever remains, however improbable, must be the truth."

Ryan frowned. "That's not an answer."

"Can I help you?" A young woman behind the reception desk looked up from her phone. A bored-looking student earning extra credit.

"DI Hale and DC Asare from the Derbyshire Police," Ryan said. "We're here to see Peter York."

Her eyes widened. "Ooh.. Police? Is he in trouble?"

"You should ask to see our warrant cards to verify we are law enforcement," Digit interjected before Ryan could answer. "While the mathematical probability of encountering an impersonator is low, good security protocols require proper identification."

The woman blinked. "Ummm... Can I see some ID?"

Digit produced his warrant card with a flourish and nudged Ryan.

Keen to see Peter before the twentieth anniversary of

Matthew Benson's death, Ryan flashed his. "Just a few questions. He's expecting us."

She slumped down and picked up the phone, her painted nails clicking on the plastic. "Peter? There are two police officers here to see you." A pause. "Yeah. They showed me their card thingies. Okay." She replaced the receiver. "He said he'll meet you in the cafe. Down there." She pointed along the corridor.

A couple of minutes later, a tall, thin young man with short dark hair entered the cafe and approached their table. "How can I help you, detectives?"

"Mr York, can I get you something to drink?" Ryan gestured to his black coffee and Digit's matcha tea.

"Just call me Peter and I'm fine. I don't drink coffee after midday." Peter held up a stainless-steel water bottle.

Digit straightened. Ryan sighed. *Here we go.*

"I pointed out to DI Hale that caffeine has a half-life of five hours and will remain detectable in his system for fifteen, but he believes its consumption has no negative impact on his sleep quality."

Peter nodded along. *Great. Kindred spirits.*

The biologist turned to Ryan. "I was told on the phone this was urgent? Something about binary data points outside acceptable parameters?"

Ryan gave Digit a long look. The DC didn't notice.

"In a roundabout way," Ryan said. "We're taking another look at an old case. Your cousin Matthew Benson's death."

The name hung in the air. Peter's gaze flickered to Digit, then back to Ryan. "Why?"

"New information has come to light."

"I see." Peter took the empty seat.

Ryan let the silence stretch while Digit pulled out his phone.

"Do you mind?" Ryan nodded to the phone Digit placed on the table.

Peter shook his head. "No."

"Were you good friends with Matthew?" Ryan asked.

"Most of the time, but Matthew was... a lot. Always getting into things he shouldn't or playing pranks, usually ones that got us both in trouble. He even lit a live rat on fire once, though he swore he didn't do it. Most of his pranks were harmless, but they wound Amos up something chronic." A small, imperceptible smile touched his lips. "We put a baby grass snake in Hannah's bed once. It released its glands when she found it. Stank her room out for a week. Her scream was so loud we could hear it from halfway down the street."

"So approximately one hundred and ten to one hundred and twenty decibels?" Digit said.

Peter blinked. "Ah..."

"Amos Benson was strict, I hear," Ryan said to move things away from family anecdotes and back to the case.

"Old school," Peter confirmed. "Amos believed it was a father's duty to discipline his son. His actual son, luckily for me." He took a shaky sip from his water bottle. "He left me alone. I wasn't his to break, I suppose. That's why Matthew always tried to pin the blame on me for any pranks that backfired, but Amos wasn't fooled."

"What about Hannah? What was she like?" Ryan asked.

"Hannah?" Peter considered this. "She was just there, I suppose. She was a couple of years older than us and did her own thing. She and Matthew fought a lot, but it was over stupid stuff. The day before he was killed, he'd cut up her fashion magazines. She was pissed off, but it was all water off a duck's back to Matthew."

"At present, Hannah Benson's whereabouts are unknown to us," Digit said. "I can find no active digital traces of her on social media, and if I can't find her, she doesn't want to be found."

Peter's gaze slid away. "She didn't have an easy time of it after Aunt Bee got locked away. There wasn't much for her to inherit besides the house." He paused. "I think she expected something more substantial given the big game Uncle Amos talked. After that, I think she just wanted to forget her life in the UK and start over, so she went travelling. Sometimes she sends me postcards. Paris, Northern Italy, Spain, New York." He fiddled with a napkin. "I got one from Buenos Aires a few months back. Saying she's having fun, you know?"

"Do the postcards include a return address?" Ryan asked.

"No, she's never emailed or phoned me either."

"Do you have any photos of Hannah?"

Peter took out his phone and scrolled through. "Only this."

The image showed Peter and Matthew wearing identical red trucker hats, their arms around each other's shoulders. Hannah stood beside them but separate. Her head lowered so her hair fell down and obscured half her face.

"She was a bit of a loner in high school. I don't remember any of her friends coming round much, but that could have been because of Amos."

Ryan watched Peter's face. "Tell me about Jacob."

Peter's brow furrowed. "Uncle Jacob? I didn't know him well. He'd only been staying with the Bensons a few weeks before... before Matthew. Kept to himself."

Ryan was about to move on when Peter added, almost as an afterthought, "Matthew didn't like him, though."

Ryan's attention sharpened. "Oh?"

"Yeah. He thought Jacob was faking his injury for a payout. He reckoned he'd seen him lifting some heavy boxes in the garage when he thought no one was watching."

A kid seeing something he shouldn't. Thin, but still a potential motive.

Ryan drained the last of his coffee and set the empty cup aside. "Could we get a photo of the postcard from Hannah? The most recent one from Buenos Aires, so we can check the postmark."

"I'll look, but I'm not sure if I kept it." Peter's manner suggested Ryan shouldn't hold his breath.

Ryan leaned back. "One last thing, Peter. Do you think Bee did it? Do you think she killed Matthew?"

Peter met his gaze. "She confessed, didn't she?"

The answer felt rehearsed.

Was it grief, or something else? Was Peter York hiding a far darker secret than a dysfunctional family past? Had Peter got sick of being the scapegoat and wielded those scissors?

"Any orders, Sir?" Digit asked as they walked to the Range Rover.

"Yeah. Forward me any info you pull up on Jacob's compensation. Then transcript what we got from Peter. Cross-reference it with Lynsey's statement. Let's check everything lines up."

CHAPTER TWENTY-NINE

SHERI WATCHED BLAISE KERRINGTON FROM ACROSS THE grey metal table of Interview Room Four. The man before her barely resembled the imperious costume designer who'd dominated the costume department at Silverheath that morning. His sculpted silver-streaked hair now fell in limp strands across his forehead, and the Derbyshire Police-issued sweatshirt and jogging bottoms hung on his frame. His tailored black designer outfit now bagged in evidence storage.

He sat with his arms wrapped around himself, a protective posture she'd observed in vulnerable people on the streets during her PC days. Nothing like the commanding presence he'd displayed in the costume room.

DS Bennett placed the digital recorder on the table. She stated the date, time, and those present and then delivered the caution. "Do you understand, Mr Kerrington?"

Blaise nodded. "Yes."

"Louder for the tape, please."

"Yes, I understand." His voice cracked.

The lawyer beside him adjusted his posture in the uncomfortable plastic chair. Sheri had already forgotten his name. He wore an expensive suit and a sneer. They probably taught that look in law school.

"My client maintains his innocence and wishes to cooperate."

Fiona laid out a series of photographs on the table. Crime scene photos of the dagger, close-ups of the notebook and poems, and copies of the photoshopped images. Blaise's gaze dropped to his hands.

"Your fingerprints, Mr Kerrington, were found on this notebook containing what could charitably be called poetry about Cyrus Wilde." Fiona pushed forward a photograph of the notebook's exterior.

Blaise stared at it, and his lower lip trembled. "I've never seen that before. I only use notebooks for sketching, and I haven't written a poem since juniors."

"Your fingerprints are all over it, Mr Kerrington."

"That's not possible. I'm being framed."

Fiona placed the next photograph in front of him. "This is the dagger we recovered from Stage Five. We believe it was the weapon used to kill Cyrus Wilde. Your thumbprint was found at the top of the handle." She paused. "If you're being framed, as you claim, how do you explain your fingerprints on the murder weapon?"

The lawyer laid a restraining hand on Blaise's arm. "Mr Kerrington handles props daily in the normal course of his work."

"The dagger isn't a costume piece," Sheri said. "It's not catalogued in any of the prop inventories."

Blaise opened his mouth, closed it, then tried again. "I don't... I can..." His composure crumbled. "This is ridiculous. I didn't do anything." His shoulders shook as tears welled in his eyes. "Even if I'm cleared, they're going to give Grace my position. Do you understand what that means? Everything I've built, my entire vision for the show..." He buried his face in his hands. "She's a talentless hack. She'll ruin everything with her half-baked, pedestrian ideas. My God, this isn't happening."

Sheri exchanged a glance with Fiona. This wasn't the reaction she'd expected.

The lawyer held up his hand. "My client needs a moment."

Sheri reached for the water jug in the centre of the table, poured a glass and slid it towards Blaise.

After the man had composed himself somewhat, Sheri leaned forward. "Mr Kerrington, can you tell us where you were last Saturday night?"

Blaise dabbed at his eyes with a tissue from the box on the table. "I was working late on the pirate queen's costume. I fell asleep on the chaise in the costume room."

"Did anyone see you there?"

"No." He swallowed hard, then his eyes widened. "My husband. I called my husband that night. Julian's in California. At a medical conference."

"What time did you call him, Mr Kerrington?"

"About nine-thirty, I think? We talked for an hour, maybe a little more."

Sheri did a quick calculation. Even accounting for the call, Blaise would have had plenty of time to slip out to Stage Five and murder Cyrus.

Blaise must have realised this too. He slumped back in his seat.

The tears escaped and rolled down his cheeks. "He'll leave me. Oh God, he'll divorce me. He's the kindest, sweetest man. How will he understand any of this?"

"Mr Kerrington, did Cyrus Wilde threaten to expose you?" Fiona asked.

The lawyer straightened. "I don't see how—"

"Perhaps Cyrus discovered the notebook and tried to black-mail you. He seems to have form for this type of behaviour." Fiona continued. "The notebook getting out would destroy the career you worked so hard to build."

Blaise's head snapped up. "What? No."

"My client doesn't have to respond to these provocative speculations," the lawyer cut in.

"They're not speculations. They're reasonable inferences based on evidence." Fiona tapped the photographs. "Your client's notebook with Cyrus Wilde's fingerprints. Your client's prints on the weapon used to kill Cyrus Wilde."

"None of this is mine," Blaise whispered. He looked at Sheri, perhaps sensing her as the more sympathetic presence. "You must believe me. I didn't kill him."

"Or maybe you misread the signals and tried to force your affections on the star," Fiona said. "Cyrus was, by all accounts, an arsehole. He wouldn't have let you down gently. Maybe when he rejected you, you flew into a rage?"

"That's preposterous." Colour flooded Blaise's pale cheeks. "I love my husband. I would never cheat on him."

The lawyer slammed his palm on the table. "Enough! I'm advising my client not to answer these inflammatory questions. This interview is over."

Fiona nodded. "Interview suspended at 16:42."

Sheri released a long breath as the door to the interview room clicked shut behind them. Fiona rubbed her forehead. "God, I hate playing bad cop. Where's Ryan when you need him?"

———

THE SKY WAS TURNING indigo while Sheri waited for a fresh chicken salad roll from the sandwich van down the road from the station. After the interview, she'd needed to stretch her legs. While she waited, she scrolled to a *Crown of Shadows* GIF on her phone. Caspian lounged on the Queen's throne with a smirk. The comments underneath were all fire emojis and declarations of "my king." She shut the app. The sight of his face turned her stomach now that she'd glimpsed behind the curtain.

She pulled out her notebook instead. The pages were filled with observations, witness statements, and the growing unease she felt as they worked Cyrus Wilde's case. She couldn't stop thinking about Isaac's dismissive wave when he'd discussed the harassment complaint or the haunted look behind Margot's defiant eyes. She thanked the girl at the counter and took her roll, then tucked it into her bag with her notebook.

A few doors down from the van, the distinctive figure of Dr Alexis Hope emerged from the door to her private practice.

On impulse, Sheri called out, "Dr Hope?"

Alexis turned with a surprised look before it softened into a smile. "DC Dewan, isn't it?"

Sheri shifted her weight. "Yes, Ma'am. I was wondering if you had a moment? It's about a case. Sort of." The words tumbled out before she could reconsider.

"Is it about Ryan?"

Sheri wondered that the psychologist's mind went to her boss, but Fiona had mentioned Dr Hope had been a good friend of Ryan's wife, and the DI did have an alarming ability to find trouble.

"No, it's nothing to do with DI Hale. The case we're working on has stirred up some old feelings I thought I'd buried, and I'm struggling to deal with them."

Alexis glanced at her watch, then back at Sheri. Whatever she saw there made her nod. "Of course. I've got a few minutes before I need to be at the station. Let's go back inside."

The quiet calm of Alexis's office settled around Sheri like a weighted blanket.

"A little something for both of us." Alexis handed Sheri a steaming mug of herbal tea. "Though after a day dealing with Major Crimes, I'm sorry I can't offer you something stronger."

Sheri managed a small smile and cradled the warmth. "This is lovely, thank you." She took a sip.

"So how can I help?" Alexis settled into the chair opposite, her own mug balanced on her knee.

"The case we're working on, there's a set decorator who filed a harassment complaint against our murder victim, Cyrus Wilde." Sheri traced the rim of her mug with her finger. "It felt familiar."

The psychologist's expression remained neutral but open. She didn't speak, so Sheri continued.

"At university..." she began, the words hesitant. She reached for her pendant for reassurance, then continued, "I was doing my undergraduate degree in business and economics. There was this professor, Dr Smyth-Hall. He was highly regarded, and his work brought in a lot of funding." She stared into her tea. "He kept asking me out. Suggesting if I went on a date with him, my grades might see a 'significant improvement'."

"He propositioned you."

Sheri nodded. "Repeatedly. I tried to laugh it off, make excuses, but it escalated. He'd 'accidentally' brush against me in tutorials. Find reasons to call me into his office." The memory made her skin crawl. "Eventually, I complained to student services."

"And?" Alexis prompted gently.

"The dean called me in." Sheri let out a short laugh that sounded hollow in her ears. "He didn't want to hear it. Said the professor was a cornerstone of the faculty. Implied that perhaps

I'd been encouraging him or misinterpreted a professor's professional interest in my success. He pressured me to retract my statement. Said pursuing it would be 'unnecessarily disruptive' for everyone involved."

Alexis listened, her gaze unwavering. "So the university protected its prestigious professor."

"Just like the production company protected its star. Margot said she's been branded as 'difficult'."

"What stopped you from pursuing your complaint further?"

Sheri shrugged. "I'm pragmatic enough to know how it would've played out. I'd be the one with an inflated ego who couldn't take a joke. The sensitive girl who accused one of the university's favourite professors." She paused. "It was easier to switch degrees. Get away from him. Criminology and psychology felt safer. More aligned with what I wanted, anyway." Another pause. "And let's be honest, I knew I'd be fighting a losing battle."

"Because of your South Indian heritage?"

Sheri looked up, surprised by the directness, but relieved. "Half the time, people treat me like I shouldn't even be there, and the other half, it's like I'm just ticking a diversity box." She hesitated. "I'm sure you've encountered the same."

"At times," Alexis replied.

Sheri rushed on. "I don't want to come across like I've got a chip on my shoulder, because I don't. I'm proud of my heritage, even if I don't always conform to every cultural expectation my parents and relatives might have."

"Do you feel the team treats you like that?"

"No," Sheri said. "Not them. DI Hale and DS Bennett, they've been welcoming, and Digit's oblivious to that sort of thing. Cal can be a bit of a twat, but he's almost an equal opportunity twat, if that makes sense?"

Alexis nodded.

"But there have been other times. On the street. In the station."

"Your experiences give you an insight that others might lack," Alexis said, her voice thoughtful. "You understand what it's like to be underestimated, to have your voice dismissed. In cases like this, with the set designer, with powerful men like Cyrus Wilde, that's not a vulnerability, Sheri. That's insight the others don't have. People will underestimate you. Let them. Use it to your advantage."

A small smile touched Sheri's lips. "At their peril, eh?"

"Precisely."

Sheri placed the cup on the coffee table and stood. "Thank you for listening, Dr Hope."

"That's what I'm here for." Alexis walked her to the door. "And Sheri? Trust your intuition. Ryan won't dismiss you for having an opinion, even if he doesn't agree."

Sheri paused at the door. "I wish I could read people the way you and DI Hale do."

"It will come with time." Alexis's face grew serious. "And be careful. This Cyrus character created ripples of fear and resentment, and sometimes, when people feel powerless, they look for justice elsewhere."

CHAPTER THIRTY

Ryan found Fiona leaning against the counter in the break room, a mug of tea beside her. Her hand shot behind her back before she realised it was him. She pulled it out again, holding a half-eaten packet of Hobnobs.

"Thank Christ, I thought you were Digit. I couldn't listen to another well-meaning but extensive lecture about the dangers of fructose syrup and oxidative stress. Personally, I don't find eating biscuits stressful at all." She winked at him as she snapped off a piece and dunked it in her tea.

Ryan made himself a cup.

"Have you reviewed the video of Kerrington's interview?" she asked before she popped the soggy biscuit into her mouth.

Ryan ran his hand through his hair. "Twice."

She swallowed. "Notice anything?"

"Ah... DI Hale?" DC Dewan said from the door before he could answer. "Can I have a word with you? Actually, both of you."

Ryan nodded, while Fiona held out the packet of biscuits. "Hobnob?"

Sheri looked around.

"Don't worry, I dropped Digit off at Beans & Greens. Apparently they do the best kale chips in town, which suggests there's more than one place in Chesterfield serving kale chips."

They all shared a collective shudder.

"Thanks," Sheri said. She took a Hobnob and nibbled at the edge.

"So how can we help?" Ryan asked.

"I don't think Blaise Kerrington is our killer," she blurted out.

"Care to elaborate why?"

"I..." Sheri's fingers clutched her notebook. "It's just... it all feels too tidy. The way he reacted when we told him Cyrus was dead—"

"He fainted," Fiona reminded her.

"Exactly." Sheri's brows furrowed. "If you've murdered someone, would you faint at the news they're dead? Wouldn't you try to act surprised but normal?"

"Maybe he fainted because he knew he'd been caught?" Ryan said.

Sheri opened her notebook at the page she'd marked after talking with Dr Hope. "When we were at the studio earlier, I asked Dominic, the stunt coordinator, if the stuntmen could faint so convincingly they'd knock themselves out on the floor. He said, not a chance. The body has a strong self-preservation instinct. Even professional stunt performers protect their heads when they fall. In a real faint, you're unconscious before you hit the ground, so you drop like deadweight."

Ryan studied her. "So you think someone's framing him?"

"I don't know," she admitted. "Maybe the notebook is real, but I don't believe he killed Cyrus. It's just a gut feeling, though."

Ryan smiled. The exact words he'd used with Lee upstairs. "I think you might be right."

Fiona's brows lifted. "Wait? I thought he was our guy?"

"The notebook's all wrong."

"In what way?" Fiona asked. "Apart from the obvious 'ew' factor."

"Fi, we've both seen real obsession. Stalkers, exes who can't let go." He sipped his tea and grimaced. It was lukewarm. The water in the kettle had been colder than he thought. "It's always chaotic. Scraps everywhere. Half-finished lines. Angry ones, then apologetic ones. It escalates. Starts with 'You're perfect' and ends with 'If I can't have you...'"

Fiona watched him over the rim of her mug of tea.

"The notebook Millie found? It's curated. Every poem is finished. There's no angry cross-outs. No scrawls. The photos are trimmed and tucked in. It reads like someone's idea of obsession. Not a private spiral."

Fiona frowned. "Grace said he's a perfectionist."

"Perfectionists still draft. Especially when they care. And if it were real, he would care." He took a couple of gulps of tea and then gave up on it. "And the knife. Blaise's thumbprint on the top of the handle. One clean print. No partials on the grip, no smear, no shift. Who holds a knife that way?"

"Maybe he got sloppy," Fiona said, continuing her role as devil's advocate. "Wore gloves the rest of the time?"

"Maybe." He met her eye. "Or it's possible this wasn't evidence we discovered, it's evidence we were meant to find."

Silence stretched until Sheri said in a voice barely louder than a whisper, "Thank you, Sir."

"So what are you going to do with your musings, oh fearless leader?" Fiona asked as she hid the biscuits at the back of the drawer.

"Tonight? There's nothing I can do. Go home, eat something that will give me a heart attack before fifty, then listen to Winston snore until I fall asleep." He left out *and likely jolt awake from a nightmare, bathed in sweat.* He emptied the remains of his tea, washed the mug and placed it on the draining board to dry. "Tomorrow, if I still feel the same, I'll take it to Lee first thing. Tell her I think I've cocked it up and think we should keep looking."

Fiona nodded. "But then the question is… where?"

———

RYAN SHUT the front door and snapped the chain across. The flat felt colder than the street outside. He should have organised someone to fix the draught coming in around the door frame, but with winter over, he'd let it slide.

Winston shot out from the kitchen like a tan and white missile. The corgi's entire backside wiggled.

"Yeah, yeah. I know," Ryan muttered.

Winston bounced against his shins, nosed at his knee, then trotted towards the kitchen.

"Food first, paperwork after. I'm aware of the schedule."

Ryan dropped his keys in the bowl on the shoe cabinet and hung his coat on the hook by the door. As he bent to ruffle Winston's ears, something on the floor caught his eye.

A plain brown envelope lay face up on the mat below the letter box. No logo, no window. The edges rough from where it had scraped through the flap.

His stomach dropped as the note left on his car flashed into his head.

He kept his hand on the dog for a moment to steady himself, then stood. A box of disposable gloves sat on the shelf above the coat hooks, next to Winston's lead and a spare roll of poo bags. He pulled a pair on. The cold rubber clung to his fingers.

Winston gave a sharp bark at the snap of elastic, then resumed his looping patrol to the kitchen and back.

Ryan crouched by the mat. No name on the front, no stamp or smudged postmark. The envelope was damp at one corner. There wasn't much weight to it.

Please, just be a pamphlet about the Lord's work.

He slid a gloved finger under the flap and eased it open along the glued seam. He reached in and pulled out the contents.

A single photograph.

His throat closed before his brain caught up.

Jaime walked down a street he didn't recognise. Two heavy canvas shopping bags dragged down her shoulders. Her blonde hair was loose, half caught in the collar of her coat. The blue one Ruth had bought for her birthday.

She'd twirled in the kitchen the night she got it, making the hem flare. The bright blue fabric had made her eyes glow like sapphires.

Ryan pushed the memory away. *Focus on the facts.* The coat meant the photo was taken within a month of her disappearance.

The surrounding street blurred the way photos did when the light was low. Shopfronts smudged to streaks of yellow and grey. No obvious signage. No distinctive building to pin down the location. Not that it mattered. Any surveillance footage would be long gone.

Jaime looked over her shoulder, her eyes not quite in focus. The camera had caught motion instead of her expression, but he knew that look. The flattened lips and the set of her shoulders. She'd heard something behind her or seen something out of place. A primitive part of her brain had tried to get her attention.

She knew someone was there.

Ryan squeezed the photo until it bent, then forced his hand to loosen.

He flipped it over.

On the back, in neat block capitals, someone had written in black ink.

SHE KNEW SOMEONE WAS FOLLOWING HER.
SHE JUST DIDN'T KNOW WHO.

He stared at the words. The lettering was straight and measured. No flourishes. No wobble.

Below it, a second line.

AND NEITHER DO YOU.

Heat prickled under the jagged scars along his cheek. They felt too tight for his face. He fought the urge to dig his nails in and scratch until the scars tore open.

Winston yipped, sharper this time, and the bark jarred him from his spiral.

Whoever had taken this had been close, but far enough away she hadn't spotted them when she turned. Or she had, but she'd dismissed them. A guy on his phone or a woman with a pram. Someone stopped at the lights, leaning over the steering wheel.

Jaime used to mock him for scanning strangers in the supermarket. She'd tease him about seeing bogeymen while everyone else saw pensioners buying custard creams. If only she'd been as paranoid as him and spoken to him about it.

He read the lines again. His phone rang in his pocket.

He jumped, and the photograph slipped from his fingers. It landed face down and slid across the floorboards.

Winston shot to full alert, ears pricked. He gave a short, questioning huff.

Ryan pulled out his phone, his heart thumping in his chest. Unknown number.

Was it the sender? Watching? Wanting to know what he thought of their gift?

He moved to the front window, his thumb hovering over the green button. He pushed back the net curtains. Outside, the street was quiet. Sodium light pooled around the lampposts. The hairdresser's sign across the road swung in the wind. A car was parked two doors down, beaded with rain, but no one peered over the seats. There was no shape in the shadows behind the trees lining the street or behind the bins.

He answered.

"DI Hale."

A woman's voice. Cut-glass vowels, but tired around the edges.

"Detective Inspector Hale?"

"Who is this?"

"Patricia Peasley."

Ryan blinked. "Mrs Peasley."

"Is this a bad time?"

He stared at the photo on the floor, then looked away.

"It's... fine. How can I help you?"

"I hope I'm not intruding. I found your card in my purse. From the other day." A slight pause. "When you... ah... stopped us from leaving."

Ryan thought of the bruises around her eye, the cold fury in Peasley's voice and the rifle in the golf bag.

"I remember."

"I watched the press conference this afternoon. With your superior. The woman with the dark bob."

"Lee. DCI Lee."

"Yes. My husband had the news on. He was... animated."

"That doesn't sound like him at all," Ryan said.

A quick breath down the line might have been a laugh, or a flinch.

"I want to tell you something before I lose my nerve, Inspector. Right now my husband is out at a function, but he's been on the phone quite a bit for the last two days. He's spoken to someone from the *Crown of Shadows* studio. And the council cabinet. He's very cross about the... disruption to filming and the negative media. Apparently, it reflects badly on the constituency."

Ryan watched his own reflection in the black glass of the window. "What has he been saying?"

"He told them it was unacceptable that... how did he put it... a 'loose cannon with a martyr complex' was heading up the investigation." Her voice lowered. "He wants you taken off the case. Says he knows people who can get it done, and he's not wrong."

"So he's leaning on them to put pressure on Toddock and Lee?"

"Yes, he thinks it's all a, I quote, 'politically motivated witch hunt' because you dared to question him about his private affairs." A small, brittle note crept in. "He spent quite some time explaining how ungrateful everyone is for his service."

What a twat.

"Mrs Peasley, why are you telling me this?"

"Because it's the only thing I can give you." She exhaled slowly. "You were... respectful to me that day. Most men aren't when they're trying to get at my husband."

"Your bruise didn't come from a cupboard door," Ryan said.

Silence settled between them for a moment.

"I didn't call for sympathy. I called to say thank you. For trying. For putting your own career in jeopardy. Because you thought I might be in danger."

"You are in danger."

"You did what you could in the moment." The armour in her voice went back on. "I recognised that. It's more than most people do."

"Mrs Peasley, I meant what I said. I can get you the help you need, put you in touch with the right people. We can still—"

"No." The word was soft but final. "I wanted you to know why they're targeting you. It's because of me. Because you saw through him."

"Patricia, please." Ryan lifted his hand as if he could stop her.

"You can't save us all, Detective Inspector."

The line went dead.

The words hung in the air.

I can't save any of you.

Winston whined from the kitchen doorway, tail low and eyes pleading. His routine had been broken for at least five whole minutes. Unforgivable.

Ryan let his hand drop.

"All right," he said to the dog. "You win."

He stepped over the fallen photograph and moved into the kitchen. Dry food rattled into Winston's bowl. The smell of meat dust and cereal filled the air.

Winston's mood flipped like a switch. He bounced up on his front paws, then buried his face in the bowl the second it hit the floor.

The chewing and snuffling as Winston hoovered up his biscuits grounded Ryan back in the room.

He leaned on the counter and pressed his palms to the cool surface. His foot caught where the cheap linoleum bubbled near the sink.

Mrs Peasley's voice echoed in his head. Lynsey begging him to help Bee Benson. Jaime, her head turned, because her instinct told her someone followed.

You can't save us all.

He pushed away from the counter, replaced his gloves with a fresh pair and picked up the photograph by the very edge.

Studying the background again, Ryan forced his brain into investigation mode. Shopfronts, but no clear signage. A double yellow line. A black bollard with a chipped band of white paint around the top. The pavement slick from the wet weather. A lamppost in the distance. It could be anywhere in Derby.

He turned it over and read the words on the back again. The handwriting seemed smug. He picked up the envelope and studied it too. No writing inside the flap. No logo in the corner. Cheap stock, the kind you bought in bulk. No smears of ink or oily thumbprints he could make out without a UV light.

Protocol said he should phone Lee immediately. Log the new contact. Let someone else bag and tag it and set the chain of evidence from the start.

He stood in the stale chill by the door but didn't reach for his phone. Not yet.

This wasn't a random crank letter to the station. It had come through the front door of his home. This was a snapshot of his wife some stranger had kept for twelve years, waiting for the moment it would hurt most.

It belonged to the case, but it also belonged to him.

Winston padded out and licked his muzzle. With a satisfied snort, he flopped on his side near the radiator in the lounge, legs splayed, belly exposed to the weak warmth. He'd already moved on.

"Wish I could as well," Ryan told the dog.

A stack of cardboard boxes he hadn't unpacked sat in one corner. He flipped open the flap of a box marked 'Work stuff' and dug through notebooks and spare evidence labels until his fingers closed round a flat packet of self-seal bags.

He pulled two out and laid them on the table by the keys. This was his space. His mess. The one pocket where he could leave people's tragedies at the door.

Ryan slid the envelope into a bag, then the photograph into the second one. The plastic swallowed Jaime's face.

The seal strip waited, white and blank.

He hesitated with his gloved thumbs on it. Once he closed it, it stopped being a taunt and a memory and became evidence. Something to hand over, catalogue and pass through other hands.

He pressed the strip down anyway.

On the label, Ryan wrote the date, the time and his initials. The pen tip paused over the space for case reference. For a second, he thought about leaving it blank, keeping it between him and the anonymous bastard who'd pushed it through his door.

He filled in the box.

CHAPTER THIRTY-ONE

ADVIKA'S TRAINERS SQUEAKED AGAINST THE WORN linoleum as she hurried towards the photocopy room. She resented Janet more with every step as the cardboard box of scripts dug deeper into her arms. Of course, Janet would insist she do the shredding at the last minute and somehow forget Advika had plans. Her mum was already halfway through preparing her famous Hyderabadi biryani. She could almost taste the cardamom and saffron already. Her mother's disappointment that she would, yet again, be late for dinner had been delivered over the phone with a gentle click of the tongue and a sigh so theatrical it could have come from Piper.

She adjusted her grip on the box. The scripts had already become unusable thanks to Cyrus's disappearance, but with Stage Five's new crime scene status, Janet considered it even more important they were destroyed. Everything felt chaotic now, uncertain. Whether any filming would happen tomorrow felt beside the point after Cyrus had been found dead in the props department.

Advika shivered. The corridors felt different at night, like school after the last bell. The usual bustle of runners carrying trays loaded with takeaway coffee, the bark of orders from impatient second ADs, and the constant static crackle from walkie-talkies was gone, replaced by an uncomfortable stillness. She shook the discomfort away. It was just because everyone sensible had gone home, a luxury not extended to lowly production assistants tasked with clean-up duty.

In the photocopy room, the shredder hunched in the corner next to reams of paper and boxes of industrial staples. She dropped the box, and it landed on the linoleum with a heavy thump. She glanced up at the overhead light. It flickered and then went out. Fitting. A dying bulb for a dying production. A fleeting surge of guilt washed through her despite the truth of her thoughts. But how long could she pretend things were fine? Even without the murder, the production had felt messy for months. Badly disguised infighting. Reshoots. Whispered conferences around Isaac's office door.

She fed scripts into the mouth of the shredder, and the machine chewed up the pages.

She still struggled to process how she felt about Cyrus's murder. His death didn't fill her with grief. She felt safer now, as horrible as it sounded. Cyrus had cornered her more than once, standing too close and crowding her into spaces with disguised threats veiled as jokes.

Recently, when she delivered scripts to his trailer, he'd brushed his fingers against hers as he'd taken the papers and held the contact longer than necessary. "You're too pretty to be running errands," he'd said, voice dropping to what she assumed he thought was a seductive register. "If you need a better role? I could put in a word. Come sit and let's chat about it."

She'd extricated her hand and backed out the door, murmuring something noncommittal about being happy with her job and needing to get back to Isaac. The interaction left her feeling dirty, then angry at herself for just smiling and hurrying away. At least now, it wouldn't happen again.

The shredder tore through pages of dialogue and reduced Caspian Drest's last scenes to confetti.

Advika fed in another script. "The entire production's going to hell," she muttered.

Grace had said the same thing that morning, and she wasn't wrong. The ratings had been sliding since mid-season, and rumours of budget cuts swirled through the crew. Isaac pretended everything was fine, all while slashing craft services and cancelling night shoots to save on overtime.

Advika knew more than Isaac realised. He tended to forget she was in the room during financial discussions and treated her like wallpaper, rather than a person with functioning ears. She'd heard enough phone calls and seen enough emails to know *Crown of Shadows* was sinking faster than the Shadow Queen's enemies in the Drowning Pools.

The shredder jammed with a metallic screech, and it jerked Advika from her thoughts. She switched it off and peered inside to view the crumpled pages caught between the teeth. She reached in and tugged at the corner.

"Ow!" she yelped as the sharp edge sliced across her index finger. Blood welled up, a bright red bead against her brown skin.

"Brilliant," she said to the empty room. She sucked on the cut and grabbed a handful of tissues from a nearby box. She wrapped them around her finger and then inspected the machine. Blood had smeared across the metal teeth and dripped onto the half-shredded pages below.

Advika dabbed at the metal with more tissues, careful to avoid the blades. The last thing she needed was another injury.

Or worse, the blame for damaging expensive equipment. As she cleaned, her mind returned to her career.

She loved *Crown of Shadows*. The story, the characters, the intricate world-building. Despite the long hours and demanding conditions, working on this set had been a dream come true. But dreams didn't pay bills, and if the show collapsed, she'd be scrambling for work on other productions with hundreds of other displaced crew members.

Maybe it was better to jump ship now with good references than to go down with it? She had enough experience now to land a junior production coordinator role on a different show. Something stable. Something where the lead actor hadn't just been murdered on set.

Advika unwrapped the bloodstained tissue and replaced it with a fresh one. The pressure hadn't stemmed the bleeding. The cut was deeper than she'd thought.

She heard a noise like a footstep behind her and spun. There was no one in sight, but her heart pounded. The copy room was surrounded by empty offices. No one would hear her scream.

"You watch too many Jordan Peele movies," she said to herself as she switched the shredder back on. Its persistent mechanical hum pushed back the silence and calmed her nerves. She leaned over, ignoring her stinging finger, and fished another script from the box at her feet.

She caught a swift movement out of the corner of her eye and gasped. The script slipped through her fingers and fell to the floor. She turned around.

A figure stood just inside the doorway.

Advika's shoulders slumped in relief.

"Oh! It's just you. You scared me..."

CHAPTER THIRTY-TWO

Ryan met Fiona in the car park at Silverheath Studios. Police lights painted the imposing quarry walls in pulses of blue. Ryan hauled himself out of the Range Rover and looked over at the forensics van and Odd Bod's forest green Jaguar parked nearby. The sight made his fingers feel stiff and his body heavy. Two murders in a week. The studio was no longer just a film set. It had become a hunting ground.

Vance met them at the entrance to the main building. His usual bluster had vanished, replaced by a drawn expression. "One of my security guards found her forty minutes ago. I've locked the place down, but over a hundred cast and crew have trailers or cabins on site."

"Any CCTV?"

Vance grimaced. "The camera in the hallway was tampered with. No one in the security wing caught it."

"Can you take us to her?" Fiona asked.

"Yeah. This way."

He led them through the deserted corridors of the administrative block until they reached a room cordoned off with blue and white tape. Ryan stepped inside while Fiona stayed in the corridor to question Vance about the night's security detail.

Dr Yates knelt beside the body, dictating notes into a hand-held recorder. Paul, head of forensics, dusted the photocopier for prints. He glanced at Ryan and nodded before returning to his task.

Advika Patel lay on her side, coiled on the floor as if she'd tried to make herself smaller. An image of her the day before popped into Ryan's mind—a soft smile on her face as she'd patted Winston on the head. Now her dark hair fanned out on the linoleum, and her animated face was blank. Odd Bod had pushed up her black t-shirt to reveal a series of narrow cuts on her blood-caked stomach. A box of tissues lay tipped over beside her, several of them clutched in her hand. One wrapped around her index finger was soaked crimson.

"Evening, Ryan," Odd Bod said without looking up. "Nasty business."

Ryan swallowed. "What have we got?"

"Multiple stab wounds to the abdomen." The doctor remained focused on his examination. "Right upper quadrant, one punctured the liver. Looks like a narrow blade, smaller than the one that killed Mr Wilde. She bled out quickly. Died holding these." He pointed to the tissues in Advika's hand. "Appears she cut herself on the shredder before she was attacked. Perhaps she was cleaning up the blood when our killer walked in?"

"Time of death?"

Odd Bod peeled off his gloves and stood. He smoothed down his purple waistcoat while he pondered the question. "I'd say approximately two hours ago."

Ryan cursed under his breath. Plenty of time for the killer to destroy evidence and disappear.

His gaze swept the room. The shredder stood silent in the

corner, a trickle of dried blood on its metal teeth. A cardboard box filled with scripts sat beneath it.

Ryan crouched beside the box, careful not to disturb the scene. "She was shredding these?"

Paul nodded. "The machine was still running when security found her. It was the noise that attracted them. Trace amounts of blood on the blades and in the collection bin."

Ryan pulled on a pair of gloves and lifted the top script from the unshredded pile. The title page read "*Crown of Shadows - Season 3 - Episode 6: 'The Lord's Demise' - DRAFT*". He flipped through the pages and stopped when a particular scene caught his eye.

INTERIOR - RITUAL CHAMBER - NIGHT

CASPIAN lies bound to the altar, blood streaming from multiple wounds as THE SHADOW QUEEN stands over him, her ritual dagger dripping.

SHADOW QUEEN

Your reign ends tonight, false king. Your blood will feed the ancient ones.

She plunges the dagger into CASPIAN's abdomen. He SCREAMS, blood bubbling from his lips.
CASPIAN
(gasping)

You can't... kill... me.

SHADOW QUEEN
(leaning close)

I already have.

CASPIAN convulses, then goes still, eyes fixed and glassy.

A chill ran down Ryan's spine. "Christ." He kept reading, skimming over the gory details of what the Queen did to the corpse after the character's death.

Fiona appeared beside him. She looked over at Advika's body and squeezed her eyes shut. "It never gets easier."

She sighed and then leaned over to see what he was reading. "Is that…"

"A script killing off Cyrus's character similarly to how he was murdered." Ryan handed her the script. "Looks that way."

She scanned the page. "Isaac Emerson wrote Cyrus out of the show."

"This changes things." Ryan's voice dropped. "Where is he?"

"Not on site, according to Vance," Fiona said. "Janet has come in, though. She's waiting outside his office for us."

"Good." Ryan pushed through the door of the photocopy room, his mind fixed on one target. "I want to talk to her now."

———

THEY FOUND Janet at her desk outside Isaac's office, lit only by her desk lamp. She hunched over her keyboard, eyes bloodshot and a pile of crumpled tissues beside her.

"Detectives." Her voice came out thin. "This is… this is just awful. I feel responsible. I asked Advika to shred the scripts. She didn't want to. Her mum was cooking her a special dinner…" Her voice trailed away.

"It's not your fault," Fiona said. She reached out to squeeze the woman's hand.

"Where's Mr Emerson?" Ryan's tone left no room for pleasantries.

Janet flinched. "He's not here."

"We know that. Where is he? At home?"

She shook her head and twisted a crumpled tissue in her hands. "I don't know. Security notified me when they couldn't get hold of him. I've called him several times, but he hasn't answered. He said he was heading home just after I left at six. Maybe he turned his phone off?"

Ryan slapped the script down on her desk. The sound made her jump. "Did you know about this?"

Janet stared at the cover, and her lower lip trembled. She nodded without meeting his eyes. "Yes."

"The writing credit says Mr Emerson wrote it."

Another nod. "He... he was unhappy with Cyrus. The constant disruptions, the threats to quit. He said the show would be better off without him." Her eyes widened. "Without his character, I mean."

"So he killed him off in the show." Ryan watched her face. "A brutal death in the Ritual Pit room. And then Cyrus disappears, only to turn up stabbed in the same location. The script goes into very graphic detail."

"He told us to shred them." Janet's voice cracked. "The moment Cyrus's body was found. Until that point, I think he believed Cyrus would waltz back into the studio. The optics... He was trying to protect the show."

"To protect the show?" Ryan echoed. "Or to protect himself?"

Janet shrank back. "I... I only know what he told me."

Fiona shot Ryan a *back-off* look over the secretary's head.

"And what else did he tell you, Janet?" Fiona asked, her tone gentle. "Do you have any idea where he might be?"

Before Janet could answer, a condescending voice cut in. "I'm afraid this interview is over."

Christopher Barnaby stood framed in the doorway, holding a leather briefcase. His face was a constructed mask of professional regret, and his charcoal suit was immaculate despite the late hour. "Must I remind you that any interviews with studio personnel require legal counsel present?"

"A young woman has been murdered on your client's property," Ryan said. "She was twenty-three. Her mother was expecting her home for dinner, and now, they'll never share another one. I'm less concerned with legal counsel and more concerned with finding the person who stabbed her."

"A tragedy the studio feels most acutely," Barnaby said, like they were discussing a dip in the share market. "We can't risk any evidence being deemed inadmissible because of procedural errors."

"How noble of you," Ryan said dryly. "I'm sure Advika's family will appreciate that her death was handled with such legal precision."

Barnaby's smile never wavered. "I regret to inform you that without proper authorisation, this interview cannot continue. Mrs Henderson is distressed. You are taking advantage of her emotional state."

Janet looked between them. "I... I don't understand. I want to help. Advika was..."

"Mrs Henderson will be available for questioning tomorrow morning with representation," Barnaby interrupted. "I'm simply ensuring her rights are protected."

Ryan stepped closer to the lawyer. "Because that's what matters most here, isn't it? Not the dead girl in the photocopy room, not the fact there's a killer walking around this place."

"We will provide what's required within the appropriate legal framework, Detective Inspector."

"Tell me," Ryan said, tilting his head, "when you were studying law, did they have a special module on how to be a complete arsehole, or is it a natural talent?"

Fiona placed a warning hand on Ryan's arm, but he shook it

off. He was done with all the lies and bullshit swirling around this toilet bowl of a show.

Barnaby's thin smile grew even thinner. "I understand emotions run high in these situations—"

"Do you? Do you understand emotions, Mr Barnaby? Because from where I'm standing, you seem about as invested in this girl's murder as you would be in a parking fine."

"My job is to protect this studio's interests."

"Your job," Ryan cut him off, "is to make sure justice gets served wrapped in red tape that only benefits the killer." He turned back to Janet. "We'll speak tomorrow."

Janet nodded, still clutching her tissue, and fled the room.

Ryan spun to face Barnaby again. "Since the studio's so keen on seeing justice served, you could speed up the release of any CCTV footage from this evening."

Barnaby straightened his already perfect tie. "Of course the studio wants the killer caught, but there are procedures to follow."

"Why am I not surprised?" Ryan said.

"We'd hate for word to get out to the press that the studio was dragging its heels releasing evidence in a murder case," Fiona added.

Barnaby's nostrils flared, but he didn't budge. "We'll have it sent through first thing."

As the lawyer escorted them to the lift, Ryan's thoughts turned from Isaac to Advika. Guilt twisted in his chest. If he'd caught the hooded figure on Stage Five. If he'd been more alert, more cautious, would Advika still be alive? The question ate at his stomach like acid.

He'd let a killer slip through his fingers, and now an innocent person was dead because of it.

CHAPTER THIRTY-THREE

THE SECURITY OFFICE DOOR STOOD AJAR, WHITE LIGHT from multiple monitors spilling into the corridor. Fiona took a deep breath. When Ryan had asked her to see if she could get anything out of Vance, she'd understood what he hadn't said. *Vance is still hung up on you, and if he'd bend the rules for anyone...* She exhaled and knocked on the metal frame.

Vance Mitchell's head snapped up from the bank of screens. His expression shifted from concentration to surprise, then wariness. But underneath it all flickered something else. The same look he'd given her at the gate when they first arrived. The hopeful glimmer made her stomach twist.

"Fiona." He straightened in his chair and adjusted his badge. Even at this hour, his uniform remained pristine.

"Vance." She stepped into the cramped room. "I thought you might be reviewing the CCTV footage."

His gaze flicked to the screens and then to her. "I am, but Mr Barnaby's been very clear about protocol. The footage goes to legal first thing tomorrow."

"Mind if I stay while you work?" She leaned against the wall.

He sighed and ran his hand over his short hair. "Look, Fi..." He caught himself and swallowed. "DS Bennett. My hands are tied. The studio legal team needs to review the footage before you lot see it."

"We've got a killer walking around."

"You think I don't know that?" His voice rose, then his shoulders slumped. "My primary duty is to the studio. Barnaby made it crystal clear what's expected. I could lose my job if he found you in here."

Through the window behind him, Fiona could see a security guard patrolling the backlot with a torch. The clean choice would be to walk away, to follow proper channels. Ryan would understand.

"Vance." She closed the door behind her. "I know things didn't end well between us. And I know you think I..." There had been too many accusations flung about in those last weeks. She regrouped. "I'm not asking you to risk your job. I'm asking if there's anything you've seen so far that has bothered you. Off the record."

He studied her, and his eyes narrowed. The wary tension between them felt like a physical thing in the room. "Why should I help you?"

"Because a twenty-three-year-old girl is dead. And because..." She met his gaze. "Because a long time ago, you wanted to become a copper for the same reasons I did."

Vance held her gaze for a long moment, then glanced away. He reached for his coffee mug, discovered it empty, and set it down with a quiet *clunk*.

"There is something," he admitted. "Probably not related, but..." He typed something on his keyboard and brought up footage of the car park. "There. The back end of Mr Emerson's Tesla."

The timestamp read 19:15.

"Mr Emerson left in a studio car with a driver at six. I thought he must have come back for something," Vance continued. "The car was gone by the time I locked down the studio at nine. So I checked the logs." He pulled out a clipboard. "The guard at the front gate recorded Isaac Emerson's name for both the entry and the exit again at 19:57."

"But?"

"Whoever parked the car avoided the main car park CCTV camera." He switched to another feed. "But there's a secondary camera the cast and crew don't know about. I placed it only a week ago. I got a tip some extras were taking home props as souvenirs."

The camera angle showed the side of the Tesla as the driver's door opened.

"That's not Isaac," Fiona said.

"No, it's Astrid Belmont."

Fiona leaned closer. The footage revealed Astrid Belmont stepping out of Isaac's car. She glanced around then headed for the main building. The timestamp placed her at the studios shortly before Advika's estimated time of death.

"Did you include this in your report to Barnaby?"

Vance's jaw twitched. "I noted it in my observations to the legal team, but I doubt it will make it into the official security report."

"Astrid Belmont on studio property at the time of a murder isn't relevant?"

"I doubt legal will think so." His look implied they both knew why.

"Can you make me a copy of the footage?" Fiona asked.

"I told you, I'm not supposed to—"

"I don't need all of it. Just this clip. If Barnaby deliberately hides Astrid's presence, we need proof."

He stared at the screen, conflict written across his face. "I'm not giving you a statement, and the footage didn't come from me. This conversation didn't happen."

Fiona nodded. "Thank you, Vance."

She turned to leave, hand on the door handle.

"Fi."

She stopped, not turning around.

"Nathan seems like a good bloke. The twins look like you."

The comment caught her off guard. He'd checked out her social media. The thought should have been creepy, instead, it was just sad. A man who'd never quite moved on, trying to lurk at the edges of her happiness.

"He is," she said. "They do."

She left without looking back.

Fiona walked through the darkened corridors, her thoughts churning. She'd got them a lead. Astrid was at the studio at the time of Advika's death. But she'd exploited Vance's lingering feelings to get information he wasn't supposed to give her, information that could get him fired.

Fiona pushed through the exit doors into the night air. She thought about how, a few hours ago, she'd kissed Nathan on the head as she slipped out of bed to answer Ryan's call and poked her nose into the boys' room on her way out. They'd been sprawled across their beds, both on top of the covers and topsy-turvy. How removed her family life felt from this reality, standing in a dark car park at a murder location, feeling queasy at what she'd just done. Was the way Ryan pushed the boundaries rubbing off on her?

She'd do it again, though. For Advika. For the justice the

girl deserved. And perhaps that justification should make her feel better, but it didn't quite wash away the sour taste in her mouth.

CHAPTER THIRTY-FOUR

RYAN PUSHED THROUGH THE HEAVY FRONT DOORS OF Chesterfield Police Station, and the warm air rushed to meet him. Sergeant Barney Goody sat at the front desk, his uniform strained across his barrel chest. His face soured when he spotted Ryan.

"Anything for me, Sarge?"

Goody shuffled some papers with profound reluctance. The fluorescent lights glinted off his thinning hair. "Don't know why everyone thinks I'm their personal message boy. Some muppet's always wanting something."

"It's a mystery, Barney. Your natural charm and helpful disposition must encourage people to ask for favours."

Goody's eyes narrowed, and he grunted, "Uniforms from Buxton called. They can't find your man. Emerson."

"Isaac Emerson still isn't at his house?"

"Vanished, has he?" Goody delivered the news with a faint smirk, as if Ryan's inability to keep tabs on a key witness was a personal victory. "People around you are making a habit of it."

Ryan's hand tightened on the strap of his bag. He kept his

voice even. "Thanks for the stellar relay of information, Barney. Your efficiency is, as always, breathtaking."

Goody grunted again. Ryan could tell the sergeant was unsure if he'd been complimented or insulted. Counting the ambiguity as a small win, Ryan swiped his key card. The door buzzed open. He felt the sergeant's resentful gaze bore into his back as he stepped through.

He took the stairs two at a time, eager to get upstairs to the relative sanity of his team.

On the main whiteboard in the incident room, a second column now stood beside Cyrus Wilde's name.

Advika Patel. Twenty-three years old. Above the name was a production headshot Digit had pulled from the studio files. Advika half-smiled at something off camera, headset askew, a lanyard cutting diagonally across the same T-shirt she'd worn yesterday.

Ryan watched Sheri as she stared up at the photo.

"We were going to compare family horror stories over a drink when this was over," Sheri said, half to herself, her face creased with grief.

Ryan settled down on the corner of his desk and addressed the team.

"Right. Advika Patel." He skipped the preamble. They all knew the headlines. "Stabbed three times in the abdomen in the studio photocopy room. Bled out on the floor between seven thirty and eight thirty last night."

Sheri's knuckles whitened. Her pen hovered motionless above her notebook.

Fiona broke the heavy silence. "Any defensive wounds?"

"Some bruising on her left arm," Ryan replied, grateful to shift his focus from the upset DC and back to procedure. He looked at the report notes on his phone. "And a cut on her right index finger. Forensics thinks she cut it on the paper shredder blades. The killer surprised her while she was cleaning up the blood."

"CCTV?" Sheri asked.

Fiona shook her head. "The killer spray-painted the camera in the corridor. They knew the layout and the blind spots."

"So not much to go on," Ryan replied.

Digit swivelled in his chair. "I bear more bad news. I have concluded my analysis of the handwriting samples retrieved from Mr Kerrington's workshop against the contents of the notebook."

He projected two documents onto one of the blank whiteboards. One was a list of fabric orders in an elegant, looping script. The other was a page of overwrought poetry. To the untrained eye, they looked identical.

"The graphemes show correlation," Digit began. "However, the allographic variations in the ligatures and terminal strokes exceed the expected deviation for a single author under varied emotional states. The probability of forgery is eighty-four percent."

Cal leaned forward. "So the notebook's fake?"

"It is probable that the handwriting in the notebook is a forgery, yes."

"The costume department is chaos," Ryan said, rubbing the scarred knuckles of his left hand. "Anyone could have walked in, picked up an order sheet, and practised his handwriting. Crew, extras, other cast members."

"Has to be Cyrus, yeah?" Cal jabbed a finger at the whiteboard. "The bloke was a world-class git. A proper puppet master. He fakes the diary to blackmail the designer, maybe to get some free outfits or for a laugh. Then the actual killer finds it after topping Cyrus and thinks, 'Happy days, here's a ready-made suspect'."

"Seems labour-intensive for Cyrus," Fiona mused. "But his

prints were on the notebook. Framing Blaise to mess with his head or gain something he wanted would fit his pattern of behaviour. He could have paid someone to create it."

"Maybe," Ryan agreed. "Mr Kerrington was in a cell when Advika was killed. It gives him a hell of an alibi for the second murder, and chances are, they're related." Ryan studied the boards and the lines connecting Cyrus to Blaise. The familiar frustration of a case collapsing settled over him. "It's likely the killer planted the notebook to give us a scapegoat. Without Mr Kerrington, we're back to the drawing board."

"Not entirely," Fiona said. She filled the team in on Astrid's presence at the studio.

"I have also uncovered information pointing towards the Emersons," Digit said. He tapped a few keys and brought up a spreadsheet on his monitor. The numbers were stark. Red. "Silver Dawn Productions, the company behind *Crown of Shadows*, is operating at a net loss of eight-point-seven million pounds for the financial year."

The figure dropped into the silence like a stone, and the entire energy of the room shifted.

"Piper Stone floated the idea that Isaac was trying to get Cyrus killed for an insurance payout, but it seemed far-fetched." Ryan turned his full attention to the tech specialist. "The studio's lawyers have refused to release a single paperclip of financial information. How did you get this, Digit? Tucked into their quarterly newsletter?"

Digit shifted in his seat. "The information was technically on a public server, just not one they intended for public access. And there's more."

Ryan nodded for him to continue.

"In Isaac Emerson's personal folders, which were also on the server, I found digital documents of life and serious injury insurance policies taken out on all the show's main cast. Including a six-million-pound policy for Cyrus Wilde."

"So the studio will get six million pounds because Cyrus is dead?"

"No, Isaac Emerson will get the payout personally. He took out the policies."

"So killing your star is cheaper than firing him," Cal murmured. He shook his head. "Showbiz, innit?"

Ryan held Digit's gaze for a long moment. He wondered how close Digit's digging had skirted legality, then let it go. He turned to the board, grabbed a red marker and drew a thick circle around Isaac and Astrid Emerson's names.

"So the life insurance payout saves Emerson's arse. His new wife, who was close to losing her child custody battle, also stands to benefit from her ex's death, especially if he's the father of her unborn child. She then turns up at Silverheath at the same time our second victim is killed. I think I need a chat with Astrid Emerson."

CHAPTER THIRTY-FIVE

R YAN TURNED HIS R ANGE R OVER ONTO THE PRIVATE ROAD
leading to the Emerson estate. The wheels kicked up small
stones that pinged against the undercarriage as he drove down
the gravel driveway lined with birch trees. The house appeared
ahead, all glass and white brick. He pulled up beside a
gleaming Tesla with personalised plates reading 'GENIUS IE'.
The car Fiona had seen in the footage last night.

The doorbell echoed somewhere deep within the house. A
few moments later, the heavy oak door swung open to reveal a
thin older woman in a neat grey uniform dress.

"Detective Inspector Hale." Ryan flashed his warrant card.
"I'm meeting with Mrs Emerson."

The housekeeper nodded. "Please follow me, Inspector.
Madam is expecting you."

She led him through a white marble entrance hall. A sculp-
ture looking like someone had dropped a bag of metal coat
hangers stood on a plinth in the centre. They continued down a
corridor lined with edgy but ugly abstract art before they
emerged into a kitchen straight out of an architectural maga-

zine. Polished concrete surfaces, copper pans hanging from a ceiling rack and a marble island that dominated the space.

"Please take a seat." The housekeeper gestured to a leather stool at the island. "Would you care for coffee?"

"Black, no sugar. Thank you."

As the housekeeper busied herself with the coffee machine, Ryan's gaze wandered to the far wall.

A wedding portrait hung in the centre. Astrid and Isaac backlit against a rugged mountain range, somewhere in Europe, perhaps? Astrid wore a flowing white dress that caught the breeze, her blonde hair forming a perfect halo. Isaac stood behind her, face wrinkles artfully photoshopped away. He had one arm possessively around her waist, his trademark turtle-neck replaced by a midnight-blue tailored suit. They both stared soullessly into the camera.

Ryan thought about the framed photo he used to keep on his bedside table. A candid shot of Jaime and him, laughing as he'd messed up the slow dance at their wedding. Her beauty had radiated from her shining eyes.

He pushed the memory away as the housekeeper placed a steaming mug before him. "Mrs Emerson will join you shortly."

After she left, Ryan studied the contents of the kitchen island. A thick paperback book titled *The Complete Guide to Baby Names and Their Meanings* sat next to an ornate crystal fruit bowl filled with perfectly arranged pears, apples, and plums. He poked a pear. It yielded beneath his finger. Real fruit, then, though he doubted anyone ate from the display.

He pulled the name book over and flipped it open, idly turning pages until he reached 'R'. His eyes skimmed down to his own name.

Ryan: Gaelic origin. Meaning "little king."

He snorted and closed the book with a soft thud.

"Finding inspiration, Detective?"

Ryan looked up. Astrid stood in the doorway. She wore a silk emerald dress, somehow managing to both showcase and disguise her pregnancy. Her blonde hair fell in perfect waves, and despite the strain around her eyes, she looked photoshoot ready.

"Mrs Emerson." He stood.

"Like I said before, call me Astrid." She glided across the room and perched on the stool next to him. "I hope Francesca offered you coffee?" she asked, ignoring the mug at his elbow.

Ryan nodded and raised the coffee.

"I apologise for keeping you waiting. Freddy was throwing a tantrum." She smiled. "Do you have children, Detective?"

"No."

Astrid reached for the baby-name book. "Isaac and I have been going through this every evening. He likes Harold for a boy." She flipped to the H section and pointed. "See? Harold: 'Powerful in war'."

Ryan glanced over at the page to be polite. "A strong name."

She shrugged one elegant shoulder. "Isaac admires Prince Harry. He likes the idea of a son with gravitas. My preference is for Milo."

Ryan decided against pointing out Prince Harry's actual name was Henry. How did he even know that? Ruth, Jaime's mum, was a big royalist. It must have come up at one of the many Sunday dinners he'd enjoyed at her house before Jaime had disappeared.

"Mrs Emerson, we're concerned about your husband's whereabouts. When did you last see him?"

She trailed her manicured fingers along the marble. "Yesterday morning. He left for the studio early, before seven. He called around lunchtime to say he was working on rewrites." She hesitated. "At first, when he didn't come home last night, I thought it was one of his creative bursts. He likes his space when the muse strikes."

"But now?"

"Now I'm worried." Her hand drifted to her swollen belly, cradling it. "He's not answering my calls, and he always answers for me. If he can't talk, he at least texts back. But there's been nothing."

Ryan took a sip of his coffee. "Astrid, I need to ask you about some rumours that have come to our attention."

Her spine stiffened. "What rumours?"

"There's talk on set you and Cyrus Wilde were having an affair before his death."

Her laugh was brittle. "Absurd. Who told you that?"

"Several sources at the studio have mentioned it." Ryan lied.

"Well, several sources are wrong." Her fingers curled around the edge of the island. "It's just jealousy about the role on the show Isaac wrote for me."

"Is it a big part?"

Her face lit up. "Hopefully, it will be. I begin filming after the baby comes. I'm the big reveal at the end of this season. Isaac wrote the role for me. The mysterious sister of Lord Drest returned from exile." Pride rang in her voice. "It's small to begin with, but Isaac says if the audience responds well, they'll expand the role next season."

Ryan noted how her face transformed when discussing the role. Much more animated than when she'd talked about her missing husband or the name for her unborn child.

"Let's talk about Freddy. I understand Cyrus was trying to gain custody through the courts?"

Her face hardened. "Cyrus dropped it." She brushed invisible lint from her dress. "He realised he had no chance of winning."

"The final hearing isn't until next week."

Astrid's eyes narrowed. "Cyrus made a lot of noise about being a devoted father, but it was all for show. I helped him understand pursuing the case would damage his precious public image."

"From all accounts, he wasn't the type of guy to back down. How did you manage it?"

She laughed, but it sounded hollow. "I guess it doesn't matter now he's dead. There's a video of him snorting cocaine and making disgusting sexual jokes about his cat. I told him if he persisted with the custody battle, I'd post it on my social media accounts. There's edgy, and then there's icky." She leaned forward. "Cyrus understood that."

Ryan set down his mug. "Were you aware your husband had taken out a six-million-pound life insurance policy on your ex?"

Her perfect composure slipped. "What? On Cyrus?"

"The policy pays out directly to your husband in the event of Cyrus's death."

She recovered quickly. "I didn't know, but it doesn't surprise me. Isaac is always thinking about protecting the show. The insurance would cover production delays if something happened to one of the leads."

"That's a lot of money for production delays."

"Do you have any idea how expensive it is to run a production like *Crown of Shadows*? Six million barely covers a week." She waved her hand dismissively. "Besides, Isaac doesn't need the money."

"The production's financial reports we've uncovered suggest otherwise."

She let out a huff.

"Mrs Emerson, why were you at Silverheath Studios last night around eight?"

She stood and rested a hand on her belly. "I think this conversation has gone far enough. I want you to leave. Now."

Ryan remained seated. "Mrs Emerson—"

"No," she cut in. "I invited you here because you said you would help me find my missing husband. Instead, you're sitting there drinking my custom Italian blend, implying either myself or my husband murdered my ex, for something as crass as money. I shouldn't be talking to you without the studio lawyers present."

"You're not technically a studio employee."

"Yet," Astrid shot back.

"We're following the evidence, Mrs Emerson."

"Then follow it elsewhere." She gestured to the door. "Francesca will show you out."

As if summoned by thought alone, the housekeeper appeared in the doorway.

Ryan kept his frustration hidden. So many avenues pointed to Isaac and Astrid, but nothing concrete. "Thank you for your time. We'll be in touch if we have any news about your husband."

"Find him." Her voice was small. "Please."

CHAPTER THIRTY-SIX

Ryan knocked twice on the glass door of DCI Lee's office before he entered.

She sat at her desk, shoulders rigid, her back to the wall of green that usually gave the room a sense of life. Today, even the plants looked weary, their leaves drooping as if exhausted by the constant pile of shit Lee had to deal with.

Lee gestured to the chair opposite her without looking up from the screen of her open laptop. "Shut the door."

He did. A stack of newspapers sat on the corner of her desk, displayed so he could see their headlines.

'SILVERHEATH SLAYING: POLICE BUNGLE?' and 'NO ARREST IN DREST MURDER,' were the two that jumped out.

He eyed the pile. "I see the press are their usual balanced selves."

She met his gaze, her face unreadable. She pushed a newspaper across the glass towards him. *The Derby Observer.* Sophie's paper. A picture of Blaise Kerrington, looking distraught as he was led from the hospital, sat above a scathing article that questioned the competence of the investigating team.

Ryan scanned the text. His jaw clenched tighter with each paragraph.

Sources close to the investigation suggest detectives have focused on a costume designer with a clean record because of flimsy evidence while ignoring more viable suspects. Does the North Derbyshire Police have the resources or competence to handle such a high-profile investigation?

Ryan dropped the paper. "Christ."

"It's not your sister-in-law's byline, but her fingerprints are all over it." Lee sank into her chair and sighed. "This is a bloody disaster. And it's not just the press. The studio lawyers have been on the phone to the chief constable all morning."

"Let me guess. They're very concerned there's been a second murder on set and now want to do everything in their power to help the investigation?"

Chance would be a fine thing.

"They're threatening to sue the EMSOU for irreparable brand damage," she said, her tone laced with contempt. "They claim losing their lead actor was bad enough, but having their production associated with a chaotic and bungled murder investigation is destroying the global reputation of their precious show."

The scars on Ryan's hands itched. "They've got a killer on set and they're worried about their brand?"

"Their lawyers are now classifying every costume and prop as 'valuable intellectual property.' They're refusing to release them for full forensic analysis without a court order for each individual item. They say we've 'compromised the integrity' of the murder weapon by handling it." A muscle worked in her jaw. "It's a pantomime, and a bad one."

She leaned back. "The local council is now involved. They're whispering in the chief's other ear about the millions the studio brings into the local economy. About how this investigation, my investigation, is putting all of that at risk. The man's getting it from all sides, and you know what rolls downhill."

"And we've got the wrong man." Ryan stated it as a fact, not a question. "It complicates things."

"It makes a mockery of our procedures," Lee countered, her voice sharp. "The press will crucify us. 'Incompetent police arrest gay man while the real killer strikes again.' Your sister-in-law's next headline writes itself."

She stood and walked over to her plants. She picked a yellowed leaf from a fern. "I'm fighting them, Ryan. I'm holding off the lawyers, the politicians, and the chief. But they smell blood in the water. They want results, something concrete to justify the resources we're pouring into this. Something to shut the papers up."

She turned to face him, the dead leaf crushed in her fist. "Which means, for now, the Benson case is on ice."

Ryan's posture stiffened. He opened his mouth, the words of protest already formed, but stopped himself. He saw the resolve. This wasn't a negotiation.

"I need you and your team focused only on Silverheath. No distractions. No side projects. We find who killed Cyrus Wilde and Advika Patel, and we find them now. Or this investigation will be taken out of our hands."

He gave a single, curt nod. A shared frustration passed between them. A silent understanding.

"Got it."

"I'm not Lampton," she said quietly. "I'm not interested in

protecting reputations or sweeping things under the carpet. But I can't protect this team if you give our esteemed superiors a reason to take you off the board. You're already on their shit list after the Peasley incident."

Ryan thought about the photo in the evidence bag still sitting in his glove box. He should hand it over, get it logged. But who would know? It's not like the killer was going to pipe up and say he got it a day earlier. He'd hand it in... but not yet.

Lee dropped the crumpled leaf into the bin beside her desk. "Find me a killer, Ryan. Go."

He stood.

"And Hale?"

He glanced back.

"Be careful. Some people are looking for any excuse to see you fail."

———

"Sir!" Digit's voice cut through the noise of the incident room as Ryan reached for his coat.

Ryan changed direction towards the tech corner, where Digit hunched over his three monitors. Each displayed different datasets. The first showed Isaac's insurance policy for Cyrus Wilde, the second tracked the studio's finances, and the third cycled through what appeared to be witness statements from the Benson case.

"I've cross-referenced the statements from Jacob Long and Peter York against Lynsey Cooper's account, and I've found several interesting inconsistencies that—"

"Hold up." Ryan glanced around the room. "Sorry, Digit. I should have told you. Lee's asked us to freeze work on the Benson case until the studio murders are solved."

Digit paused. "Unfortunate timing. I arranged for you to

interview Beatrice Benson at HMP New Hall tomorrow morning at seven. Before regular visiting hours."

"How did you manage that?"

"The governor owes me a favour. Well, technically, he owes EMSOU a favour after I recovered his hacked email account last year and prevented several..." He shook his head. "It's irrelevant. It took considerable negotiation, including a promise to fix his daughter's laptop before her university coursework deadline. Do you want me to cancel?"

Ryan hesitated. Lee had been clear about prioritising the Silverheath murders, but the appointment was set and Digit's tense posture suggested he didn't want to cancel. A tiny voice whispered if he'd already committed the offence of disobeying orders by starting the Benson investigation, what difference did one more interview make?

"No, keep it in the diary since it's scheduled."

The guilt of going against Lee's direct instruction less than an hour after he'd promised not to tugged at him, but he pushed it aside. If this interview revealed something crucial, it might be worth the reprimand.

"I also arranged a walkthrough of the Benson house with the estate agent, but I will cancel that. Do you still want to hear what I've uncovered so far?" Digit asked.

Ryan nodded. Digit had put hours into this.

"Go on, then."

Digit clicked to enlarge the third monitor. "I've been examining Amos Benson's death in the car crash three years after Bee's imprisonment." He brought up scans of a police report and medical examiner's findings. "The official report lists multiple injuries, with a severe fever as a contributing factor."

Ryan frowned. "So he was ill when he crashed. Was he driving?"

"Yes. According to his daughter Hannah's statement, Amos refused to let her fetch him flu medication from the pharmacy. His exact words were, 'I am stronger than the devil inside me'." Digit's face remained impassive as he relayed the bizarre detail. "The pathologist notes signs of acute pneumonia."

"Stubborn bastard," Ryan muttered.

"Indeed. Hannah's account and the pathologist's findings align. However..." Digit tapped the keyboard and brought up a witness statement. "I found an overlooked statement from a roadside witness who claimed to see someone wearing a red baseball cap walk away from the crash site before emergency services arrived."

Ryan leaned closer. "Why wasn't this followed up?"

"The witness, Ernest Hamper, was known to local police for reporting suspicious activities that amounted to nothing. He'd previously claimed to have seen aliens in Chesterfield Market." Digit adjusted his glasses. "The investigating officer deemed his statement unreliable. It was filed but never investigated further."

"Could be nothing, could be something," Ryan mused. "What about Jacob's compensation claim?"

Digit switched tabs and pulled up medical records.

"Do I want to know how you got these?" Ryan asked.

Digit grimaced. "No, you do not. There were discrepancies according to the insurance company. Two specialists contradicted each other about the severity of his injury." He highlighted sections of the reports. "The first assessment indicates significant impairment requiring lifelong ongoing support. The second, conducted six months later, suggests he had more mobility than he claimed, but the first specialist was adamant, so the claim was approved."

"Which lines up with what Peter told us. That Matthew

had seen Jacob lifting heavy boxes despite claiming he couldn't."

"Precisely." Digit pulled up another file. "Jacob also received a suspended sentence for aggravated assault when he was twenty-six. A bar fight where he injured a man who had insulted his sister, Beatrice."

Ryan raised an eyebrow. "Protective of his sister and with a history of violence."

"Court records show three men had to restrain him."

"What about Peter York? Anything beyond what we already know?"

"Limited digital footprint beyond academic publications. However, I found Reddit posts under the username PY_Bio-Chem2001. Given the user's post and comment history and the fact Peter York's birth year is 2001, I'm eighty-five percent confident it's him. He mentions receiving intensive therapy for PTSD following what he describes as 'a dramatic life experience that shattered my understanding of family'."

"Tracks with being in the house while your cousin's murdered."

"He also commented on true crime threads discussing Matthew's case. In one post, he wrote: 'None of you knows the full story'."

Ryan's interest sharpened. "When was this posted?"

"A month ago, on a thread about a documentary on Derbyshire's most shocking crimes airing on Channel 4."

"And Hannah? Anything new on her?"

"I still can't find a digital footprint after she left the country six years ago. No social media, no employment records, no banking activity, no passport use. It's as if she disappeared."

"Or changed her identity."

"A possibility that would explain the complete absence of data."

"Good work, Digit. Thanks for digging into this, but don't let it interfere with the studio murders. They're our priority for now."

CHAPTER THIRTY-SEVEN

THE CONCRETE AND BRICK EXPANSE OF HMP NEW HALL towered in front of him. Ryan checked his watch as the damp chill seeped through his wool coat. 6:50 am. Ten minutes early. Lee would have his head if she knew he was here instead of pursuing the Silverheath murders, but Lynsey had little time and he knew how fast people could go in the end.

Inside the building, Ryan surrendered his mobile, warrant card, and keys to a guard with hard eyes, receiving a visitor's lanyard in return. The guard didn't bother to hide his annoyance at the visit outside normal hours.

"Belt as well."

Ryan dropped the belt into the tray. His trousers sat fine without it, but he felt undressed all the same.

"Open your hands."

He showed his palms, the scars white as chalk under the strip lighting. The officer ticked a box.

"Interview room three," the guard said. He gestured towards a reinforced door. "Officer Kelly will escort you through."

Officer Kelly turned out to be a stocky woman with close-cropped hair and a no-nonsense stride. She led Ryan through a series of heavy doors. Each one closed with a loud *clang* before the next would open.

"You're from Chesterfield CID?" She punched a code into a keypad.

"EMSOU. Major Crimes."

She raised an eyebrow. "Unusual for a Major Crimes DI to interview a lifer."

Ryan said nothing. The fewer people who knew about his investigation, the better.

"Beatrice is one of our model inmates," Kelly continued as they walked down a sterile corridor. "Never gives us any trouble. Keeps to herself. Works in the library."

"Has she had many visitors over the years?"

"Not that I recall. A handful in the beginning, but none for a while now."

They reached a drab interview room with institutional beige walls and a simple table bolted to the floor. Two plastic chairs faced each other across its scratched surface. A camera's red pinprick flashed above the door.

"She's being brought over now," Kelly said. "Knock when you're done."

The door closed behind her with a heavy *thud*. Ryan was alone in the silent room. He pulled out his notebook and laid it on the table. On the wall, a clock ticked loudly.

Five minutes later, the door opened. A prison officer guided in a small woman with brown hair shot through with silver and pulled back in a neat bun. Bee Benson walked with her slim shoulders back. She wore her grey sweatshirt and joggers with a certain dignity, the white trainers on her feet scrubbed clean. Her face carried deep lines around her eyes and mouth, but there was a serenity that seemed out of place.

"Fifteen minutes," Officer Kelly said before she withdrew.

Bee sat down and folded her hands in her lap. Her gaze met Ryan's without fear or expectation.

"Mrs Benson, I'm Detective Inspector Ryan Hale from EMSOU Major Crimes. Thank you for agreeing to speak with me."

She nodded.

"I'm investigating the circumstances surrounding your son Matthew's death."

If she was surprised, she didn't show it. Her expression remained placid.

"I've come because of your neighbour, Lynsey Cooper. She asked me to look into your case. She's in hospice now. End stage cancer. She wanted to do one thing right before, in her words, the 'final curtain'." He kept his voice level. "She told me about the morning Matthew died."

Bee's hands clutched together, but her face betrayed nothing.

"According to Lynsey, she had tea with you that morning, then watched you in the garden. You went into your kitchen, and she heard you scream."

No reaction from Bee. She could have been waiting for a bus.

"Mrs Cooper swears there wasn't enough time for you to have killed Matthew. She heard you scream the moment you went inside the back door. When she eventually told DI Lampton, he didn't want to hear it. After all, you'd confessed."

He let the statement hang.

Bee didn't respond.

"It's okay. You don't need to speak. She told us about your husband, Amos," Ryan continued. "She described a man who liked control. A man who ruled his house through fear. We heard similar things from your brother, Jacob. Amos had a Bible in one hand and his belt in the other. Jacob also told us you spent your life keeping the weather off your children's heads." Ryan leaned forward. "I doubt you know this. There was a witness at Amos's accident scene. Someone reported seeing a person in a red cap leave just after the crash. The police never followed up. I'll sort that out. But this is about Matthew."

A slight tremble passed through her shoulders, there and gone.

"Your daughter Hannah sold the family home and disappeared. No one's heard from her in years except for the occasional postcard with no return address. And then there's Peter, your nephew, the boy you took in and treated as your own. He says you did it, by the way. Killed Matthew. But his answer sounded rehearsed. He doesn't believe his own words. I wonder why?"

A door banged in the corridor. Bee flinched.

"Here's what I think," Ryan said. "You walked into the kitchen and screamed because you were a mother finding her boy bleeding out on the floor. You went to him, and your neighbour found you. Then Amos came in, and in two sentences he told you what story he will allow to stand. And you chose in that second to swallow it. Because you thought if you carried that burden, someone you love wouldn't have to."

His eyes bored into hers. "Am I right?"

"I'd rather not say, dear." Her gaze remained steady.

That famous line. The same words she'd repeated throughout her original interrogation and trial.

He leant forward. Not far. Just enough to make sure she saw the lines of his face and the tiredness in his eyes.

"Love makes people do strange things," he said, the words feeling rough in his mouth. He wasn't looking at her anymore, but at a space somewhere over her shoulder. A space filled with memories.

He thought of Jaime. The scent of her shampoo on the pillow, the way she'd hum off-key when she cooked. The 'His' and 'Hers' mugs they'd received as an anniversary gift he'd dragged to London and back. Twelve years, and sometimes it still felt like yesterday. He bet she felt the same.

He hadn't planned to take this tack, but something about her quiet dignity compelled him. "My wife disappeared twelve years ago. The police, my direct colleagues, suspected I was involved."

She remained silent, but a flash of genuine sympathy crossed her face.

"Every day I wake up hoping today might be the day I find her. Some people move on. They're the lucky ones." He paused and swallowed against the tightness in his throat. "But I can't. Not yet. Not till I know. It just sits there inside me."

He leaned in again, his voice raw. "Tell me what happened that day. For Matthew. Let him have the truth. It's the only thing you can give him now."

A single tear escaped her right eye and traced a shining path down her weathered cheek. Another followed, then another. They fell and left dark spots on her sweatshirt.

Bee's tear-filled eyes met his. "I killed my son, Detective Inspector. I've served ten years for it, and I'll serve at least ten more as my punishment."

He let out a breath and nodded. No point pushing now. You didn't batter a shield down. You made it safe to lay it aside.

He closed his notebook and stood. His chair scraped across the floor. "I know you don't want me to, but I'm going to keep looking into this," he said. "Thank you for your time, Mrs Benson."

"Detective?"

He turned back.

"Some of God's burdens are meant to be carried alone."

Ryan recognised the shape of her sacrifice and wondered if either of them was helping anyone at all.

She gave him a small, sad smile. "I hope you find your wife."

CHAPTER THIRTY-EIGHT

Ryan pulled up outside a detached brick house on a quiet street in Tansley and questioned what the hell he was doing. It was like the photo in the evidence bag still sitting in his glovebox was pushing him on, challenging him to follow his instincts and damn the consequences.

He shrugged. *Well, I'm here now.* He got out of the car and stretched his back.

Boxwood hedges bordered the path leading to the front door and starched net curtains hung in the windows. A blonde woman stood next to a bright yellow 'For Sale' sign, her trench coat straining across broad shoulders. Keys fanned in her hand like a bouquet.

"DI Hale?" she asked, her lips fixed in a plastic smile. "Brenda from Carter & Jones Estates."

Ryan offered a brief handshake. "I appreciate you showing me the house at such short notice. I won't need long."

"Well, you said you were very interested in the place."

"It's a professional interest." He flashed his warrant card.

"Oh." The estate agent's smile faltered. "Ah... follow me."

Ryan followed Brenda up the path to the front door.

"It's a lovely house. Great bones. The current owners have redone the kitchen and the bathrooms," she said, as if she couldn't turn off the sales pitch. "They're in Spain. The house has been on the market for three months now. It's a great property, but the market's difficult at present."

She unlocked the door and pushed it open, and Ryan followed her into a hallway stripped of all personality. The stale air smelled faintly of paint and wood polish.

"I'll be outside making some calls if you need me." She handed him a business card.

Ryan waited until she disappeared, then went to the kitchen at the back of the house. Somewhere in this ordinary space, a twelve-year-old boy had bled out.

He surveyed the remodelled kitchen. Laminate countertops, tiled splashbacks in dove grey and chrome taps. All traces of the room's violent past erased by layers of paint and new flooring.

Ryan stood at the back door and tried to picture the scene from Lynsey's description. Pretend he was Bee as she entered the kitchen and saw Matthew on the floor next to the now-missing kitchen table.

He moved through the empty dining room and into the front room. Sanded floorboards and the ghost of a rug sun-faded into a rectangle. He stood where he guessed the telly had been, trying to visualise Jacob, Bee's brother, dozing on the sagging sofa while a tragedy unfolded down the hall. Had he really not heard anything that day?

The staircase creaked under his weight as he climbed to the first floor. Four doors led off a square landing. Three bedrooms and a bathroom. The small fourth room at the end of the hall had been Amos's reading room, according to the case file. A small bathroom stood at the centre, accessible from every room.

Traces of Matthew's blood had been found in the bathroom sink. Bee claimed he'd cut himself the day before, and a plaster on his finger backed up the story.

Ryan entered what must have been one of the children's bedrooms, judging by the size. Bare floorboards. A divot in the wallpaper at hip height marked where a wardrobe doorknob had knocked for years. Standing at the window, he pushed the floral curtains open further and looked across at Lynsey Cooper's house next door. How had she felt living there all these years, seeing this house from her kitchen window, knowing Bee's confession couldn't be true, yet unwilling to do anything about it until her own death approached?

He stepped away from the window, and a floorboard shifted beneath his foot. Ryan crouched and pressed against it. Nothing happened. He pressed harder, and one end raised a fraction. His shoulder protested as he worked his fingers under the edge and lifted the board away.

A small cavity lay beneath, and inside it, a few concealed treasures. Ryan took a pair of latex gloves from his pocket, then lifted out the items one by one.

First, a gold medal from Highfields School for the 100 m sprint, the blue ribbon still bright. Next, a pair of well-thumbed copies of Vogue magazine with runway looks circled in pencil. Their pages were dog-eared and slashed with a criss-cross of cuts. *Matthew's work?* And last, a word puzzle book, half the puzzles completed in neat handwriting, with a photo of three girls tucked between the pages. The two on the outside grinned, but the girl positioned between them wore a smile that stopped at her lips. Hannah.

A girl's dreams and diversions, hidden away from a father

who would have deemed them frivolous. He placed the photograph inside his notebook and put the rest of Hannah's things back. As he went to replace the board, something caught his eye. On the underside, a smear of rust brown. Faint, but unmistakable to his trained eye.

Blood.

Ryan photographed the stain with his phone and set the floorboard back in position. He'd need Eloise to take proper samples, but his gut yelled at him to pay attention.

Downstairs, Brenda leaned against her car, her phone to her ear. She ended the call when she spotted him. "All finished? Find what you were looking for?"

Ryan nodded. "Who owned the house before the current sellers?"

Her smile faded. "That would have been the Benson family. The daughter, Hannah, sold it. A private sale, I believe. Mr and Mrs Cartwright bought it directly from her seven years ago."

"Right." Ryan pulled his phone out. "You'll have to cancel any viewings for the rest of the day. I've found something I'd like a forensic officer to examine. No one else is to enter the property until they've finished."

Her face fell. "A forensic officer? Is there a problem?"

"That's what I need to find out," Ryan said. His tone left no room for negotiation. "Lock up after me and wait for my team to arrive. They'll let you know when you can resume viewings."

She nodded, her sales patter deflated.

Ryan unlocked the car and slid into the driver's seat. He dialled Digit.

"Digit, get hold of Eloise for me," he said as soon as DC Asare answered. "I want forensics at the old Benson house. I'll text you the address. Ask her to bring a Haema test and swabs.

There's a board upstairs I need her to process. Get her to call me when she arrives."

"Eloise hates being told what kit to bring, but I'll frame it as a polite suggestion."

Ryan turned onto the main road. "Thanks, Digit. There's also one other thing I need you to do."

CHAPTER THIRTY-NINE

The catering room at Silverheath Studios reeked of fish fingers and melted cheese. The hum of the extras' conversations washed over Ryan as he carried two Styrofoam cups of what the sign optimistically called 'coffee.' Fiona trailed behind as he scanned the room for an empty table.

"There's one over by the window," she said.

As they crossed the mottled linoleum floor, Cyrus's name cut through the background chatter.

Ryan stopped. Colin, the extra, sat hunched over a cup of tea at a corner table with another extra, half hidden by a fake potted palm. Their ragged black soldier's uniforms made them look like a pair of crows picking over a carcass. Neither had noticed the detectives.

Ryan caught Fiona's eye and tilted his head to a table within earshot. They slid into the metal chairs. Ryan angled his body to keep the pair in his peripheral vision.

"I'm just saying," the other extra said as he stirred a sachet of sugar into his milky tea, "Millie told me herself, right here in this room. She said Grace asked her to check Cyrus's Porsche for a missing belt buckle on Wednesday morning."

Colin scoffed and pushed his empty cup away. "So?"

"Then Millie finds the notebook, and Grace's boss gets arrested. Pretty convenient."

Colin shook his head. "Come on, mate. You think Grace planted it? Millie feels guilty, that's all. The notebook got Mr Kerrington falsely arrested, and now she's making stuff up in her head to feel better. Christ, these things are itchy today." He touched the fake wound on his cheek, then leaned forward. "Anyway, Grace has been dead decent to Millie. Gave her that Balenciaga scarf she's always wearing. Found her a load of designer stuff on this secret website. She's Grace's pet project. It's bloody ungrateful of her to spread stories."

Bit rich coming from Crown of Shadows's number one gossip, Ryan thought as the other extra shrugged and drained the dregs of his tea.

"Just telling you what she said." He scraped his chair back and stood. "I'm off. Got to get this beautiful mug turned ugly." He pointed to his makeup-free face, then patted Colin on the shoulder. "See you on the battlefield."

After the man left, Colin remained at his table, fishing around in the top of his boot. He pulled out his phone and typed out a message. Then he picked up his tea, his gaze drifting across the scattered lunch trays and half-empty water bottles until his eyes landed on Ryan and Fiona two tables over. The extra's body went rigid.

Before Ryan could call out, Colin bolted from his chair. He weaved between tables, almost taking out a pirate with a tray of food, and hurried out the exit.

Fiona met Ryan's gaze across the table. The same thought hung between them.

"Did Grace Bonnes frame her boss to get his job?" Fiona said. They stood to follow him when Cal appeared at their side.

"Boss, you need to see this." He held out a piece of paper inside a clear evidence bag. "A security guard found it in the crew car park."

Ryan took the bag. Inside was a letter scrawled on a piece of paper.

Cyrus,

You destroyed my life and my reputation. You took everything from me and smiled while you did it.

I think about how satisfying it would be to watch you suffer the way I have. To make you feel as powerless and small as you made me feel. Sometimes I imagine wrapping my hands around your throat and squeezing until you finally stop talking. Taking one of the prop axes and cutting off your hands so you can't hurt anyone else.

You deserve to die for what you did to me. And one day, you will.

I hope it hurts.

M.

Margot? Before Ryan could question Cal further, his phone vibrated against the tabletop. Digit's name flashed on the screen. He answered. "What have you got?"

"I've gone through the CCTV backups for Stage Five," Digit's voice crackled. "The camera covering the set was disabled on Saturday night, but I uncovered a motion-activated clip from another night at a similar time over a month ago."

"And?"

"It shows Cyrus Wilde in a heated argument with an individual. The angle is poor, and the subject is in shadow. However, I've run an enhancement algorithm."

A notification pinged on Ryan's phone. A video file. He opened it. The footage was grainy, with white highlights from the key lights. Cyrus stood near the pit, his gestures sharp and angry. The other person was a silhouette, but as they turned to leave, their face caught the light for a fraction of a second.

Fiona leaned in to see the screen. "Grace."

It was her. The jagged bob hairstyle was a dead giveaway.

"She told me she had nothing to do with Cyrus," Fiona added.

Ryan disconnected the call. "We need to find her."

They left their cups on the table and moved through the warren of covered walkways. The costume department was empty, the costume assistants in the extra's green room, getting the actors ready for the upcoming battle scene.

Ryan's eyes fell on the set of drawers with the 'KEEP OUT' sign, and something popped into his head. Blaise's sketchbooks. He pulled on the bottom drawer, hoping it remained unlocked. It did.

Sliding the drawer out, Ryan lifted the sketchbook on top. He flicked through the pages until he came to a sketch detailing the Shadow Queen's robe. He held it out for Fiona and pointed to the signature at the bottom.

"I thought the initials were 'BK' for Blaise Kerrington," he said, tracing the signature with his finger. "But look closer. I think it's 'GB'."

Fiona's eyes widened. "You think Blaise was passing Grace's work off as his own?"

"It would explain a few things." Ryan placed the sketchbook back and closed the drawer.

Ryan radioed DC Pine. He told the detective what he and Fiona had overheard and asked him and Sheri to check the soundstages and backlot for Grace. He and Fiona would take the main building and the extra's green room.

As they walked back into the main corridor, a familiar, imperious figure swept past them, her heavy silken robes whispering against the floor. Piper, dressed as the Shadow Queen in full regalia, her face beneath an elaborate horned headdress with a half mask. She looked back at them and paused, as if to say something, then changed her mind. Ryan thought about detaining her to question her more about the insurance policies, but with the studio lawyers breathing down his neck about delays, he decided it could wait until after she finished filming.

Ryan's phone buzzed again. The gods of cellular service were smiling down on him today. The message contained the image file from Digit he'd had requested outside the Benson house. Ryan zoomed in, his wild guess confirmed. He pocketed the phone.

The extra's green room was filled with soldiers adjusting their uniforms and make-up artists painting artful smudges of dirt and touching up wounds, but Grace was nowhere in sight. A young wardrobe assistant knelt beside a rack of period costumes, pins held between her pursed lips like metal thorns.

"Have you seen Grace?" Fiona asked.

The girl shook her head, careful not to dislodge the pins.

Ryan scanned the chaos for a production assistant with a radio, someone who could track Grace down across the sprawling set. The usual cluster of clipboard-wielding coordinators had vanished.

He pushed open the door to the small break room near the principal cast's trailers. A kettle whistled on the counter. Piper Stone stood beside it, adding a spoonful of honey into a mug. She wore a simple cashmere jumper and jeans. No prosthetics. No headdress.

Ryan did a double take. "I thought you were heading to set."

Piper raised an eyebrow. "Hardly. I'm not in make-up for another hour." She took a delicate sip of her tea.

"Do you have a body double who does the camera positions and lighting on set?" Ryan only knew it was a job because the wife of a detective on his London team had been the body double for Keira Knightley on the set of Pride and Prejudice, and the detective was still dining out on it years later.

She shrugged. "My stand-in did the blocking yesterday."

"Would they redo it? Do they do it in costume?"

"No one is allowed to touch my costumes but me." She spun to face him. "Why, what have you heard? Surely those absurd replacement rumours have been put to—"

Ryan shut the door. He stared back down the corridor in the direction the costumed figure had gone. If it wasn't Piper or her stand-in, it had to be Grace. Colin must have warned her they were looking for her.

His phone rang as Fiona reappeared with a shake of her head. DCI Lee.

"Hale. We have a problem." Lee's voice was tight. "The studio's lawyers have served the department with an injunction application. They're claiming procedural misconduct and demanding we provide a valid warrant for every officer on the premises. You need to vacate. Now."

Bloody Peasley.

Ryan walked a few steps. "Sorry, boss, you're breaking up. The reception in here is terrible." He made a series of crackling noises with his mouth. "Losing you..." He ended the call and shoved the phone back in his pocket.

A moment later, Fiona's phone rang. She pulled it out, and her face paled as she saw the caller ID. She looked at Ryan.

"Don't answer it."

"She's not going to love that."

"Let it ring out."

Guilt twisted his stomach as her thumb hovered over the screen. Fiona hated breaking the rules.

She sighed, and her phone fell silent. "I hope you know what you're doing."

CHAPTER FORTY

"She played us." Ryan grimaced. "She's using the costume to get around the studio without being recognised."

Fiona's phone went silent. A moment later, his buzzed. He left it.

"And she's heading where?" Fiona asked as they jogged past a trio of soldier extras who strolled down the corridor.

They burst through a set of double doors onto the backlot. Ryan scanned the bustling scene. Film crew moved equipment. Extras milled about on the edges in their battle gear while make-up artists darted between them with brushes and sponges. The horned headdress was nowhere to be seen.

"There." Fiona pointed to a side door on one of the massive warehouses housing a soundstage. A flash of ornate fabric disappeared inside as a crew member emerged with a pair of spotlights.

Ryan dodged a golf cart loaded with heavy cables and sprinted across the yard. He tugged at the stage door handle. Locked. Nearby, a harried assistant shouted something about clearance. He ignored her and searched for a way in.

"Here," Fiona called out. She gestured to another door with 'CHROME HILL' written above in rusted metal letters. An enormous red light flashed above them next to a sign reading 'LIVE FILMING - NO ADMITTANCE'.

Ryan shoved the door open and stepped onto a gantry over-looking a vast set. Below them, a scene of crafted carnage unfolded. The blasted ruins of a medieval village sprawled across the studio floor. A battle raged under a stormy, artificial sky. A hundred extras in black armour clashed with a smaller group of silver-clad soldiers. Their prop swords rang against shields.

"There she is." Fiona yelled over the din of the battle and pointed down. The Shadow Queen, a flash of deep purple against the grey and black, moved through the fake rubble towards the far side of the set.

Ryan looked for a route down as the world exploded in noise. A colossal crack of recorded thunder shook the build-ing, powerful enough for him to feel it in his teeth. Industrial-sized fans kicked in and whipped up a gale that sent dirt and loose props skittering around the set. Then came the rain. Not the standard Derbyshire drizzle, but a torrential down-pour from the overhead rigs that soaked everything in seconds.

The Shadow Queen faltered. Her hands went to the horned headdress as if to steady it against the wind. Ryan spotted a metal staircase fifty feet away. Too far.

Fuck. Trying not to think too hard, he swung his legs over the railing, hung for a second and dropped twenty feet into a pile of what he hoped was hay. It was foam matting. The fall still knocked the wind out of him.

He looked back to see Fiona sensibly heading for the stair-well. The noise was deafening. The thunder, the soldiers yelling over the clashing of swords. Then a new sound. The director's voice boomed over a megaphone, though the maelstrom broke up the words.

Ryan ploughed into the fight and shoved extras aside. They were too absorbed in their choreographed battle to pay much mind aside from the occasional grunt as he pushed through their ranks. The ground was a treacherous soup of fake mud and slick cobblestones. He slipped and caught himself on the arm of a dead-eyed mannequin propped against a crumbling wall.

Ahead, the Shadow Queen navigated the village streets with a strange, stumbling grace. She wasn't running like a fugitive. She moved like someone lost in the dark, her hands held out, the heavy robes tangled around her legs. Ryan shouted her name. A useless gesture.

He saw her disappear through the skeletal remains of a burnt-out tavern and followed, leaping over a fallen cart. A couple of crew members in black waterproofs now ran parallel to him, shouting and pointing. They weren't looking at the Shadow Queen. They were looking at him.

"Hey you! Stop!" one of them yelled.

Ryan ignored them. His focus pinned on his quarry. She was twenty yards ahead, trying to climb a small hillock of rubble at the base of a ruined watchtower. Her foot slipped, and she went down hard. Her horned headdress skittered away into a puddle.

He closed the distance as his lungs burned and his damaged shoulder pulled tight. The crew members were close behind. Their heavy boots splashed through the water. He reached the figure as she pushed herself onto her hands and knees.

He grabbed her arm. "Grace. It's over."

She flinched and twisted to face him. Her face was smudged with dirt and streaked with rain. Lashes clumped together. But the hair wasn't electric, jagged blue. It was plain, mousy brown, plastered to a pale, terrified face.

Millie Higgins.

Ryan stared. The adrenaline drained out of him, replaced by a wave of confusion.

Millie's eyes were panicked. "I'm so sorry. I got lost. The stupid headpiece. I couldn't see a thing. Then all the noise started, and I realised I was in the middle of a scene. I was trying to get out of the way before anyone saw me."

The megaphone voice cut through a lull in the thunder, closer now. "CUT! FOR THE LOVE OF GOD, CUT! WHO IS THAT MAN? AND WHY IS HE ACCOSTING THE QUEEN? SHE ISN'T DUE TO APPEAR UNTIL AFTER THE GATES ARE BREACHED."

The rain and wind machines sputtered and died. The clash of swords ceased. A hundred pairs of eyes turned to them.

A crew member caught up, panting. "Right, you. What do you think you're doing, mate?" he said as he grabbed Ryan's arm.

"Police." Ryan gasped and fumbled for his warrant card.

Millie cried quiet, hiccupping sobs. "Please don't get me fired. I was doing a favour for Grace."

"Grace?"

"She... she said they were filming a behind-the-scenes thing," Millie stammered. She wiped her nose with the back of her hand. "Like a special for the streaming service. She said Piper wouldn't do the walk-through, and they needed some shots of the Queen moving through the village. She told me to use the side door. They weren't supposed to be filming."

Ryan looked at the set. Grace had deliberately sent Millie into a live-action shoot.

Fiona appeared at his side. Her raincoat dripped.

Ryan let go of Millie's arm. He ran a hand over his soaked

hair as the pieces clicked into place. Colin had warned Grace about what the detectives had overheard, so she'd created a diversion. A perfect little puppet show with poor impressionable Millie as the star, while she slipped out the back. She was probably long gone.

A short, bald man stomped over with an air of importance and a megaphone pressed to his lips. "GET THE HEAD OF SECURITY HERE NOW! WHAT PART OF LIVE SEQUENCE DO YOU PEOPLE NOT UNDERSTAND? WHERE'S MY FIRST?"

A first AD appeared. "We were shooting the hero tracking shot, Jim."

"I KNOW," the director roared. "EVERYONE KNOWS. THOSE CHICKENS OVER THERE BY THE WELL KNOW."

Up close, the director's cheeks were crosshatched with broken veins. He used the megaphone inches away from Ryan's face.

"DOES ANYONE WANT TO TELL ME WHY THIS MAN IS PLAYING TAG WITH THE QUEEN IN THE MIDDLE OF MY TEN MILLION POUND BATTLE SEQUENCE? BECAUSE I CAN ASSURE YOU, IT'S NOT IN THE SCRIPT."

CHAPTER FORTY-ONE

RYAN CROSSED THE BACKLOT, HIS SHOES SLIPPING ON WET concrete and his ears still ringing from the director's yelling. Fiona matched his stride. Vance, the head of security, trailed behind with a tight jaw and muttered complaints about protocol. Ryan's radio crackled.

"DI Hale? Sir?"

Sheri. She was breathless, but he made out the words.

"Go."

"Cal intercepted Grace trying to leave the studio lot with a group of extras. Something about Alexander McQueen boots? He went after her, but she got away. We've followed her to Stage Five. She's forced Colin into a stunt rig and suspended him over the pit. She's threatening to drop him. Sir, you need to get here now."

Fiona's head snapped round.

"Armed?" Ryan asked.

A beat of static. "The only thing I can see is her scissors. She's up in the rigging at the gantry control box. The pit's full of blades. If she drops him..."

"We're on our way. Don't engage her." Ryan turned to Vance. "What's the quickest route to Stage Five?"

For once, the head of security didn't argue. "This way."

They tore down the corridors, dodging coils of cables and hard cases. They passed a pair of grips hauling sandbags and a runner who flattened herself against the wall with a squeak. The stage door loomed ahead.

They burst into the Stage Five warehouse. Emergency strips and two harsh work lamps lit the space, carving stark shadows into the alcoves.

In the middle of the stage, the pit yawned. The neon green screen disc had gone. In its place lay a bristling collection of swords, daggers, and blades positioned points up. The weapon racks decorating the set walls stood empty.

Above them, Colin Rogers dangled face down in a stunt harness, arms yanked tight behind his back and a rope binding his wrists. The rig's cable ran up to the gantry high above the set, where a small box hummed and clicked.

Sheri and Cal stood on the stage floor, necks craned. Relief washed across their faces when they saw Ryan and Fiona.

"Oh, detectives, thank God," Colin called, his voice wobbling between bravado and panic. "Is this part of the documentary too? I know Mr Emerson requested me, but I'm not sure I'm the right choice for this scene. Is this harness rated for prolonged suspension? My arms are going numb..."

"I keep telling you, Colin, this isn't part of filming," Cal shouted up.

Ryan stepped forward as Vance slipped backstage. "Everyone stay clear of the pit in case he drops."

Sheri took two slow steps back. Cal shuffled sideways.

"What do you mean, drop?" Colin shrieked. His body twisted in the harness, and the cable swayed.

On the gantry above Colin, Ryan made out Grace Bonnes

leaning against the stunt coordinator's control box, her electric blue hair slicked back from her forehead. She wore a soldier-extra's leather cuirass over a mud-encrusted tunic and breeches, all smeared with fake mud and streaks of stage blood. In one hand she swung a lank brown wig by its netting like something freshly scalped.

Her lips pulled back into a snarl. The fake blood on her face made her fury feral. In her other hand, a pair of costumer's scissors caught the light.

"Colin, I need you to stay still," Ryan said.

The extra looked ready to argue, then glimpsed the blades below. His legs convulsed against the straps.

Grace rolled her eyes and let the wig drop. It slumped across the gantry railing like a skinned animal pelt and fell to the floor beside the pit.

"He wouldn't stop squealing when I hooked him in," she shouted down. "You'd think a supposed professional would know his upstage from his arse."

Her fingers flicked a lever.

A motor whined. The cable released and dropped Colin half a metre.

He screamed. The harness jerked at his waist and made the whole rig bounce. The metal gantry creaked.

Ryan could see the moment Colin's belief that it was all a prank evaporated. "Oh God, oh God, oh God."

Grace rested her wrist on the lever as if testing how much weight it would bear. "If anybody comes up these stairs or tries to override these controls, I'll let him fall the rest of the way. If the drop doesn't kill him, the props department will."

Vance appeared from backstage. "The rig's rated for a full stunt load," he muttered, eyes fixed on the cable. "But the fail-safes... I don't know what she's done. She's bypassed the safety lock." His jaw clenched. "She's a wannabe actress with a pair of sewing scissors. I can end this." He gestured to the closest set of stairs leading up to the gantry.

Fiona rounded on him. "Stand down. You go near those stairs, you'll get him killed."

He bristled. "It's my bloody studio."

Ryan stepped into the pool of light cast by the work lamps, close enough for Grace to see his face clearly but far enough back he could have a run-up to throw himself at Colin if the worst happened. The blades glinted at the edge of his vision.

"Grace."

Her gaze flicked to him. "Detective Inspector," she called, her voice echoing. "So glad you could make it to the final act."

"You know we can't let you walk out of here," he called. "Not after Cyrus. Or Advika."

"Oh, I'm not walking anywhere." Her lips curled. "Running into the mist, maybe."

Ryan kept his eyes on Grace. "You're good at disappearing when things get uncomfortable, aren't you? Changing your name and your hair." He paused and let the silence stretch. "A girl learns early the best way to survive is to make herself invisible. Then she gets tired of cowering and fights back. She creates a character people can't ignore. One who doesn't get pushed around or locked in her bedroom and told to repent."

Grace's grip on the gantry rail tightened.

Ryan let it hang there, then gave her the name sitting in his throat since the Benson House in Tansley.

"Hannah."

No smirk. A blank, stunned stillness. "Wrong girl," she said at last. "I get mistaken for people all the time. Apparently, everyone with blue hair looks the same to you lot."

"You didn't have blue hair then."

"Then?"

"When Amos Benson laid hands on you to drive out the

devil." Ryan's voice stayed level. "When you killed Matthew in a fit of rage with your dressmaking scissors."

"Shut up. I'm not Hannah Benson." The words cracked out. Her hand twitched on the lever, and the cable jerked. Colin yelped.

Fiona sucked in a breath. "Grace, listen. Think about where you are. You drop him, there's no coming back from that."

"You don't know anything," she yelled.

"I know your mother took the blame for your actions," Ryan went on. "Confessed to a murder she didn't commit. She sacrificed her freedom out of love for you."

Something raw flashed across Grace's face, replaced by icy anger. "Shut up, shut up, shut up!"

"Was it because Matthew destroyed your fashion magazines?"

"It wasn't about the magazines," Grace screamed back.

"My designs," she said, her voice raw. "Amos threw my sketchbook into the fire. Hours and hours of work gone up in flames because that snivelling little tattletale wanted to impress Daddy. Amos made me pray in penance on my knees on the wooden floor for hours."

"So you killed Matthew." A statement, not a question.

"I didn't..." She stopped. Her jaw worked.

"You didn't mean to," Ryan said. "But you did."

Grace's face contorted. "He laughed the next morning. Said I deserved it. Said I was a sinner and a whore for drawing women in short skirts." Her voice climbed. "He was ten years old and already a perfect little copy of that monster."

"So you made him stop laughing. You stabbed your brother with your scissors, and he bled out on the kitchen floor."

"I made him quiet." The words came out like a hiss. "One thrust, right here." She pointed to her chest with the bloodied scissors. "He looked so surprised. Like he couldn't believe I'd fought back."

Ryan let the confession hang in the misty air for a beat.

"And your mother found you standing over his body. She told you to go upstairs and clean up."

Grace's face cracked with grief, then the mask slammed back into place.

"And Amos?" Ryan asked. "That was you?"

Grace gave a brittle laugh then nodded. "I was quite proud of that one. A one-way trip down a cliff face for daddy dearest."

Ryan nodded. Wearing Matthew's red trucker cap like a tribute.

Something moved in his peripheral vision. Vance sidled to the bottom of the gantry stairs, taser in hand.

Grace saw him too. "I see you, Vance. Don't try to be the hero."

Ryan tried to catch his eye, a subtle warning to stand down, but the man was locked in his own mission. Ryan and Fiona shared a look. She nodded and moved in Vance's direction.

"Maybe we could workshop this in therapy instead?" Colin squeaked. "Please?"

"Stop moving," Ryan barked.

"I'm not moving!"

"You're flailing. Keep still."

Before Fiona could react, Vance charged up the narrow metal staircase, his boots clanging against the steps. He reached the walkway as Grace spun. In a fluid motion, she danced forward and drove the point of her scissors into his thigh.

Vance's eyes flew open, and his knees buckled. His body smashed against the gantry rail. For a sick second, Ryan thought he'd tip over it. Instead, Vance toppled sideways, limbs tangled as he bounced down the metal stairs.

The taser flew from his grip, skittered along the gantry

grating and tipped through a gap. It clattered onto the stage and spun to a halt in the shadow of an alcove.

Vance landed in a heap a few steps up.

He roared in pain and grabbed at his leg.

Not dead yet, at least.

A pool of blood spread out from his trouser leg.

"Vance!" Fiona rushed over and dropped to her knees beside him. She ripped off her raincoat, bundled it up, and clamped it over the wound with both hands.

Grace staggered back to the control panel, breathing hard, one hand smeared red. "I told you what would happen if anyone tried to interfere." She jabbed at a button.

Ryan went to leap, but instead of Colin plummeting, the set came alive. An eerie chant sounded, and theatrical fog billowed across the floor and curled around their legs.

"Look for something to cover the pit," Ryan muttered out of the side of his mouth to Cal, who stood a short distance away.

The detective constable nodded and backed into the darkness until he was out of Grace's line of sight.

"Disappearing is easy," Grace called down over the chants. "If you know how to change your hair, your name and your entire personality." She leaned over the railing. "Maybe it's what your wife did, DI Hale? Started fresh somewhere else, far away from you."

Ryan's stomach dropped at the mention of Jaime, but he didn't give her the satisfaction of a reaction. "There's no disappearing this time, Grace."

He heard Fiona speak into Vance's radio, requesting the doctor.

Out of the corner of his eye, Ryan noticed Sheri had moved across the stage, hidden by the shadows. Mist wrapped around her and swallowed her in the gloom. She reached the far staircase, the one opposite Vance and Fiona, and climbed, placing each foot with deliberate care.

Ryan's throat tightened. He could live with Vance bleeding out on the stairs. But Sheri? Should he give her an order to stop?

Grace's fingers rested on the lever, her attention fixed on him. She hadn't seen the shadow climbing through the mist.

Ryan held his breath and prayed Sheri had a plan.

CHAPTER FORTY-TWO

"How did you let Cyrus get close enough to blackmail you?" Ryan raised his voice above the creepy chanting.

Grace paced along the gantry. One hand trailed over the control panel while the other gripped the scissors, streaked red from Vance's blood. Even from below, Ryan could see her hands were steady.

"Like I had a choice." The clatter of her boots grated on his nerves. "He recognised me in those stupid Highfields year-books." She almost spat the school's name.

"He knew who you really were?"

"Oh yes. Cyrus never forgot a face, especially one attached to a juicy scandal." Her voice hardened. "He realised exactly what that secret meant to me. In this industry, optics are every-thing. No one would want to hire the daughter of a murderer, let alone promote them to head costume designer."

"What did he want?"

She stopped. "He told me he'd keep my dirty secret if I messed with Piper's costumes, make her look difficult."

Ryan heard Vance yell as Fiona applied more pressure to his leg.

"At first I didn't care," Grace continued. "If Piper were replaced, what was it to me? But Cyrus kept pushing me, testing how far I'd go. I realised he wasn't going to extract the claws he'd dug into me until I was fired, or exposed."

Grace twisted a knob. The rig juddered. Colin swung in a nauseating arc, his face green.

"Oh God, I'm going to be sick," he moaned.

Ryan saw Cal bending low as he tried to lift a piece of backdrop. "Boss, nothing's loose or wide enough."

Grace's hands hovered over the controls. "Every story has to end somewhere, I guess. I'm done letting other people manipulate me."

Ryan looked up through the drifting fog. Sheri had made it up the stairs and was halfway across the gantry, stepping carefully to avoid making it sway. Their eyes met. He gave the smallest nod.

"What about Advika?" Ryan asked. "Why kill her?"

Grace's expression flickered between pride and regret. "Advika. Sweet, nosy Advika. She couldn't resist having a look at gawky teenage Cyrus in the yearbooks when that idiot Millie dumped them on her."

"Advika found your picture too?"

"She found Hannah Benson's face."

Ryan kept his eyes on Grace. He avoided tracking Sheri's slow advance. "So she confronted you."

She snorted. "Hardly. She came to me all wide-eyed, remarking on the resemblance and asking if I'd ever heard of the case. Apparently, she'd watched a documentary about it recently." Grace's laugh was brittle. "Such a helpful girl, always wanting to please. I couldn't risk her connecting the dots or sharing her little discovery."

Grace spun and spotted Sheri on the metal walkway.

Her lip curled. "Well, look at you. Another Paki girl eager to die."

The words hung in the air, ugly and sharp. Sheri stopped. Artificial fog curled between them. She planted her feet on the grating and raised Vance's taser.

"I'm not a Paki." Sheri's voice rang out clear and steady. "I'm a police officer."

On the last word, she squeezed the trigger.

The cartridge fired with a sharp crack, and the probes caught Grace in the chest. Her body snapped rigid as her mouth flew open in a silent scream. She reached for the controls, but her arm spasmed away from her body.

Grace collapsed onto the metal grating. The scissors clattered from her grasp and tumbled into the pit below.

Sheri rolled her onto her stomach and snapped cuffs around her wrists before Grace could recover from the charge. She crossed to the control panel and studied it for a moment. The motor whirred to life, and Colin descended slowly.

"At least let me say something profound if this goes wrong," Colin whimpered. "Cal, if I die, clear my browser hist—"

"I've got him," Ryan called up as he pulled the extra away from the pit.

Cal joined him, and together they guided Colin down until he lay on the stage. Once free of the harness, Colin collapsed to his knees.

"I didn't know," he babbled between gulping breaths. "She promised it was part of this behind-the-scenes documentary. She said it could lead to a permanent role on the show."

Ryan squeezed his shoulder hard enough to ground him. "You're alive. Breathe through your nose. Try not to throw up on my shoes."

The soundstage doors burst open. Shaun, the studio doctor,

barrelled in with a trauma bag over one shoulder and two of Vance's uniformed guards on his heels. More security followed, radios crackling.

"Over here," Fiona shouted from the base of the stairs.

Shaun veered towards her. Vance lay where he'd fallen, propped against the metal steps, his skin a waxy grey. Blood soaked the raincoat Fiona had pressed to his thigh and dripped down onto the stage below.

"He's lost a lot of blood," she told Shaun.

Shaun dropped beside them and ripped open dressings with his teeth. "We've got you, mate. Stay with me." He waved a guard closer. "Lift his leg. Higher."

Ryan straightened. Cal had moved to the far stairs.

Sheri appeared at the top, one hand on the railing, the other holding the back of Grace's borrowed cuirass. Grace's legs wobbled, her muscles misfiring from the taser. Her mascara had run, and black streaks carved through the fake blood on her cheeks.

"Need a hand?" Cal called up.

"I've got her," Sheri answered, breathless but controlled. "She's slippery, but she's not going anywhere."

She walked Grace down, the woman's chunky boots ringing on the metal. At the bottom, one of the security guards moved in.

Sheri shook her head. "No. She's ours."

She brought Grace to a halt in front of Ryan. The costume designer blinked up at him, dazed, but there was still a layer of fury simmering under the stupor.

He looked past her to Sheri.

Sweat plastered her hair to her forehead, and her pupils were huge, but her gaze was direct.

"Nice work," Ryan said. "You might have saved his life." He jerked his chin at Colin, still huddled on the floor.

Sheri glanced down at Colin, then back at Ryan. "Like I said, I'm a police officer. It's my job."

CHAPTER FORTY-THREE

RYAN STOOD BEFORE THE WHITEBOARDS, A MUG OF espresso in hand. A mugshot of Grace Bonnes occupied the centre, circled in red. Beneath it, Cal had written in neat block capitals: 'AKA HANNAH BENSON'.

DCI Lee perched on the edge of Fiona's desk, her jacket off and sleeves rolled. The rest of the team sat at their desks with their faces turned towards him.

"Two cases." Ryan rapped his knuckles against the board. "One killer."

"Hannah Benson became Grace Bonnes." Lee folded her arms. "And nobody spotted it for ten years."

Ryan nodded. "She'd changed her appearance drastically. Dyed her hair blue, wore coloured contacts and cultivated a distinct style."

"How did you make the connection?" Lee asked.

Ryan crossed to his desk and retrieved two clear evidence bags. Inside them lay the sliced-up Vogue magazines and the word puzzle book he'd discovered beneath Hannah's floorboards.

"When I searched the Benson house, I found these under a floorboard in Hannah's old room, along with blood that likely transferred from the clothes she wore the day she stabbed Matthew." He placed the bags on an empty desk. "If Hannah'd hidden the fashion magazines from Amos, they must have been important to her. She would have been furious when Matthew slashed them up the day before he died."

He tapped the bags. "The magazines made me think of the postcard locations Peter mentioned. Paris, Milan, New York. All major fashion capitals. I wondered if fashion was Hannah's calling and whether the sewing scissors Matthew had been stabbed with belonged to Hannah, not Bee. Turns out Peter suspected Hannah of killing Matthew and Amos all along, and he was terrified he might be next. The postcards were her way of letting him know she was keeping tabs on him while she was away studying. He never got a postcard from Buenos Aires, he was just trying to put us off the scent."

"That's still quite a leap to Grace," Fiona said.

"It is. I knew Hannah's face in the photo I found in the back of the puzzle book was vaguely familiar, but I didn't know why."

Sheri leaned forward. "That's why you asked Digit to create an age progression?"

Ryan nodded.

Digit spun his monitor so the others could see the split screen. On the left, the grainy photo of teenage Hannah Benson with her two friends. A girl with mousy hair and wary eyes. On the right, a professional headshot of Grace Bonnes.

"I used a standard facial ageing algorithm," Digit explained. "Factored in ethnic background, family traits from Bee and Amos's photos, environmental stressors. The output profile for twenty-eight to thirty-two years had a ninety-two percent match with Grace Bonnes' staff photo from the Silverheath database."

The program cropped in on the photo to show only teenage Hannah and then aged her to a woman in her late twenties. If you took away the blue bobbed hair, the blunt fringe and the long fake eyelashes, it was obvious they were the same person.

"Note the brow line," Digit said. "Jaw, orbital spacing. It's improbable for two unrelated people to share that configuration."

Ryan continued. "At first, I thought of Millie. She fit the profile. She was the right age, knew Cyrus's movements, was interested in fashion and allergic to cats. Just like Hannah.

"But then on the drive from Tansley to the studio, I remembered the baby name book in Astrid's kitchen. I'd been thinking about the Benson case on my way out to the Emerson's, so when Astrid looked up 'Harold', I noticed Hannah on the opposite page. The name's meaning was 'grace of God'." He raised an eyebrow. "Like me, Hannah was fond of wordplay." He gestured to the puzzle book. "So I focused on Grace's surname. Rearranged the letters mentally. 'Bonnes' is 'Benson' reshuffled. Then it all came together."

"Bet you wish you'd worked it out before she nearly turned Colin into a human kebab," Cal muttered.

Ryan shot him a glance. "Digit confirmed my suspicions when he sent the age progression."

Cal leaned back. "So when you got that through on your phone..."

Ryan gave a single nod. "I already thought of her as Hannah before I walked into the costume department. Kids from Tansley often go to school in Matlock. Hannah and Cyrus went to Highfields School together."

"So he clocked her," Cal said.

"He was a classically trained actor with strong observational skills. There was a high chance he would recognise a former schoolmate, even with her altered appearance."

Ryan wrote another name beneath Grace's on the board, the scrawl much harder to read than Cal's handwriting. 'CYRUS WILDE - HIGHFIELDS'.

"Cyrus threatened to expose her connection to Bee Benson unless she sabotaged Piper's costumes. Eventually, he pushed her too far."

"So Grace killed him before he could reveal who she really was," Fiona said. "She was also the one who left the note on Ryan's windshield. To try and point the finger at the people we were already investigating."

"Which brings us to Mr Kerrington's confession," Lee prompted.

Ryan looked at Fiona, who'd conducted the follow-up interview.

"He has admitted he'd been passing off Grace's designs as his own for the past two seasons," Fiona explained. "Her talent exceeded his, but she lacked the connections and pedigree to advance. He rationalised it as mentoring. In reality, he'd appropriated her work."

Sheri frowned. "He stole her credit."

"She tolerated it while using the studio rumour mill to paint Blaise as obsessed with Cyrus. She'd been crafting the notebook to discredit him and take his job, then when she killed Cyrus, she realised she'd created a fall guy." Ryan paused. "Blaise often fell asleep in the wardrobe department, and he was working late Saturday night. Easy enough for her to press Cyrus's dead hand onto the notebook, then sneak in and touch the sleeping man's fingers to the dagger handle and the notebook cover. She planted everything in Cyrus's unlocked Porsche, and Millie 'finding' the notebook gave us what Grace wanted. A neat suspect in a tidy package." He glanced at Sheri.

"Not that you need me to admit it, but your instincts about Blaise were right."

She smiled. "I'll get it in writing and frame it later." Her smile faded. "What about Advika? Was it really just an innocent observation about the yearbooks that got her killed?"

Fiona's face softened. "I'm afraid so."

Lee's gaze shifted to the crime scene photos. "And Isaac Emerson? The studio's been breathing down my neck about his whereabouts."

Fiona straightened. "We located him this morning. He wasn't abducted or lying in a ditch. He was in his guesthouse on the estate. He didn't even tell his wife he was there."

Cal snorted.

Fiona flicked through her notes. "Locked himself in with a bottle of whisky and a burner phone. Had one of the gardeners bring him food and leave it at the door. Turned his main mobile off so Vance couldn't track him. When we persuaded him to open up, he shook too much to light his own cigarette."

"He thought Grace was coming for him?" Lee asked.

"He thought someone was," Fiona replied. "Kept insisting, 'You don't understand, there's a killer on set, picking us off.' He couldn't articulate why he believed he was next. Kept bouncing between the insurance policies, the stunts he'd pushed and the script where he killed off Cyrus."

"Couldn't believe it wasn't all about him," Cal said.

Lee considered the news. "So legally, Isaac's exposure is creative accounting and the insurance mess. Not murder."

Digit consulted his screen. "The financial irregularities remain significant, but there's no evidential link between Isaac's policy checks and the timing of the murders beyond coincidence."

"So why was Astrid at the studio the night Advika was killed?" Sheri asked.

"She thought Isaac was cheating on her with Piper, so she snuck in to catch them in the act but found Piper with a camera grip instead."

Lee cleared her throat. "And Margot's letter? The one found in the car park?"

"A healing exercise set by her therapist," Sheri explained. "She was on her way to an emergency session when she dropped it. The letter wasn't a threat or a confession, just part of her recovery process after the harassment and lack of action from the studio."

"Narrative Exposure Therapy," Digit supplied. "If you'd like to know more?"

"No, we're good, DC Asare," Lee cut in. She studied the boards, expression unreadable. "The media are already spinning this as a family tragedy spanning a decade. The detective who cracked a cold case while solving a murder." She shot Ryan a pointed look. "The news agencies are making you out to be some kind of hero."

Ryan grimaced. "It was a team effort. We followed the evidence."

In the room's corner, a muted television played a news clip of Cyrus as Caspian Drest. Ryan wondered whether they'd recast the role or write the character out of the script.

Somewhere, an editor was sitting in a dark room cutting scenes, smoothing over the gap, and pretending a tyrant had never stood at the centre of it all.

Real life was less tidy. The ritual pit set on Stage Five would always be a crime scene now, even after the set dressers scrubbed away the blood. Would the show continue or go under?

Lee pushed away from the doorframe. "Bee Benson spent ten years in prison for a murder her daughter committed." She shook her head. "What a waste."

The room fell silent. The weight of two interconnected tragedies hung in the air.

"Right," Lee said. "I want full reports on my desk by tomorrow morning. Forensics is still processing evidence from Silverheath and the Benson house, but we'll need formal statements from everyone involved." She surveyed the team. "Good work, all of you. Especially you, DC Dewan."

Sheri looked up, startled.

"Quick thinking with the taser," Lee continued. "You saved Colin Roger's life, not to mention potentially Vance Mitchell's."

A flush spread across Sheri's cheeks. "Thank you, Ma'am."

After Lee departed, Ryan sank into his chair as the exhaustion of the last two days caught up with him.

"The papers will have a field day with this one," Fiona said, gathering her things. "Family secrets, a celebrity murder, a wrongful conviction, Hollywood drama. It's got everything."

Ryan took a sip of coffee, now lukewarm. "I'm more concerned about what happens to Bee Benson now."

CHAPTER FORTY-FOUR

Ryan poked at the ham and cheese toastie on the plate in front of him. It bore more resemblance to the brown cardboard folder beside Fiona's elbow than to any recognisable food group.

The cafeteria was quiet in the mid-afternoon lull. Three uniformed officers occupied a table on the far side, bent over their phones. A pair of admin staff queued at the servery, where Nancy, who'd served the same jacket potatoes and wilted salads for fifteen years, wiped down the counter with efficient swipes.

"I can't believe you paid five pounds for that," Fiona said.

"The feeling's mutual." Ryan waved a hand at her carton of limp lettuce and soggy tomato, claiming to be a seasonal salad. He took a bite of the toastie to prove his point, then wished he hadn't.

Fiona put down her fork and opened the folder. "Sign here." She held out a pen and the final summary sheet for the Bee Benson case review. "Then it'll be officially in the system."

Ryan scanned the summary paragraph once more and then signed his name with a decisive stroke.

"You're sure about this?" Fiona took back the form. "Lampton won't take it lying down."

Ryan swallowed the lump of plastic cheese. "Let him come. If he'd done his job properly ten years ago, an innocent woman wouldn't have spent a decade locked away for a crime she didn't commit."

"Speak of the devil." Fiona glanced over his shoulder.

Chief Inspector Stuart Lampton stood in the doorway, his hands bunched into fists at his sides. The fluorescent light caught his domed forehead and gave him the look of an agitated egg.

He marched over. "DI Hale. A word."

Fiona rolled her eyes and collected the remains of her salad. She mouthed "Good luck" over Lampton's shoulder and retreated to the incident room.

"Chief Inspector." Ryan kept his tone neutral. Now wasn't the time to pretend to forget Lampton's rank. The man looked seconds away from an aneurysm.

Lampton's nostrils flared. "What the bloody hell is this!" He thrust a printout at Ryan's chest.

Ryan glanced at the case review confirmation notification for the Benson case, taking the paper.

"It's what it looks like."

"You've submitted a formal request to review the Matthew Benson murder." Lampton's voice shook, his face mottled with angry red patches. "On what grounds?"

"On the grounds that Beatrice Benson didn't kill her son."

"The woman confessed!" A spray of spittle hit the table. Lampton glanced towards the uniformed officers in the corner and lowered his voice to a furious hiss. "She confessed, and you know it. I ran my investigation by the book."

Ryan folded his arms. "Did you? Because our re-examination uncovered a witness statement you took no further. You overlooked forensic evidence and you convicted a suspect who lacked both motive and opportunity."

Lampton's face darkened to a dangerous shade of purple. "Are you accusing me of misconduct, DI Hale?"

"I'm saying you got it wrong." Ryan stood, forcing Lampton to tilt his head back. "Same as you got it wrong with Jaime."

Lampton's eyes narrowed to slits. "I followed the evidence. It pointed to you."

"The evidence pointed wherever you bloody well wanted it to." Ryan's fingers flexed. "You never even looked at any other suspects."

"Because there weren't any."

"Did you even look? You couldn't see past your own bloody ego."

Sheri appeared in the doorway, a stack of papers in her hand. She saw Lampton and hesitated, her eyes darting between them before she turned and left.

Ryan took a steadying breath.

"I'm warning you. Pursuing this Benson review will not end well for you," Lampton said.

"Is that a threat?"

"It's a professional courtesy." Lampton looked down his nose. "I have friends in this station and outside it. People who remember how you used to operate and don't like how you operate now."

Ryan gritted his teeth. "People like Gerald Peasley?"

Lampton's lips pressed together, and Ryan knew he'd hit the mark. The MP could make life difficult for him, but only if DCI Lee and DCC Cliffe stepped out of his corner.

"Here's what's going to happen, Chief Inspector. The review will proceed. If the evidence supports it, the conviction will be overturned. And when Bee walks free, you'll be the one facing questions about your investigation. You're a man who made a call based on limited imagination and laziness, and now you're scared of the fallout."

"Scared?" Lampton gave a wet sniff. "I've outlasted better detectives than you. I'll outlast this little crusade too."

Ryan held his gaze. Up close, the lines around Lampton's eyes were carved deeper than he remembered.

"Bee's done ten years for something she didn't do," Ryan said. "You can either help put it right, or you can keep pretending your conviction record is more important than her freedom and make the department look stupid in the process."

"You think you're so bloody clever," Lampton hissed. "But I know what you are. A man who leaves destruction in his wake and then tries to blame everyone else for the mess."

"The truth matters more than convenient confessions, Chief Inspector." Ryan said in a steady voice despite the anger bubbling beneath the surface. "It mattered twelve years ago, and it matters now."

"My job is to protect the integrity of the investigations I've led." Lampton ground the words out. "I won't let you drag my name through the mud to polish yours. Lee might indulge your little crusades for now, but she won't protect you forever."

The click of shoes on the floor behind them made both men turn. DCI Lee stood there, phone in hand, her expression hard.

"Everything all right here, gentlemen?" Her tone made clear it was anything but.

Lampton straightened, his demeanour shifting from confrontational to deferential. "A professional discussion, Olivia."

Lee's eyebrows rose. "Is that right, DI Hale?"

Ryan met her gaze. "The chief inspector has concerns about our case review."

"Concerns he should have brought to me directly." Her voice was arctic. "Stuart, my office. Ten minutes."

Lampton's mouth opened and closed like a stranded fish. "I was merely expressing—"

"Ten minutes." Lee continued past them towards the counter.

When she was out of earshot, Lampton leaned in close enough that Ryan could smell the sickly-sweet scent of liquorice on his breath.

"This isn't over," he hissed. "You want to dig up the past? You'd better be prepared for what might crawl out." With a final huff, he turned on his heel and stalked away.

CHAPTER FORTY-FIVE

SHERI ADJUSTED HER BURGUNDY BLOUSE AND WILLED HER hands to stop trembling. The lecture hall hadn't changed much since she'd last sat in it. Same uncomfortable chairs arranged in a gentle slope down to the podium. The faint mix of floor polish and sweat brought her straight back to her student days.

In her first year, she'd walked these halls as a different person, anxious and diminished. She was none of these things now.

"Need any help with the PowerPoint?" A student volunteer from the Criminology Society hovered nearby, laptop in hand.

"No, thanks. I've got it." Sheri smiled and plugged in her USB stick. Her presentation slides appeared on the screen behind her. Minimalist and professional, with the Derbyshire Constabulary crest displayed.

While the students filtered in, Sheri arranged her notes at the podium and then glanced up to gauge the crowd. It was mostly students, a few faculty members, and Alexis, who'd insisted on coming for moral support, settled into a seat in the middle row. She gave Sheri a subtle thumbs-up.

Sheri's gaze drifted to the back row, then froze.

Professor Arthur Smyth-Hall slouched in the corner seat, arms folded across his chest. Older now, his hair greyer, but his profile was unmistakable.

Her throat tightened. She didn't know why he was here, but he looked relaxed as he scrolled on his phone. He was clearly unaware of who the speaker was.

The Criminology Society president approached the podium. "We'll begin in about two minutes. Good turnout."

Sheri nodded, not trusting her voice. She took a sip of water and stared down at her notes, unseeing.

Breathe. You deserve to be here.

She squared her shoulders and looked up just as Smyth-Hall raised his head. Their eyes met across the room. His expression shifted from boredom to shock, then rearranged into careful neutrality.

Too late. She'd seen the flash of panic, and for some reason, it calmed her nerves.

The society president tapped the microphone. "Good afternoon, everyone. Today we're delighted to welcome Detective Constable Shriya Dewan from the East Midlands Special Operations Unit. DC Dewan graduated from our university four years ago with a degree in criminology and psychology and has already established herself on one of the region's most prestigious investigative teams. She's here to talk about careers in policing, especially for those interested in detective work."

Sheri leaned into the microphone. "Thank you for that kind introduction." She smiled at the audience but deliberately avoided looking at the back corner. "It's strange being back where it all started for me, though I should point out I didn't begin in criminology. I switched from a business degree midway through my first year."

She clicked through to her first slide. A photo of her team outside Chesterfield Police Station.

"When I sat where you are now, I never imagined I'd become a detective. Many paths lead to policing, and mine was unconventional." She paused, surprised by her own steadiness. "Today I'll talk about how I got in, what the job actually looks like and what I wish someone had told me when I sat in your seat."

She ran through the basics. When she mentioned her first murder case, a few pens paused, then started again.

"Now I'd like to talk about something that isn't in the official recruitment brochures." She clicked. The slide title was blunt: 'What I Didn't Know At Nineteen'.

"This isn't the part where I drop inspirational quotes and tell you to follow your dreams," she said to a ripple of quiet laughter. "So I'll be specific. When I was a first-year here, a member of staff suggested my grades might improve if I were... more accommodating."

A stillness settled. Even the shuffling at the back stopped.

Out of the corner of her eye, she noticed Smyth shifting in his seat.

"I reported it," Sheri went on, voice steady, "and I was told I was being 'culturally hypersensitive'. That phrase stuck with me for years, because it was designed to make me feel silly for trusting my own instincts."

She didn't look at the back. She didn't need to.

The next slide wasn't numbers. It was a short list.

"If something like that happens to you. Here, at work, or anywhere—do two things immediately." She held up a finger. "First. Document. This means dates, words used and any messages or screenshots." She added a second finger. "Second.

Tell someone who isn't invested in keeping it quiet. There are ways to report that don't involve walking alone into the lion's den."

She scanned the crowd. A student in the third row swallowed hard and nodded once, like she'd been waiting for permission to breathe.

Smyth stood and edged towards the door. Sheri refused to track his movement, keeping her focus on the students as she listed the different ways to report harassment. A few heads turned anyway. The movement at the back pulled their eyes like a magnet.

"Last thing," Sheri said, as the door opened. "If you're considering policing, Women in Justice and I are setting up a mentoring network. It's not therapy, just practical support."

The door at the back of the hall clicked shut.

She wrapped up and opened the floor. The questions came fast. Training, interviewing, whether TV ever got anything right.

One girl in a hijab raised her hand. "Do you ever feel you have to work harder to prove yourself because of your background?"

"Sometimes," Sheri admitted. "But I've found what felt like disadvantages, things like being underestimated, have become strengths. Observation and adaptation are core detective skills, and I've been practising those my whole life."

Another hand, male and hesitant, half-raised and dropped, then rose again. "If it's... someone senior. Like staff. What if they're..." he glanced at the lecturers, "untouchable?"

Good. Name the fear. Sheri kept her tone even. "Then you treat them like any other suspect. You preserve evidence, and you widen the circle. You don't go alone, and you don't let the first dismissal be the end of it. But it's also okay not to come forward. Each individual has to do what's right for them."

By the time she packed up her materials, she felt drained but satisfied. Something had shifted inside her. The weight she'd carried for years felt lighter.

Alexis met her at the door. "That was brilliant. Especially how you kept it grounded."

"He was there in the audience. He scarpered the minute I started talking about my first year," Sheri said as they walked across campus.

"Probably scared you were about to name and shame him."

They found a quiet corner in the university cafe, away from the afternoon rush. Sheri sipped her chai latte.

"Did you plan this all along?" Alexis asked. "Using the talk to flush him out?"

"No." Sheri shook her head. "I didn't even know he still taught here." She traced the rim of her cup with her finger. "But I guess I finally found my voice." Then she added, mostly to herself, "And it turns out it carries further than I realised."

CHAPTER FORTY-SIX

RAIN BEAT AGAINST THE WINDSCREEN AS RYAN NAVIGATED the narrow country roads towards HMP New Hall. In the passenger seat, Lynsey Cooper sat huddled beneath a thick tartan blanket, her oxygen canister tucked between her knees.

She adjusted her nasal cannula. "Thank you for this."

Ryan squinted through the wipers' swipes. Today's variety of rain fell somewhere between biblical deluge and drowning hazard. "We don't have to do this if you're not feeling up to it," he said.

"I've reached the end of my story, Inspector." Her laugh turned into a cough. "This can't wait for better weather or one of my good days. Time has run out."

Ryan turned down the tree-lined street, which led to the prison's entrance, and followed the green fencing crowned with coils of razor wire.

"I need to see Bee one last time," Lynsey added. "So I can see her face and explain why I did it."

He waited for the gates to open, then parked as close to the entrance as possible. He retrieved the wheelchair from the boot and set it up, then he helped Lynsey from car to chair, keeping the umbrella over her. Her bones felt like twigs beneath his hands, like they would snap if he held too firmly. The oxygen tank settled into the pouch behind the seat.

"Ready?"

She nodded, her translucent skin grey in the weak daylight.

The process of entering took half the time of Ryan's previous visit, thanks to Officer Kelly. The guard had looked at Lynsey with kind eyes, then expedited their entry and organised a private room.

"Twenty minutes," she murmured to Ryan. "Best I can do."

The interview room was the same as his last visit. Ryan positioned Lynsey's wheelchair at the table, then paused, uncertain whether to stay or offer privacy.

"Please stay," Lynsey said, reading his hesitation.

He nodded and stood back.

The door buzzed and Bee Benson entered, escorted by a guard Ryan hadn't met. She wore the same shapeless prison-issue clothing as before with her grey hair pulled back in its customary bun. For a heartbeat, she maintained her usual impassive expression. Then her gaze fell on Lynsey.

Her eyes widened and her lips trembled. "Lynsey," she whispered. The word escaped like a prayer.

The guard guided Bee to her seat, then retreated to stand by the door.

"Hello, Bee." Lynsey's voice quavered. Her hand, spotted with age and illness, inched across the table. "It's been a long time."

"Too long." Bee stared at Lynsey, at each visible sign of her illness.

The silence between them stretched, taut with unspoken history. Ryan felt like an intruder.

"I'm sorry," Lynsey said, "that I spoke up after all these

years when I knew you wanted the truth to stay buried, but I couldn't carry the burden on my soul. Not when..." She gestured at her body. "Not when I'm running out of time."

Bee reached across and took Lynsey's hand in both of hers.

"It's all right," Bee said, her voice steady despite the tears gathering in her eyes. "You did what you thought was right."

"Did I?" Lynsey looked uncertain. "You sacrificed so much to protect her, and now it's for nothing."

Bee's gaze dropped to their clasped hands. "I should have got Hannah the help she needed when I first saw the signs. The cruelty to animals. The fires. The lies. She'd blame it on Matthew but a mother knows." A single tear tracked down her cheek. "I told myself it was a phase. She'd grow out of it. That she was acting out because of Amos and the way he treated her."

Ryan shifted his weight, careful not to disrupt the moment. This was the confession he'd been seeking, unfolding without a single question from him.

"But it wasn't only that, was it?" Lynsey prompted gently.

"No." Bee shook her head. "There was something in her I didn't want to see. Something broken that I couldn't fix with love or patience." Her voice caught. "And because I couldn't fix her, all I could do was protect her. Now Amos... and that actor and that poor girl. They're all dead because I wouldn't let her face the consequences."

Lynsey's thin fingers squeezed Bee's. "We do what we must for our children."

"She killed my son," Bee whispered, the words torn from somewhere deep inside her. "My sweet Matthew. I thought..." She swallowed. "I thought if she got help, if she understood she had a second chance, to live her life right..."

"That she'd be a better person," Lynsey finished for her.

Bee nodded, tears flowing. "Instead, she became someone

else. Changed her name and her appearance. But not what she was inside."

"You couldn't have known."

"I should have." Bee withdrew her hands and wiped at her face. "I spent ten years in here hoping she was healing and building a new life. Instead, she continued to hurt people."

Ryan cleared his throat. "Mrs Benson, I'd like to send someone to formally take a new statement from you regarding Matthew's death, when you're ready."

Bee looked at him and something washed over her face. A mix of relief and bone-deep grief. "Yes. It's time." She turned back to Lynsey. "Thank you for making me face the truth."

Lynsey smiled, though her eyes brimmed with tears. "We were good friends, weren't we? Before it all went wrong?"

"The best," Bee agreed. "You brought me tea when I couldn't leave my bed after Hannah was born. Remember?"

"Earl Grey with honey. You said it tasted like kindness."

They spoke for several more minutes, exchanging fragments of memories from a time before tragedy rewrote their lives. Ryan stepped back and gave them space for this reunion that would also serve as their goodbye.

The rain had cleared by the time Ryan helped Lynsey back into his car. She'd declined his offer to take her straight to the hospice.

"I'd like to see the sky a bit longer," she'd said.

So he'd detoured along the reservoir, where the still water mirrored the cloudy sky. Lynsey stared out the window beside him, white-faced but relaxed. He'd drop her off soon, but for now, the quiet humming of the engine and her soft breaths brought him his own temporary respite.

Sometimes, love blinded people to the darkness in those closest to them. He contemplated his own certainty about Jaime. That she would never leave, despite what others believed. His stubborn insistence had pushed against Lampton's equally stubborn suspicion, mirrors of distrust reflected at each other.

But unlike Bee, Ryan knew there was no neat confession coming to explain Jaime's absence. No sacrifice he'd made to shield someone else. He thought of the photo he'd given to Lee, now filed away as fresh evidence in his wife's case. All he had were questions. Questions that still needed answers.

Ryan glanced at Lynsey, her head tilted against the window, breath fogging the glass. She'd found peace.

Maybe someday soon, he would too.

WANT MORE?

Keep an eye out for

EMPTY NEST

Book 3 in the DI Ryan Hale Crime Thriller series.

Want more Ryan and Fiona?
Join my newsletter to get my FREE prequel novella 'Cradle of Lies' about Ryan and Fiona's last case together before Ryan's world is shattered, and a BONUS prequel short story about the case that went sideways for Fiona.
Sign up now on my website.
rklynottbooks.com

ABOUT THE AUTHOR

R. K. Lynott is a crime thriller author writing mystery and crime fiction featuring compelling, quirky characters and stories packed with suspects, clues, and unexpected twists.

She lives in the South Island of New Zealand with her husband, two young children, and a grumpy Australian terrier who knows where all the fictional bodies are buried.

rklynottbooks.com

@rklynottauthor

ALSO BY R. K. LYNOTT

The DI Ryan Hale Crime Thriller Series

BURY THE TRUTH

LAST TAKE

EMPTY NEST